PRAISE FOR MARK PAWLOSKY'S NIK BYRON SERIES

"Written with all the speed and blunt force of a high-speed car chase, Mark Pawlosky's debut, *Hack*, is a thrill ride you don't want to miss. Part Jim Crumley, part Don Winslow, Pawlosky's prose is delivered with the confidence of an old pro. A killer thriller, to be sure."

—Vincent Zandri, *New York Times* bestselling Thriller and Shamus Award–winning author of the *Dick Moonlight PI* series and *The Girl Who Wasn't There*

"*Hack* by Mark Pawlosky is a heart-pounding novel and nearly impossible to put down. It's a compelling storytelling with hairpin twists. Not for the fainthearted."

—Jon Bassoff, author of *Beneath Cruel Waters*

"Nik Byron is flawed, charming, and always flirting with being down on his luck. But tell him he can't get a story and his smarts and ambition take over. Mark Pawlosky's clever plotting and affection for the craft of journalism and its rituals barrel through every page. Don't let this book's title fool you— Nik and his creator are first-rate storytellers."

—Joe Drape, *New York Times* bestselling author of *The Saint Makers, American Pharoah* and *Our Boys*

"With fluid prose and a journalist's keen eye for detail, Mark Pawlosky's *Hack* delivers a rich and fast-moving tale populated with a fascinating collection of characters that readers will find equal reason to love and loathe. Hack will keep you up even after you stop flipping the pages."

—Bryan Gruley, Edgar Award–nominated author
of the Starvation Lake Mystery trilogy.

"A propulsive conspiracy tale with a credible and capable hero. Pawlosky has a deft touch in conveying character."

—*Kirkus Reviews*

FRIENDLY FIRE

MARK PAWLOSKY

FRIENDLY FIRE

— A —

NIK BYRON

INVESTIGATION

GIRL FRIDAY BOOKS

 **GIRL FRIDAY BOOKS**

Published by Girl Friday Books™, Seattle
www.girlfridaybooks.com

Produced by Girl Friday Productions

Cover design: Emily Weigel
Production editorial: Bethany Davis
Project management: Sara Spees Addicott

Image credits: cover © Shutterstock/Frontpage

ISBN (paperback): 978-1-954854-62-8
ISBN (e-book): 978-1-954854-63-5

Library of Congress Control Number: 2022905924

First edition

To the memories of Joseph W.,
Margaret A., and James E. Pawlosky.

AUTHOR'S NOTE

Friendly Fire, the second novel in the Nik Byron series, is set in Washington, DC, where I once lived and worked and which I still remember fondly. The city and its environs have changed considerably since my days there, but, out of a sense of nostalgia, I've resurrected several long-shuttered establishments for the telling of this story. I have attempted to remain true to the more iconic landmarks, but, for my purposes, I have altered some locations and institutions and conjured up whole entities—the Northern Virginia County Sheriff's Department among them—where none exist.

Likewise, part of the action in *Friendly Fire* takes place in South Florida. My descriptions of the area are inspired by my travels there over the years, but they are not meant to be true-to-life representations. The baseball academy in Islamorada, for example, lives only in my imagination.

PART I

THE INTRUDER

CHAPTER 1

March 17, 2019

Had she still been living in the crumbling Adams Morgan apartment building with the shabby lobby, broken elevator, rickety staircase, and foul-smelling courtyard, she would have heard the rasp on the jamb as the window was forced open, felt the air's cold sting on the back of her neck, noted the creak of the floorboards, but as it was, this new twenty-five-thousand-square-foot house was airtight, with reinforced concrete floors overlaid with old-growth timbers and thick Persian rugs, the ambient murmur of mechanical equipment drowning out any sound.

She didn't hear a thing. Until he was on her. And then all she could hear was the thundering of her heart exploding in her ears.

One moment, she was at the bathroom sink gently cleansing her face, brushing her hair, softly humming a tune from *Wicked*, her favorite Broadway show; turning down the covers, looking forward to starting a new book. And the next, she was fighting for her life, the intruder's hands at her throat, a knee shoved up in her crotch, a man's body pressing down on her with all its weight.

She couldn't think, let alone breathe, then survival instincts kicked in. She dug her nails into the intruder's back, neck, and scalp and, when he momentarily loosened his hold, raked his face and drove her knee into his nuts. He groaned, and she slithered partially out from under him and clutched for the bedside table. She yanked out the drawer and thrust her hand inside just as he grabbed a fistful of her hair and kicked the drawer shut on her wrist. She screamed in pain, or at least she thought she heard herself scream.

He had a stocking over his face, and she could hear him panting hard. He tried to lever himself up on his elbow to get a better purchase but only wound up sinking deeper into the soft bedding, his foot slipping from the table. When it did, she withdrew her hand from the drawer. In it, she held a .38 Special stainless-steel revolver and shot him, point-blank, twice through the chest. She rolled out from under him, dropped the gun on the floor, grabbed her phone off the bedside table, ran down the stairs, out the front door, and dialed 911.

———————

A female deputy for the Northern Virginia County Sheriff's Department was consoling her when Sheriff Jake Korum, investigator Samantha Whyte, and a heavyset detective walked out of the Georgian-style mansion, with its six twenty-foot columns, down the sloped lawn, past rippling fountains, to expansive gardens where the pair stood silhouetted by flashing blue emergency lights.

"You holdin' up okay, Mrs. Tate?" the sheriff drawled, putting a reassuring hand on her shoulder, tilting back his signature wide-brimmed off-white Stetson, and bending over so he could look her in the face. She was fighting back tears, eyes red and watery, nostrils leaking, a heavy blanket draped over her back.

"I don't know," she said between whimpers and wiped her nose with the back of her hand, the blanket sliding from her shoulders to reveal a bloodstained lace negligee. A cold rain had fallen earlier in the evening, and the air was chilled, the ground wet, her slippers soggy, mud caked. "I think so. Is he dead?" she asked and closed the blanket back around her neck.

"Oh, yeah, he's dead awright, Mrs. Tate," the sheriff assured her. "Business end of a .38 at that range does the trick every time. One round would have gotten the job done."

"Mrs. Tate," the detective asked, "you call anyone else after dialing 911?"

"My husband, Geoff. He was on his way back from a business trip in Europe. His jet should have landed by now."

The detective nodded his tree stump of a head knowingly. "That's what I would've guessed, Mrs. Tate," he said. "That's what most people would do in a situation like this, I suspect. Call a loved one, or spouse, if they're married. That's what I'd have done. Called Patsy. You get ahold of Mr. Tate?"

"No, he didn't answer his phone."

"Figures."

"Why's that?" she sniffled.

The burly detective swept his eyes over the manicured gardens, stone paths, statuary, tennis courts, koi ponds, and said, "Mr. Tate, he's lying up there on your bedroom floor, two slugs through his breadbasket. You killed your husband, Mrs. Tate."

She wailed and collapsed.

"Your bedside manner needs work, *Dee-tec-tive*," the female deputy spat angrily, struggling to support the slumping body as Mrs. Tate's dog, a cockapoo with little red ribbons pinned to its ears, ran laps around her legs, yapping incessantly.

"Careful now, Deputy. You're holding on to what just might be the world's richest woman," the detective said over the dog's barking and tucked a pinch of Copenhagen tobacco in his lower lip. "And somebody better muzzle that goddamn mutt before I shoot it."

CHAPTER 2

March 17

He hated crowds and preferred to work behind the scenes, un-detected, but tonight was different. It was important he stood out, be seen. The Georgetown bar was packed and noisy with Saint Patrick's Day revelers, and he had already bought the house one round of drinks to celebrate. Two drunk brunettes, in matching short green skirts and sequined tops, had him hemmed in as he stood facing the rowdy gathering, back to the bar, elbows propped up against the railing.

The heavier of the two flashed him a green thong she was wearing under her skirt. The other pulled him closer and whis-pered in his ear, "I don't own green panties, so I'm not wearing anything at all." She belched softly in his face and giggled. Her breath smelled like licorice.

He remained in the bar for another fifteen minutes, set-tled his tab, and ordered up an Uber, but not before buying a second round of drinks and engaging in some heavy petting with the two females, running a fleshy hand up the skirt of the pantyless one while the other massaged the inside of his thigh.

He downed what was left of a mug of green beer, slipped the bartender a fifty-dollar tip, and escaped the claws of the two women.

The Uber driver was wearing a Washington Nationals baseball cap and kept up a running dialogue on the team's chances to get back to the World Series as spring training approached. "I still can't believe they got rid of Harper," he said, referring to the perennial all-star and two-time MVP Bryce Harper. "Who would have thought."

When he reached the entrance to his building, one of the new high-rise luxury towers off upper Wisconsin Avenue, he made sure to pause and chat up the doorman.

"Karl, my main man, how come you didn't tell me about the hottie who moved into 2A? You been holding out on me?"

Karl smiled. "You plenty busy as it is awready, Mr. Mack. You not careful, your manhood like to fall off."

"I do like the ladies," he boasted.

"Good night, Mr. Mack."

"Good night, Karl," he said before taking the elevator up to his twelve-room apartment on the fifth floor.

Dwayne Mack kicked off his sneakers in the entryway, padded to the kitchen, poured two fingers of rye whiskey into a cut-crystal tumbler to wash the beer taste out of his mouth, dropped in ice cubes, selected a Fuente robusto from the humidor on the counter, and made his way to the living room. He flipped on the television and started scrolling through the stations to catch the local news, all the while monitoring Twitter.

The lead story on all three programs was about a gangland shooting that had left four people dead and six others wounded in southeast Washington. "That brings the number of murders to forty-four this year, and we're only in March. At this pace, we will surpass last year's record homicide rate," the newsman said somberly.

Shame it was only four, Dwayne thought to himself and muted the sound.

He checked his watch. In an era of iPhones, he still preferred wristwatches and owned an expensive collection—Rolex, Cartier, Patek Philippe—because it was his experience that luxury sent an important message.

He was careful not to overdo the extravagance, lest he be considered vulgar, and offset the five-figure bracelets dangling from his plump wrist by purposely dressing down in flannel shirts, blue jeans, sneakers, baseball caps.

He was a good twenty pounds overweight, a fold of belly draped over his beltline like a water balloon, and looked like he belonged behind the wheel of a Peterbilt semitruck. Instead, he drove a restored 1966 Ford Mustang, canary yellow, hardtop. He avoided the sun, his skin as white as the underbelly of a fish.

Clients were intrigued by Mack's eclectic style, but that's not why they hired him. They hired him because he got results. Always. That, and he carried scores of politicians and judges in his pocket like loose change.

Most lobbyists and crisis communication firms in Washington, DC, are what those in the industry refer to as "relationship specialists." Not Dwayne Mack. He was a cage fighter, and he didn't give a damn who he crawled into the octagon with as long as their checks cashed. Technology monopolists, tobacco companies, industrial polluters, dictators, they all came knocking at Blue Sky Consulting's door, and they always found it wide open.

Mack booted up his laptop and started surfing the web. It was one minute past midnight. On the third news site, *Hush Now,* a crime and political gossip rag that Mack often secretly spoon-fed tips, he saw the story. He clicked on the headline, and it took him to a page with scant details.

Yukon CEO Shot, Killed at Home

Geoffrey Tate, CEO of Yukon, the
world's largest artificial intelligence
company, and one of the planet's
wealthiest individuals with a net worth
estimated north of $150 billion, was
shot and killed in his McLean, Virginia,
home late this evening.

"At this time, we are still trying to
determine the sequence of events that
transpired prior to Mr. Tate's death.
We will release further details as they
become available," Samantha Whyte,
chief spokesperson and lead investigator for the Northern Virginia County
Sheriff's Department, said in a prepared statement.

This is a developing story. Check
back for updates throughout the night.

Mack unmuted his television. The local stations had now
picked up the story and were broadcasting news of the shooting. They didn't have many more facts than *Hush Now*'s online
report, but they did have a dated mug shot of Tate, circa 1994,
when he had started Yukon in his garage; aerial photos of his
new walled-in ten-acre McLean, Virginia, estate; and a picture
of Yukon's distinctive headquarters building in downtown DC
with its thirty-eight-foot steel sculpture of a mechanical prospector mining for gold, the pickax in his hand hypnotically
striking a blow on rocks every seventy-five seconds.

Mack continued to monitor Twitter and waited five minutes before making a call. When a sleepy woman answered,
he announced in a wounded voice, "This is Dwayne. Have you

heard the news? It's all over the media. Geoff's dead. He's been shot and killed."

The woman gasped and said something, but Mack wasn't paying attention. He was too busy calculating what impact the news of Tate's death would have on the company's stock price when markets opened on Monday. He figured it'd shave 20 percent off the market cap on the high side, or about $200 billion. He'd be sure to load up on the dip.

He turned his attention back to the blubbering woman on the phone and told her to pull herself together and start calling Yukon's board of directors to notify them of the news. He hung up the phone, picked up his laptop, and pecked away at the keys, tapping out a statement for the board to release to the press that read, in part:

While tragic, Geoffrey Tate's passing will in no way jeopardize or interfere with Yukon's work on the $500 billion Bullwhip contract to provide the Department of Defense with advanced artificial intelligence capabilities for our nation's fighting men and women. The company is on track to deliver state-of-the-art technologies on the initial phase of the project, which, when completed, will usher in the world's first unmanned and autonomous fleet of war machines capable of seeking out, engaging, and neutralizing enemy forces in the field and skies without human intervention or risk.

Let this be Geoff's everlasting legacy.

When he was satisfied with the statement, Mack clipped the tip of his cigar, lit it with a gold lighter inscribed with "The best is yet to come," refilled his tumbler with the bottle of rye he carried in from the kitchen, and reclined back on the couch. Minutes later, the encrypted app on his phone signaled the arrival of an incoming text message with a piiiing.

He specifically chose this particular app because it didn't store any bread crumbs in the cloud and contained no GPS monitoring code. He glanced down at the message. The text contained no words. Just an emoji. It was a four-leaf clover. The Irish symbol for luck.

CHAPTER 3

March 17/18

"Slow down, Nik. This ain't a fuckin' cattle auction. Now, you're mumbling. E-nun-ci-ate."

When news of Geoffrey Tate's killing broke, reporter Nik Byron was barricaded deep inside the bowels of *Newshound*'s Washington, DC, basement studios wrapping up a late-night recording session for *The Front Page*, the company's signature investigative podcast, on the mysterious disappearance of a cryptocurrency mogul and $125 million in Bitcoin.

Nik's twentysomething producer, Teofilo Mezos—Teo to colleagues—was a taskmaster. He insisted on Nik's undivided attention during these sessions and declared a total news blackout, literally locking Nik in the suffocating studio with a cot, seizing his cell phone, and feeding him Chinese food from the Asian market down the block until he was satisfied with the final product.

Aliens could have invaded Washington, and Nik, sealed off from the outside world, would never have known it.

Teo constantly harangued Nik on elocution, pacing, and

the art of creating a compelling audio story. His needling ran-
kled the seasoned print journalist, who, despite a number of
first-rate podcasts under his belt, remained uncomfortable
with a format that placed the reporter at the heart of the story,
rather than on the outside looking in as a detached observer.
Nik's instinct was always to remove himself from the equation, as quaint as that idea might seem in the current media
landscape.

Their sessions, often contentious, could last days and run
nonstop for hours as the pair butted heads and bickered over
every programming detail.

That's why it surprised Nik to hear Teo's voice boom
through the headset, summoning him to the production booth
shortly after the final recording got underway. "Shut it down,
Nik, and come on up. We got a situation."

Nik had barely set foot inside the cramped booth when
Mia Landry, *Newshound*'s executive producer and Teo's manager, blurted out, "Geoffrey Tate's dead."

Nik was as bewildered by the news as he was by Mia's late-
night presence in the studio. He stammered, "The Yukon CEO?"

"Yeah. That Geoff Tate. Rich as Croesus. World's biggest
AI company. Why, you know another?" Mia asked.

Nik considered Mia for a moment. Judging by her wardrobe, she must have been at home when she got the news and
rushed to the office. She was wearing an orange puffy jacket;
Ugg boots; and sweatpants from Northwestern University, her
alma mater, its name emblazoned on one leg. Her normally
unruly hair was plaited in a long weave and draped over her
shoulder like a pet boa constrictor.

Barely five foot two and still in her twenties, Mia had
earned the respect of much older colleagues with her relentless drive and innate digital media skills. She had proven herself an enterprising reporter, and officials who equated youth
with naïveté often came to regret their miscalculation.

"No, of course not. I'm just trying to process it. It's a little jarring. It's like saying the president got shot. What the hell happened?" Nik said.

"Unclear, but what is clear is that it's going to have huge consequences for Yukon, the Department of Defense, the artificial intelligence industry, and this region."

Teo had confiscated Nik's cell phone during the recording session, and it was now buzzing with incoming messages. Nik snatched it off the soundboard and started skimming through the calls and texts.

"They're from Sam," he said, referring to Samantha Whyte, his current girlfriend and the lead investigator for the Northern Virginia County Sheriff's Department. "Says they're taking Mrs. Tate to the county courthouse. Doesn't say what for or if she's a suspect."

"We gotta jump on this," Mia said as she pulled out her cell phone and started scrolling through her contact list for other *Newshound* staffers she might be able to enlist. "I've already left a few messages, and I'm waiting to hear back from Mo," she said. Patrick "Mo" Morgan was Mia and Nik's longtime associate and *Newshound*'s new deputy editor.

"Whoa, Mia," Teo protested. "Our job is to produce long-form audio-documentaries. We're not equipped or staffed to cover breaking stories, that's what the news department on the sixth floor is for."

"Sorry, Teo, but we're flipping the script," Mia said.

"Mia, that's crazy," he pushed back. "We have a half-dozen podcasts in the pipeline that need to be produced."

Mia held up her hand to cut off his protests. "They'll have to be shelved for now. This story's too big to wait another six months to start reporting."

It was music to Nik's ears.

When Nik moved to Washington, DC, he had been promised *Newshound*'s chief editor position, but even before his first day on the job, he was demoted to deputy editor and senior reporter, the result of a hastily arranged media merger.

The new editor, Richard Whetstone, felt threatened by Nik and would later fire him for insubordination after Nik refused Whetstone's direct order to drop an investigation into OmniSoft Corporation, a Washington-based technology company that had developed state-of-the-art surveillance software that rogue operatives stole and offered for sale on the black market around the globe.

The story's tentacles reached deep into the US Department of Justice, the military's Defense Intelligence Agency, and China's Ministry of State Security. More than a dozen people lost their lives during the course of the story, and Nik was badly beaten and hospitalized.

Mia had tossed Nik a career lifeline and offered him a job on her small but feisty podcast team, which bypassed the local chain of command—including the vindictive Whetstone—and reported directly to corporate headquarters in the Midwest.

Nik was grateful for the work, but podcasting did not come naturally to him, and he longed for the rhythm and camaraderie of a daily news operation. He had started his career in newspapering, but joined *Newshound*, a digital media juggernaut, when he was shoved out of his job because of a botched investigative project he was conducting. He worried constantly that his best reporting days were behind him now; indeed, he brooded that the whole media industry was in an irreversible decline, despite *Newshound*'s success.

Now closer to forty than thirty with a shock of sandy hair, John Lennon–style wire-rimmed glasses, an impish smile, and perpetual three-day stubble, Nik still appeared youthful, but that belied a weariness he'd felt deep in his bones ever since the aftermath of the brutal beating he had received while covering the OmniSoft story.

"Let me see if I understand," Teo said in a mocking tone. "You're proposing we throw everything out the window that we've worked on for the past six months to chase a lurid news story when we don't have any idea where it's going and certainly don't have the staff or resources to cover it. That about right?"

"Pretty much," Mia said. "We'll report, write, produce, and stockpile stories as they come in, and then we'll air them when we think the time is right. At least, that's the general idea, Teo, subject to change. Come on, I'm winging it here. Cut me some slack. I only found out about this an hour ago."

"Suit yourself, but it ain't gonna work," he said dismissively.

"Why not?"

"Because Nik here's no Usain Bolt when it comes to writing, and he still hasn't gotten the hang of podcasting," Teo argued. "And on top of that, he's discipline challenged."

Nik quickly jumped to his own defense. "I'll freely admit I'm not the world's fastest writer or God's gift to podcasting," he said, aware of his well-earned reputation as a plodder who labored over every word, sentence, and paragraph in stories, "but I've never missed a deadline."

It was getting hot in the stuffy production booth, and tensions were flaring along with the temperature as Nik and Teo glared at one another over Mia's head.

"Calm down, both of you," Mia said sternly. "This is no time for squabbling. We have plenty to do. First thing we have to tackle is to locate our old Yukon notes and scripts."

Earlier, Nik and Mia had spent weeks working on a story about Geoff Tate and Yukon after tabloids had published pictures of Tate and a former beauty contestant on a nude beach together in the Caribbean. Tate was married when the scandal erupted, and it threw Yukon's future into question.

The reporters had collected extensive material on Tate, the young woman, and Yukon, but *Newshound*'s corporate lawyers intervened and convinced management to hold off publishing the stories until after *Newshound*'s planned initial public stock offering, fearful Tate would sue the company and effectively derail the IPO and the millions of dollars it would generate for the media operation.

The offering eventually came off without a hitch, but by that time, the Yukon story was old news and Mia and Nik had decided to mothball the material.

Nik used the Freedom of Information Act to pry several volumes of documents out of the Pentagon on Yukon's $500 billion Bullwhip contract, but he had no idea what the material contained since he had never bothered to look at it after the decision was made to pull the plug on the story.

"Now that the IPO is behind us and Tate's no longer around, there shouldn't be a problem with reviving the stories," Nik said.

"If we can find the damn notes," Mia responded.

"Right," Nik said. "That might be a problem."

Hackers thought to be working for China's Ministry of State Security had accessed *Newshound*'s servers and emptied them of all content connected to Nik—notes, podcasts, recorded interviews—after he had disclosed China's role in hijacking OmniSoft's surveillance technology. Thankfully, Nik, being an old-school reporter, had kept hard copies of much of his work.

All the Yukon notes and files had been packed up and shipped to a storage unit when *Newshound* moved to its new location and were now buried under mounds of old desks, used copy machines, and worn-out office furniture. It would require digging through stacks of boxes and piles of discarded equipment to unearth the files.

"I'll head over to the storage unit in the next couple days

and start digging around," Mia volunteered. "Once I find what I'm looking for, I'll piece together a story and then kick it to you to take a crack at, Nik."

Nik pulled on his coat and began packing up his bag. "Great. Think I'll go to the courthouse and see what I can learn."

"You're not sticking around to finish the podcast?" Teo asked sullenly.

Nik shook his head. "You know why you don't see the best reporters hanging around the office schmoozing and drinking coffee?" he asked as he slung his bag over his shoulder, placing a hand on the doorknob.

Teo looked at Nik blankly.

"Because there's no news in a newsroom, Teo, only desk jockeys," Nik said, paraphrasing a quote from a novel he once read. "You should try to remember that."

CHAPTER 4

March 18

Nik was slumped in a chair in Samantha Whyte's modest but tidy second-floor office in the Northern Virginia County Courthouse. He was thumbing through a dog-eared copy of the National Sheriffs' Association magazine with her boss's picture on the cover, trying and, for the most part, failing to pry information out of Whyte about the Tate shooting when Sheriff Jake Korum breezed through the door.

"Oh, Nik, didn't realize you were here. Past your bedtime, in'nit?" said the sheriff, dropping into the chair next to Nik and snapping open a laptop computer he was carrying. Korum was dressed, as always, in his nut-brown uniform, cowboy boots, and off-white Stetson hat.

"Sheriff." Nik nodded.

It was approaching two a.m., and Nik knew precious little more about the shooting than when he'd first arrived, other than that Mrs. Tate had been released after some routine questioning.

"When did they put you back on the news beat?" the sheriff asked.

"They haven't. I'm covering this for our podcast channel."

Korum looked at him quizzically. "I thought you told me your podcasts were meant to be documentaries, like Ken Burns but for audio, no pictures."

"That's right, they are," Nik said, shifting in his chair uncomfortably. "We're trying something a little different this time. It's experimental."

"Mmm, good luck with that," the sheriff said, swishing the ever-present toothpick around in his mouth. "What have you told him, Sam?"

Nik closed the magazine and tossed it back on Sam's spotless desk. It landed with a thwack. It puzzled Nik how someone who rarely made her own bed, left toiletries scattered all over the house, clothes in the dryer for weeks on end, and whose closet looked like a discount bin in a bargain-basement store could maintain such a pristine and uncluttered office. Sam only shrugged when Nik brought it to her attention.

"I'll answer that, Sheriff," Nik said with a yawn. "Zero. She's given me nada."

Sam, a strawberry blonde with a ribbon of freckles that ran across the bridge of her nose, cheekbone to cheekbone, flashed Nik an embarrassed smile.

"We trained her well, then," the sheriff said with a nod.

Korum had defeated incumbent Tubby Charleston, an incompetent public servant and glad-handing career politician, for the sheriff's job. For his efforts, he inherited a bloated, mismanaged, and resentful staff that he immediately set about overhauling. While many rank-and-file members applauded Korum's efforts, just as many tried to undercut him at every opportunity.

One of Korum's early decisions was to hire Sam, a former

political and investigative reporter for the *Washington Post*, to handle communications, beef up investigations, and bring some vitality to the staid office.

The sheriff casually crossed his legs, removed his Stetson, and dangled the hat on the toe of his snakeskin boot. Korum liked to cultivate an image of a slow-witted hayseed for public consumption, but the truth was he was an ex–Army Ranger, previous FBI special agent, and Rhodes scholar who had graduated at the top of his class from West Point. Korum, who had been introduced to Nik by a former Israeli special forces operative, had been one of Nik's best sources during his time in Washington.

The sheriff took a moment to gather himself and then proceeded to relate to Nik Mrs. Tate's story about being attacked in her bedroom by a masked intruder, the ensuing struggle, and, finally, the two gunshots that ended Geoffrey Tate's life.

When Korum finished, Nik remained silent, dumbstruck. He eyed the sheriff skeptically before momentarily turning his gaze on Sam, who was slowly nodding her head up and down in agreement.

Nik removed his glasses, rubbed his forehead, and then repeated what he had just heard. "Geoffrey Tate—one of the world's richest men—comes home from an overseas business trip, pulls a mask over his face, breaks into his own home, tries to strangle his wife, who, as they wrestle, produces a handgun and shoots and kills him?"

"Appears to be the nub of it," the sheriff said.

"In self-defense?"

"Yup. That's her story."

"And you buy it?"

"Dunno." Sheriff Korum shrugged. "We don't have much to go on at this point other than the victim's version of events. A young wife kills her older wealthy husband—certainly raises a lot of questions. But then again, there is evidence he did break into his own home and assault her."

"People are going to naturally assume she killed her husband to get her hands on his fortune," Nik said.

"S'pect you're right, but it'll be up to the prosecuting attorney ultimately to make that determination," the sheriff said, referring to Northern Virginia County Commonwealth Attorney Lance St. Mary.

"Any idea which way Lance is leaning?" Nik asked.

"Lance don't lean," Korum said levelly. "He blows with the wind. It'll be all about the politics for him. He's got his eye on a run for the state attorney general's office come the fall, and Geoff Tate's death, it's the biggest case of his career. He's not about to let this opportunity go to waste. He'll milk it for all the publicity it's worth, if I know Lance."

"I heard he's already hired a campaign manager," Sam offered.

The sheriff swiveled his head toward Sam. "That so. Sam, why don't you go ahead and describe Mr. Tate's getup to Nik. He might get a kick out of it," he said as he continued to swirl the toothpick from side to side in his mouth.

———

Sam's feet were tired and sore after standing most of the day, and she now scooched her chair forward in stocking feet. From a neat stack, she selected a slender blue folder with the sheriff's department seal on the cover, flipped it open, and began reading its contents aloud.

"The alleged perpetrator's body was discovered in the couple's second-story bedroom on the bed, dressed head to toe in dark clothing. The deceased wore a black watch cap, black calfskin gloves, and had a stocking pulled over his face, concealing his identity," she recited.

"Pantyhose?" Nik asked, not looking up from his note-taking.

"Yes," Sam said.

"Black?"

"Yes. Wolford."

"Wolford?"

"A high-end brand. It's what Mrs. Tate wears. We assume he took them from her lingerie drawer sometime prior to the attack."

"Okay. Go on."

"Upon a search of his person, deputies discovered a half-dozen white zip ties, a red bandanna, and rope in his pockets. The deceased was wearing black cargo pants, a black belt, black zip-up windbreaker with a black T-shirt underneath."

"So you figure he was going to tie her up and gag her?"

"It appears that was his intention, but he's no longer here, so, naturally, we aren't able to ask him any questions."

"Gotcha. What kind of shoes was he wearing?"

"Moccasins. Black."

"Did he have a weapon?"

"Other than the handgun, which Mrs. Tate said belonged to her husband and she claims was in the bedside table, no, none that we've been able to locate. Mrs. Tate doesn't recall seeing one."

"That seem weird?"

"Everything about this case is weirder than weird."

"How about a cell phone?"

"We've located two, but we have reason to believe there are others. We're trying to track those down now. The two we have are locked. We're in contact with the manufacturer to see if they will assist us in unlocking the phones. We don't hold out much hope they will honor our request."

"Silicon Valley assholes," Korum murmured without looking up from his laptop.

"What about security—his personal bodyguard and home alarm systems? They live in a fortress. How'd he get in without setting off alarms, triggering sensors, getting caught on camera?" Nik asked.

"He sent his bodyguard, Shaka Wulf, home after his private jet landed from Europe. As for the home security system, Mrs. Tate said her husband could control it with an app on his mobile phones. It appears everything was disabled prior to the attack."

"So, no video showing him entering the house in his cat-burglar getup?"

"Correct, but there is video of him pulling up to the front of the estate just before. That's the last video we have."

"How'd he get in?"

"It rained most of the evening, and we found what appear to be partial muddy footprints on a window seal that leads to their bedroom. There's a tree outside that window, and we believe he climbed it and got onto the roof from there. You saw those pictures of him and Jewel on the nude beach from a while back. He's pretty buff for a geek. We sent pictures of the footprints to the lab for testing. The window wasn't jimmied."

"Meaning?"

"Meaning someone left the window unlocked from the inside."

"Okay, but why climb up to a second-story window when he could have walked right through the front door and knocked her on the head?"

"Then it wouldn't have looked like someone broke in and assaulted his wife," Sam said.

"Right. Sorry, a little tired. Anything else?"

Sam shot Sheriff Korum a quick glance.

"Go on. Don't be shy," Korum said and shifted the tooth-pick from one side of his mouth to the other as he sucked on his teeth. "Tell 'im. Nothing he hadn't seen or heard before, I reckon."

"Tell me what?" Nik said and stopped taking notes momentarily. Sam blushed.

"Okay, but you have to promise not to use it," she said.

Nik crossed his arms and scowled. Sam tilted her head to one side and fixed him with an unblinking gaze. Korum clucked his tongue and went back to his computer.

"Okay, what is it?" Nik said.

"Promise not to use it?"

"I promise."

"He was wearing a black leather jockstrap with studs, and he has no body hair."

"Like he shaved his privates?" Nik said.

"More like waxed," Sam said.

Nik got a sour look on his face and appeared to be weighing a smart-ass retort to that last piece of information when the sheriff said, "Then there's the sister."

"Whose sister?"

"Geoff Tate's. Marianne Tate," Korum said, closing down his laptop, placing the Stetson back on his head, and standing to leave. "Next of kin and only living relative. She's not buying Mrs. Tate's story. Thinks it was a setup."

"She got any proof?" Nik said.

"Theories," the sheriff said, and slowly walked toward the door, looking weary. "She's got theories, s'all."

He stopped and turned back toward the pair. He pulled the toothpick from his mouth and pointed it at Sam. "Prosecutor's press conference is at half past. You best be there."

After he left, Nik asked, "Theories?"

Sam rolled her eyes as if to dismiss it. "You know, I haven't eaten anything since breakfast and I'm starving," she said as she pulled a brown paper bag from her desk drawer. She peeled open the top and retrieved a turkey sandwich on whole-wheat bread and a handful of baby carrots.

"Want half?" she offered.

"You go ahead." Nik chinned toward Sam. "What's Geoff Tate's motive?"

"Hypothetically, not hard to guess," Sam said, taking a bite of the sandwich, chewing hungrily, and washing it down with a flat Diet Coke. "Sure you don't want anything?" she said and pushed the carrots toward Nik.

"No, thanks."

"Tate," she said, briefly pausing to nibble on a carrot, "wakes up one morning, realizes he made a huge mistake marrying an unemployed yoga instructor two decades younger than himself, and wants to cut her out of his fortune."

"Buyer's remorse?"

"Biiiigtime," Sam said, bobbing her head up and down, and dabbed the corner of her mouth with a finger to wipe away a splotch of mustard.

She pushed her chair away from her desk, wiggled her feet into her shoes, stood, and stepped toward Nik. She bent at the waist, her ginger hair falling in his eyes, her presence soaking into his skin, and gave him a quick, wet kiss on the lips. She stood, straightened her skirt, and said, "I'll help you where I can, Niky, but I hope this story doesn't come between us."

So far, Sam and Nik had managed to successfully navigate the personal and professional minefield that surrounded their conflicting jobs, but Sam sensed this time might be different, given the Tates' notoriety and Nik's single-mindedness once he sank his teeth into a story.

Sam desperately wanted to avoid an exhausting cat-and-mouse game with Nik and made up her mind to tread carefully, but as a former reporter herself, she instinctively worried the story would test the boundaries of their relationship.

"Why would it?"

"No reason. I gotta go now, and so do you. Can't have a reporter in my office unattended."

"Not even one you're sleeping with?"

"Especially not one I'm sleeping with," Sam said.

"I remember this desk," Nik said, rapping his knuckles on its top as he stood to leave. "Solid as an oak tree. A night I'll always cherish."

"I don't know what you're talking about," Sam said, winked, and patted Nik on the rear before shooing him out the door.

CHAPTER 5

March 18

Nik stood outside the front entrance of his apartment building just as the sun edged over the treetops, the morning sky slipping off its gray overcoat. A street sweeper inched down Columbia Road buffing the pavement, sending dust and grit flying in all directions. Nik ducked inside the ornate walled-in portico just in time to avoid getting peppered by the debris.

Nik's pre–World War II condominium with its nine-foot ceilings, working fireplace, sunporch, rooftop garden, and a lobby sheathed in burled walnut and floors covered in pearly marble was one of the few indulgences he had allowed himself after *Newshound*'s successful IPO.

Newshound's founder, a wealthy Midwestern technology entrepreneur, had awarded Nik a generous stock option package, in part as compensation to Nik after he was unfairly demoted when he moved to DC. When *Newshound* went public, Nik's net worth increased more than thirtyfold, and for the first time in his life, he stopped worrying whether he had enough money in his checking account to cover both his monthly car payments and rent.

The building, once home to President Dwight and Mamie Eisenhower, was located in what real estate agents referred to as Kalorama Triangle, a wedge of land between Connecticut and Wyoming Avenues and Columbia Road. The location was close enough to the heart of the swanky Kalorama neighborhood and Embassy Row to make it desirable but not so close that residents were overrun by crowds of sightseeing tourists and foreign dignitaries whose black limos prowled the streets both day and night.

Nik was greeted at his door by Gyp, his copper-colored Hungarian vizsla, and a note from the dog walker, who said Gyp did a four-mile walk at six p.m. and was let out again at nine o'clock. While Nik's three-bath, four-bedroom condo was spacious, it was also virtually empty with the exception of a bed in the master bedroom, a couch, coffee table, and a couple of overstuffed chairs in the living room, and a desk and bookshelves in a spare bedroom that he had converted to a study.

Nik had missed dinner and was famished. He opened his refrigerator and fished a Budweiser out of the otherwise empty appliance, dug through the freezer for a Beecher's Mac & Cheese with ham, popped it in the microwave above the stove, and shuffled off to the living room, where he flopped on the worn red-leather couch. He was dead tired after sticking around for Lance St. Mary's press conference, but, for once, he was glad he had.

The prosecutor was known for staging choreographed briefings that revealed little of value and only served to provide fawning media exposure for the attention-seeking attorney. The early-morning event appeared, at first, to be right out of the same playbook.

The press conference was held in a claustrophobic, overheated anteroom off the courthouse's main corridor on the first floor. The air in the room was stale, the drab putty-colored walls cracked and peeling, the worn greenish carpet musty, and the mood of the reporters surly. They had been kept waiting for what felt like hours for St. Mary and his small entourage of assistant prosecuting attorneys and clerks to show up.

The prosecutor stood at the front of the room behind a tabletop lectern, Sheriff Korum and Sam off to one side. St. Mary looked remarkably scrubbed and fresh-faced for three thirty in the morning, his dark-blue pin-striped suit, with the small American flag pinned to his left lapel, unrumpled; his candy-cane-striped tie perfectly knotted; his white shirt crisp; his unnaturally yellowish hair lacquered and glued into place.

St. Mary scanned the gathering. He would have preferred to wait and hold the press conference closer to the morning news shows, but when one of the world's richest individuals is gunned down by his wife in their home, some events are out of your control. He cleared his throat and began reading a prepared statement:

"At around ten forty-five p.m. last evening, Jewel Tate was at home alone preparing for bed when she was assaulted by a masked intruder and fought to defend herself. During what appears to have been a life-and-death struggle, Mrs. Tate managed to retrieve a handgun from a bedside table and fire two shots, killing the attacker, who, it was later discovered, was her husband, Geoffrey Tate, CEO of Yukon. Mrs. Tate fled the house and called 911. A unit from the Northern Virginia County Sheriff's Department was on the scene minutes later. We discovered Geoffrey Tate's body in the master bedroom dressed in black, a nylon stocking over his head, several restraining articles in his pockets that we believe he intended to use to bind and gag his victim. Mrs. Tate was brought in, questioned, and released. At this time, no charges have been filed. We have not yet established a motive for Geoffrey Tate's actions. I am now going to play a portion of the recording from Mrs. Tate's call to the police."

One of St. Mary's young assistants pressed a key on her laptop computer, and long, shuddering sobs poured out of the speakers that were mounted on walls around the room.

———

Uh, huuuh, huuuh, huuuh, huuuuh . . .

This is the nine-one-one dispatcher. Caller, are you in a safe location?

Uh, huuuh, huuuuh . . .

This is the nine-one-one dispatcher. Caller, are you in a safe location?

Uh . . .

Caller, are you there?

I, uh, uh, just shot somebody. He was trying to kill me. Oh my God.

Okay. Try to stay calm, ma'am. Are you in a safe location?

I don't know. I think so. I'm outside my house. In the gardens. He attacked me while I was getting ready for bed. Huuuuuh . . .

Okay, I'm able to geo-locate your cell. A unit is on its way. Stay where you are. It will be there momentarily. Do you have serious injuries?

No, I don't think so. Oh, God, please make them hurry.

They are going as fast as they can, ma'am. What is your name?

What?

Ma'am, what is your name?

Oh, Jewel.

Your full name.

Jewel Tate.

Where do you live, Ms. Tate?

Here. Fernbrook Estate, Chain Bridge Road, McLean.

Okay. Is anyone with you now, Ms. Tate?

Toby.

Okay. What's Toby's last name?

Toby's not a person. He's my dog, a cockapoo. Are they going to be here soon? I'm terrified he's going to come out and try to kill me again.

They are almost there. Who did you shoot?

I don't know. An intruder. A man, I think. His face was covered.

Is anyone else in the house, ma'am?

No.

Where is the gun now?

I must have dropped it upstairs in the bedroom after I shot him. I don't remember.

Hold the line, please, Ms. Tate. Unit 229, there is a wounded perpetrator believed to be in the home, potentially armed. Extent of injuries unknown. The victim is outside. Unarmed. Ms. Tate?

Yes.

The unit's arriving now. You should see them any second. They've turned off their sirens.

Thank God.

You're going to be okay, Ms. Tate.

Here. I'm over here.

Yap, yap, yap, yap.

———

When the recording finished, a dozen hands shot into the air. St. Mary ignored all except the television reporters. "Yes, Lizzy," he said and pointed at Elizabeth Blake, a dishwater blonde from Channel 13 with a weathered face stretched taut as a trampoline from Botox injections. She was the only television reporter that Nik not only admired but feared. She broke more stories than any other reporter in DC, hands down.

"When's the preliminary hearing, Lance?"

"Good question," St. Mary replied, turning to face the camera and flashing two rows of teeth as white and straight as painted stripes on a highway. "We don't have a time line yet, but we'll want to get this in front of the district court as soon as possible. I'd guess a couple weeks, three at the most."

"What about the grand jury?" Blake followed up.

"That will depend on the prelim. Case of this magnitude, stands to reason, but it will be up to the judge to decide that."

St. Mary swiveled his head to the left. "Todd," he said, calling on Todd Lacy, a boozy, florid-faced reporter from Channel 6 with doughy jowls the size and consistency of soft-boiled eggs, who, everyone suspected, was openly auditioning for a spot on St. Mary's communication team when the prosecutor officially announced his run for the Virginia attorney general's office.

"How is Mrs. Tate holding up?" Lacy asked in a patronizing voice, amid a chorus of boos and hisses that erupted from the back of the room.

"I appreciate that question, Todd," St. Mary said, ignoring the grumbling and directing his attention to Channel 6's camerawoman, a pained look on his face. "As you can tell from the nine-one-one call, she is hysterical and distraught. Given that, she is doing as well as can be expected. You can imagine, she's in shock, as we all are."

Peter Glenn, a reporter with the alternative *City Paper,* tired of his raised tattoo-covered arm being ignored, shouted out: "Sheriff Korum, it sounds like the prosecutor is hinting at justifiable homicide. Do you agree?"

"You haven't been called on," St. Mary snapped at Glenn. "Don't feel like you need to—"

"We've made no determination," Korum cut St. Mary off. "We've got a lot of questions, and we have teams at the Tate residence and Yukon's offices conducting thorough investigations." Sam's chin was pinned to her chest, but if the reporters could see her face, they would realize she was smiling. Korum wasn't going to be railroaded by St. Mary.

"I resent that question. Of course, there's more work to do. I never implied that I had made up my mind," St. Mary jumped back in, attempting to reassert control.

But it was too late. The questions came at the prosecutor fast now, like slap shots.

"We understand Jewel Tate has been seen at a local shooting range recently. Can you confirm that, Lance?" one reporter asked.

"Is there any reason to believe Geoff Tate was having an affair?" another chimed in.

"Any truth to the rumors that Yukon is in financial trouble?" asked another.

"Do you see this case impacting your plans to run for the state attorney general's office?" a mousy radio reporter wanted to know.

St. Mary had lost control of the briefing. Worse yet, it was all being broadcast live and would be replayed over and over again in the days to come.

"That's it," he declared, slamming his leather-bound notebook shut, his face as red as a stop sign. "This press conference is over." And with that, he stormed off the stage.

Nik chuckled to himself, recalling the scene, as he stretched out on his couch, fully clothed, an empty bottle of Budweiser resting on his chest; a plate of half-eaten mac 'n' cheese on the coffee table; Gyp curled on the floor, back legs quivering and tail wagging, deep in a dream about chasing squirrels or rabbits in Rock Creek Park.

Nik knew he should already be working the phones, calling

sources, and that he had endless days ahead of him of knocking on doors and running down leads. His eyelids were heavy and he fought to stay awake. He was struggling to recall the last question he heard fired at St. Mary as the man fled from the room, a pack of howling reporters fast on his heels.

Something about a sleigh, he thought as he dozed off, *and a ruler.*

CHAPTER 6

March 22

"You're not supposed to be here," Mia said and slid a bulky pair of headphones off her ears, her dark, unruly hair exploding as if spring-loaded. "I thought today was a diamond day."

Nik dropped dejectedly into a chair next to Mia in *Newshound*'s recording studio. He had just spent several frustrating days and nights pursing tips and leads on the Tate shooting, and he had nothing to show for his work. "It is"—he sighed—"but our game got pushed back until four p.m. because the captain of the other team has to submit a brief to federal court by noon."

Nik was the second baseman and sometimes backup catcher for the Washington Cannons, an adult baseball team for players thirty to forty years old. He had played baseball throughout high school, at the club level in college, and joined adult leagues wherever he could find them post college.

Quick-footed, sure-handed, with a strong throwing arm, Nik was a contact hitter but seldom a long-ball threat. It was his defense that landed him starting spots on rosters.

This was his second season with the Cannons, his first having been cut short by his hospitalization, and he was hoping it would be a bounce-back year for the struggling team after going 9–21 the previous season.

Mia toed a chair over to Nik. "Take a load off. Something smells good."

Nik opened his shoulder bag and retrieved a box of freshly baked Sugar Shack donuts, his go-to breakfast choice most days. He popped the lid and offered it to Mia.

She peered into the box, crinkled her nose, and nabbed a cinnamon roll coated in white gooey frosting as thick as paste. "You're lucky Teo's not here. He absolutely forbids food in the control booth."

"Too bad. He could stand to be a little sweeter. Whatcha doing?" Nik asked and scooted his chair closer to Mia to look at the paperwork in front of her.

"I finally got my hands on hard copies of some of our old Yukon notes and scripts and am trying to freshen them up a bit. Luckily, I still had the taped interviews on a flash drive."

"Let me see," Nik said and picked up the script and began reading. "Yeah, I remember this. It explains how Jewel and Geoff first met online. Pretty juicy stuff."

"Of course you'd say that, since you did most of the work on it."

Nik set the script back on the desk and picked up another batch of papers and began skimming through them while he sipped coffee from a thermos. "Ah, forgot about this one. A snapshot of their wedding day. That's your handiwork. This is good."

"I'm almost done with the first script. I'll send it to you when I'm finished. You should narrate it. I've tentatively titled it 'Heaven Sent.' I'll record the second, which I'm calling 'The Bride Wore White.'"

"I'm good with that. Should be able to get to it later today, tomorrow for sure."

"It took a few days," Mia said, biting into the pastry, "but we finally got over to the storage unit, and I'd swear someone was in there before us. The lights were on and I found some of our files, but I couldn't locate any of the material on Yukon's big contract with the Department of Defense."

"The Bullwhip documents are missing?" Nik said, bewildered. "They gotta be there. The Pentagon released a shitload of material just before we put the project on ice."

"I'm telling you, they're not there. We looked high and low, and I went back and looked again. Nothing."

"It's a big place. I'm sure they're in there somewhere. I'll go over and take a look. Maybe I'll have better luck."

"Mmm, mm, mm. These cinnamon rolls are better than sex. I'd eat 'em every day if they wouldn't make me look like a stuffed penguin," Mia said, noisily sucking a thick coating of frosting off her fingers.

"I'm not quite sure how to respond to that," Nik said.

"I'll give you a hint. You don't."

Nik let it drop and told Mia about his unsuccessful reporting efforts so far.

"What're your next steps?"

"I need to get to Jewel Tate somehow. She'll be surrounded by an army of lawyers and corporate handlers. Then I'm going to try to track down Geoff Tate's sister, Marianne. I also need to get up to speed on Yukon and the Bullwhip project."

"Oh, that reminds me. Yukon put out a press release about the Bullwhip contract," Mia said and slid a copy of it to Nik. He studied it briefly and crammed it into his bag.

Mia started to slip the headset back over her ears when Nik tapped her on the shoulder.

"What is it? I gotta get this done before Teo gets back and chews me out. And don't leave that box of donuts lying around for him to find or for me to devour."

"You ever hear of something called a sleigh ruler?"

"A what?"

"Sleigh ruler."

"No, don't think so," Mia said, shaking her head, her hair vibrating like it was electrified. "What is it?"

"Dunno. Someone asked St. Mary about it as he was being chased from the room."

Mia shrugged, clamped the headset back over her ears, and turned up the volume on the soundboard.

————

The Washington Cannons lost 16–3 to the Washington Supremes, the league champions, in nine innings. The game was tied 3–3 going into the seventh when the Supremes broke it open with an onslaught of offensive firepower aided by four fielding errors, two hit batters, and three walks by the Cannons' pitchers. Going into the bottom of the seventh inning, the score was 14–3.

The game was played at West Potomac Park's field seven, adjacent to the National Mall. If there was a more picturesque setting for a recreational ball field in the continental United States, Nik wasn't aware of it.

Ringed by the Tidal Basin and Potomac River on one side, the Jefferson and Washington Memorials on the other, and hundreds of Japanese cherry trees everywhere covered in billowy clouds of white and pink blossoms, the diamond had a certain Zen quality to it.

Nik's play, however, wasn't nearly as idyllic. His box score read: five at bats, one hit, two walks, two outs, and six men left on base. That last stat was particularly galling. Twice, he came to bat with bases loaded with two outs, and flied out weakly to left field the first time and hit a dribbler back to the pitcher the second, stranding all six runners.

Nik always had a problem hitting off-speed pitching, and

that's all that Chase Hurley, the Supremes' pitcher who also happened to be a *Washington Post* Lifestyle columnist, served up to him.

"Trouble with the curve, Byron?" Hurley taunted when he saw Nik sitting at a table with other ballplayers after the game at Duke's, the default watering hole for pols, journalists, and lobbyists on Capitol Hill. Hurley paused to refill his beer mug from a pitcher on the table, foam mushrooming over the top and down the sides that he loudly slurped up, and then added with a smirk, "Not to mention the changeup, slider, and sinker."

Nik and Hurley weren't only baseball and media rivals, but there was a personal history between the two as well. Hurley had once dated Sam when they were both reporters at a paper in Maryland, and on more than one occasion, Nik had seen him outside Sam's office at the Northern Virginia County Courthouse.

"Heard they clocked your blazing fastball at thirty-two miles an hour today, Ace."

"Fuck you, Byron. You couldn't hit it if I rolled it up there."

"You should try it next time. Might just get there faster."

CHAPTER 7

March 22

Nik slipped out of Duke's and into his car with a bad taste in his mouth, and not just from Hurley's tormenting. His teammates always insisted on ordering pitchers of microbrews after the games. Nik knew other people raved about craft beers and IPAs, but anything besides traditional beer gave him a headache and left a metallic coating on his tongue.

"I'm sure it's just in your head," a doctor once advised him when Nik described the symptoms.

"No, Doc, I'm pretty sure it's in my mouth," Nik responded and never bothered to make another appointment with the guy again.

On the drive to his apartment, Nik replayed the day's game over and over in his head. He was beating himself up about his last at bat when his cell phone flashed and vibrated on the passenger seat with an incoming text. It was from Mia. She had sent him the Yukon material she had promised.

The text read: Let me know what you think of the script. I'm going to record The Bride later today.

Nik momentarily thought about heading to *Newshound*'s studio to work on the podcast but then decided against it. He could record it at Abbey Road in London, and Teo would still find a reason to criticize him. He went to his apartment instead.

When Nik got home, he took Gyp for a quick walk around the block, filled a kettle with water, boiled it, and poured the contents into his French press. He then settled into his study, propping a printout of the script on a reading stand, and laid his iPhone on his desk, screwed in his earbuds, hit Record, and began.

———

Producer's introduction: This is the first installment in the new podcast from *The Front Page*, exploring the life and death of Geoffrey Tate, one of the planet's richest individuals at the time of his passing, and the founder of Yukon Inc., the world's largest artificial intelligence company. The podcast is narrated by reporter Nik Byron.

Heaven Sent

Nik Byron: On the Christian dating app Heaven, one of a handful of online singles communities that Geoff Tate secretly belonged to, he went by the alias Kirk James, a nod to his boyhood idol, Captain Jim Kirk of the starship *Enterprise* and the television series *Star Trek*. Tate was a sci-fi nerd and devoted "Trekkie" and named his first two companies, both spectacular failures that brought him to near ruin, after *Star Trek* episodes.

Socially awkward, reclusive, and legally separated from his wife, Tate wasn't a particularly active Heaven user, but he liked the anonymity the site offered, and he privately got a thrill finding invitations waiting for him from attractive, churchy female members when he visited his page. His profile described James as thirty-nine, outdoorsy, fun-loving, dog owner, fit, and looking for the same. Except for his health, none of it was true.

He had a handful of meetups, always in out-of-the-way dimly lit bars and restaurants, over the course of several months with nearly a half-dozen women he met online, but none of the encounters amounted to anything. When rating him afterward, several of the women described James as "aloof," "plain," "strange," and one even "creepy." No one pegged him as wealthy, relentless, or CEO of Yukon, the world's largest artificial intelligence company, but why would they, since he wore disguises and kept those details secret? And none found him the least bit interesting or attractive.

None, that is, except Jewel Dean, a twenty-five-year-old unemployed yoga instructor and former beauty pageant contestant from Pascagoula, Mississippi.

She would later tell friends, "I knew he was the one for me the minute I laid eyes on him."

If Geoff Tate wasn't who he appeared to be online, neither was Jewel Dean. Her profile described her as a churchgoing Christian, monogamous, nondrinking, straight female, when, in fact, she was a hard partier who had enjoyed multiple sexual partners, occasionally at the same time, according to former roommates. They were both, in the parlance of dating sites, "catfishing," creating false online identities.

After chatting online, the pair met briefly for a drink, liked each other's company, and agreed to meet a couple days later for coffee at a Starbucks in Dupont Circle. On a chilly Saturday morning, they spent the better part of two hours getting acquainted. In the past, most of Kirk James's dates, if you could call them that, were concluded in less than thirty minutes.

Jewel confided in friends that she flirted openly with James that morning and told him he had kind eyes. They made plans to meet the next day, and within a few weeks, they were actively texting each other and exchanging selfies, each one more revealing and risqué than the previous.

One, in particular, seemed to have bewitched James.

It was of Jewel in a yellow string bikini, the strap of her left shoulder sliding teasingly down her arm, revealing a plump, deeply tanned breast, her Brazilian-waxed body glistening like a '67 Corvette in a classic car show.

James saved the picture to the home screen on his cell phone, which, to the casual observer, was hidden behind a forest of icons and apps, but he knew it was there, and colleagues would later report that they often caught him marveling at the photo. Occasionally, in meetings and in other inappropriate settings, he'd flash the picture at stunned managers. It got to the point that his own HR department had to ask him to refrain from showing off the picture on company property.

It was only a matter of days after receiving the candid portrait that James divulged his true identity to Jewel. She acted surprised, but, truth be told, she had pegged him as wealthy from their first meeting, she'd told friends.

Later, when asked how they met, the couple would joke that their encounter was a match made in heaven.

CHAPTER 8

March 22

Teo sulked in the airless booth, sipping harsh yerba maté from a gourd with a metal straw, his dark eyes hooded, when Mia's voice rang out from below in the recording studio: "How'd that sound?"

"What?" Teo said, snapping out of his reverie. "Eh, not half bad. I've heard worse."

"I swear, Teo, you could make a child cry on Christmas morning."

"It's a gift."

"More like a curse," Mia said, collecting her notes before heading up to the production booth, where she found Patrick "Mo" Morgan, *Newshound*'s deputy editor, waiting for her.

Mo, an avid weight lifter with biceps the size of cannonballs, had managed to wedge his massive frame into a small plastic armchair, various body parts spilling out over the sides and back of the sagging piece of furniture. From a distance, he looked like a giant boulder that had rolled down a mountainside and settled in the middle of the tiny glassed-in room.

"I thought it was pretty good," Mo complimented Mia.

"Gee, thanks, Mo."

"But what the fuck do I know about podcasts?" he added.

Mia ignored that and said, "So, what brings you down to the dungeon?"

"I wanted to tell you in person that your request for additional staff on the Yukon story is a no-go. Whetstone turned it down and said, I quote, 'Tell 'em to go piss up a rope and leave the reporting to real journalists.'"

"Class act," Mia said.

Richard Whetstone, *Newshound*'s Washington, DC, chief editor, resented Mia after she had interceded to salvage Nik's career when he fired Byron. Mo inherited Nik's old newsroom position, and ever since, he'd been saddled with carrying out Whetstone's unpopular decrees.

Most of the *Newshound* staff derisively referred to the barely five-foot-seven Whetstone as Li'l Dick behind his back and were in open rebellion after he sacked Nik. Whetstone only managed to tamp down the insurrection by appointing Mo, Nik's protégé, deputy editor.

"I appreciate you giving me the bad news firsthand, Mo," Mia said, "but it still sucks."

"I'll try to assist where I can, Mia, but I can't promise anything. Li'l Dick is sure to be watching like a hawk," Mo said, backing out of the room and ramming a speaker with a thigh the size of a side of beef, sending the equipment crashing to the floor. Mo bent over to set it right and flipped over a small table.

"Leave it. Just leave it before you trash the place," Teo beseeched, coming out of his seat and throwing up his hands. "I'll take care of it."

"Sorry 'bout that," Mo said with a sheepish grin, his pale Irish complexion turning pinkish, and exited the door.

"Fuckin' wildebeest," Teo complained after Mo had closed the door and was well out of earshot.

"So, what's missing from the podcast, Teo?"

"Plenty. We need to wrap music around it, drop in sound bites from the sources, tack on an intro and exit. Then we'll see. We might have something." He sniffed, still clearly upset by the abrupt change to the podcast team's mission.

"You work your magic on the sound, and I'll listen to it again to see if there're areas I can improve," Mia said.

Teo hoisted the speaker from the floor and reset it on its stand. "Looks like we've been orphaned by the sixth floor."

"Mm-hmm. Appears that way. Not the first time," Mia said and fitted the headset back over her ears and pressed Play to listen to the podcast one more time.

Producer's introduction: This is the second installment of *The Front Page* podcast exploring the life and death of Geoffrey Tate and his company, Yukon Inc. The podcast is narrated by *Newshound* host Mia Landry.

The Bride Wore White

Mia Landry: Not long after Geoffrey Tate and Jewel Dean met online, they were married on a cloudless, eighty-degree day just off the coast of Saint Barthélemy in the French Virgin Islands. The brief ceremony was conducted by Captain Thomas Kidd aboard the *SeaStar*, Tate's $400 million, eight-deck mega-yacht with its two heliports and onboard submarine, and was attended by a small handful of guests, including Geoffrey Tate's personal bodyguard, Shaka Wulf, the best man; and Jewel Dean's childhood friend, Noelle Clooney, the maid of honor; in addition to the ship's crew.

Pictures from the sunset wedding show the bride wore a deck-length white veil over a white thong bathing suit. Her maid of honor donned a coral-colored string bikini, and the groom and best man were dressed in tropical swim trunks, no shirts. The captain was attired in dress whites. The bride held a small bouquet in one hand and a flute of champagne in the other.

Notably absent from the guest list was Marianne Tate, Geoff Tate's sole sibling, only living relative, personal confidante, and executive vice president at Yukon, Geoff Tate's artificial intelligence company. That was by design. Jewel insisted she not be invited, and Geoffrey Tate, not wanting to upset his young bride on her wedding day, agreed.

The feeling was mutual. Marianne was suspicious of Jewel Dean from the beginning, opposed her brother's relationship with the young Mississippian when it became public, and refused to have anything to do with her.

Over Marianne's objections, Geoff Tate installed Jewel as Yukon's newly created director of employee wellness shortly after the marriage, ensconced her in an office on the executive floor, provided her a company limo and driver, a $375,000 salary plus annual bonus, and allowed her to attend executive retreats and board of director sessions. Before long, Jewel was making lavish presentations at the company's mandatory all-hands meetings and inserted herself into key hiring and firing decisions.

At the office, she wore Lululemon yoga pants, form-fitting tops, and Jimmy Choo Impala shoes and Hawaii sneakers. Wherever she went, she was accompanied by Toby, her cockapoo. Once, when asked by an employee at a new-worker orientation what she did at Yukon, Jewel replied: "Anything I damn well please." When queried about what she knew about artificial intelligence, she cupped her hands under her breasts and lifted them up and said, "You don't think these are real, do you?"

The exchange quickly became company lore, and Marianne Tate would tell acquaintances shortly thereafter that Jewel would be the death of her brother and Yukon.

CHAPTER 9

April 2

The click-clack cadence of Jewel's leather soles slapping polished mahogany floors rolled down the corridor ahead of her like a marching band, reaching Maggie Stone's ears well before she did.

Moments later, Rose, Maggie's ancient legal assistant, confirmed her arrival. Rose rapped softly on Maggie's half-open door and announced, "She's here. Shall I put her in the executive conference room?"

"Yes, thank you, Rose, and ask her if she would like anything."

Rose stood glued in the doorway, a troubled look on her pinched face. She cleared her phlegmy throat. "Ahem."

"What is it, Rose?"

"She asked if we have any vodka," Rose said, pursing dry, wrinkled lips, tightly cinching the threadbare blue cardigan draped across her bony shoulders. Feeling a need to clarify, she added, "To drink."

Maggie looked up from the yellow legal pad she had been

filling with notes and turned away from Rose to gaze out the window of her tenth-floor K Street office.

It was a far grander office than the one she had abandoned at the Department of Justice, but now, instead of admiring the Capitol's famous dome framed perfectly through her window when she looked out, she stared at a nondescript concrete office tower painted a dingy battleship gray with smoked-in windows. She wondered what the people in the office building did. Lobbyists, she suspected.

The new setting wasn't nearly as inspiring as the old, but she consoled herself with the $1.2 million salary, end-of-year partnership bonus, and unlimited interior design allowance the firm offered.

Maggie furnished her office with two downy-white leather couches from Italy, a Baker Paris writing desk, and a Steelcase worktable with four matching padded side chairs for colleague conferences. A series of colorful abstract paintings by a female artist she had discovered at a small gallery in Charleston, South Carolina, hung above the couches. Total redecorating invoice: $202,425.

Turning back to Rose, she said, "What we're going to charge her, she can have whatever she likes."

"But it's not even eleven a.m.," Rose harrumphed, "on a Tuesday morning." Rose's hair was swept up in a bun and sat perched on the top of her head like a silvery bird's nest, a pencil sticking out at an odd angle. Agitated, she removed the pencil and started gnawing on the eraser.

"Rose, she's a recent widow and probably just needs a small drink to settle her nerves, is all."

"She requested a double. 'On the rocks.'"

"Do we have any vodka in the office?"

"Yes. Left over from the holiday party. I've locked it away."

"Well, please get it and serve her a drink, and inform her I am on my way."

Rose stepped back into the corridor, shaking her ossified head, tsk-tsking loudly.

———————

When Maggie entered the room, Jewel Tate was sipping her drink, a rust-colored Birkin bag at her elbow, in her lap a small white dog with yellow polka-dot bows tied to its ears and a bobtail tuft, dyed pink, sprouting from its forehead like a unicorn's horn. The air in the room was heavy with a raw, earthy odor that seemed to seep from Jewel's pores, causing Maggie's nose to twitch involuntarily.

Jewel's face was partially obscured by oversized black sunglasses, the boxy lenses concealing her cheekbones and the lower part of her eyebrows. She was wearing a scooped-neck black top, jade necklace, a gray scarf around her head and knotted firmly under her chin. A short black leather jacket hung from the back of her chair, and she was dressed in a skin-tight black skirt and black stockings. When she stood to greet Maggie, Jewel listed slightly sideways on her high heels, and the dog spilled from her lap and scampered away.

"Thank you for coming today, Mrs. Tate, and I'm sorry it's not under better circumstances." The glassed-in conference room was outfitted with an eighteen-foot distressed Douglas fir table, two dozen chairs tucked underneath, and, scattered along the walls, a big-screen TV at one end, a credenza with assorted bottles of sparkling water and canisters of herbal tea at the other.

"C'mon 'ere now. Don't be a brat for Mommy," Jewel said, bending low under the table to look for the dog. Jewel scooped up the pet and plopped back in the chair.

"What's your dog's name?" Maggie asked, even though she knew the answer.

"Toby. You have a dog?"

"No," Maggie replied, pulling out a chair, "but from time to time, I pet sit my ex-husband's dog, Gyp, a vizsla. He's not altogether there."

"Your ex?"

"No, the dog. But now that I think about it, the comment could apply equally to both."

Jewel unknotted her scarf, releasing an avalanche of wavy golden ringlets that piled up on her shoulders like sand dunes. She pushed her sunglasses up to the top of her head, revealing a bronzed face as round as a pie tin, button nose, and wide-set coffee-colored eyes. Jewel had an untamed quality about her, and she wasn't dressed as much as she was decorated.

"You remarry?" Jewel asked.

"No, I haven't. Not yet, anyway."

"What's your ex do?"

"He's a reporter."

"Here in Washington?"

"Yes."

"What's his name?"

"Nik Byron."

"I know that name. He's been calling me and snooping around. Doesn't he know I'm grieving?"

"Sounds like Nik. I'd advise you not to talk to the press."

"You seeing anyone?"

"Off and on," Maggie replied hesitantly.

"Good, 'cause I prefer to be represented by a woman who knows a thing or two about men. Know what I mean?"

Maggie nodded.

"But that's not why I want you to represent me," Jewel said, stroking the dog. "I want you to represent me because I hear you're a real badass."

A thin smile creased Maggie's lips. She was a grade A badass, and everyone knew it.

When she was an attorney for the Department of Justice,

Maggie was one of her office's top criminal litigators, successfully prosecuting Wall Street financiers, Mexican drug kingpins, crooked pharmaceutical executives, and corrupt politicians. It was why Woodward, Stallworth, and Moran, as well as a half-dozen other prestigious DC law firms, had aggressively bid on her services when she left the US attorney's office for private practice.

"I met with the attorneys Yukon's lawyers suggested. They're a bunch of old farts who were more interested in looking at my tits than they were in hearing what happened."

"Well, let's talk about that, Mrs. Tate."

"Jewel."

"Of course, Jewel. You're certain you want to retain my services?"

"That's why I'm here, ain't it? Can I get a refill?" Jewel said, lifting her empty glass and shaking it at Maggie, the ice rattling around inside like dice.

Maggie punched the intercom button on the desk phone. "Rose, can you please bring Mrs. Tate another drink."

Silence.

"Rose?"

"Yes," Rose answered peevishly. "Perhaps Mrs. Tate would like something different. Have you offered her coffee or water?"

Maggie gave Jewel a quizzical tilt of the head.

Jewel scrunched up her nose. "Hmmm, just have her bring the bottle and a cup of ice."

"You get that, Rose?"

"I heard."

Moments later, Rose entered the conference room and set the bottle down on the table just out of Jewel's reach. "Anything else?"

"I'm good," Jewel said and leaned forward for the bottle and refilled her glass with vodka.

After Rose departed, Maggie said, "I think it would be

beneficial if I explained how the legal process is likely to unfold." Several of the firm's junior male associates were routinely parading past the conference room, straining to steal glances at Jewel. Maggie pressed a button under the table and lowered a set of dark shades.

"Don't you want to hear what happened?" Jewel asked. "It was awful."

"Of course I do, and we'll get to that, but just so you know, I've read the sheriff's report, watched the press conference, and listened to the 911 recording. I think it important that you be fully aware of what awaits you. It could be a three-ring circus, and I predict it's going to move at warp speed since the prosecutor is a publicity hound and wants to keep his face plastered all over the media."

"If you say so. You're the lawyer. I met that sheriff. He was nice enough, but that detective of his is mean."

Jewel dug into her handbag and came out with an expensive-looking paddle brush and a small bag of kibble for Toby, who greedily gobbled up the treats from her outstretched hand.

"In criminal cases in Virginia, there are potentially three initial stages to the judicial process—a preliminary hearing to determine if the case will be referred to the grand jury, the grand jury proceedings, and, depending on if the grand jury finds evidence of a crime, a trial." Maggie paused. "You follow me so far?"

"I think so," Jewel said, brushing the dog and teasing out small knots of hair on its coat. It struck Maggie that Toby and Jewel shared similar facial features—dark eyes, pug nose, round face.

"Good. The district court judge could theoretically dismiss the case after evidence is presented in the preliminary hearing, but that's not likely to happen here. The prosecutor could also decide to bypass the preliminary hearing and go directly to the grand jury. I'm almost certain your case will be forwarded to the grand jury, one way or the other. If there is a preliminary hearing, it will be short and pro forma."

"Why's that?" Jewel pouted. "The prosecutor all but said I acted in self-defense on TV."

"Sort of, but I wouldn't put much stock in what Lance St. Mary said. If there is a preliminary hearing, the district court judge won't want the responsibility of dismissing such a high-profile case and be second-guessed the rest of her career. No, her safe bet is to kick it to the grand jury as fast as possible."

"'Tain't faaar," Jewel said, her Southern accent thickening from the vodka, and poured herself another drink.

Maggie then explained to Jewel that the grand jury meets in secret and that she, as Jewel's attorney, would not be allowed to attend or participate in the process. Jewel could opt to plead the Fifth Amendment against self-incrimination and refuse to answer the prosecutor's questions.

"Either way, we need to prepare as if this case is going to trial. There's a chance you could be charged with second-degree murder," Maggie said and stopped to let that sink in for a minute.

Maggie was surprised when that news didn't elicit any response from Jewel, who continued to brush the sleeping Toby. Maggie continued. "If that happens, I believe the facts are on our side, Jewel."

"No foolin', and I got the choke marks to prove it." Jewel lifted her chin to expose faded purplish bruises on her neck that were masked under a thin layer of makeup.

Maggie winced, but she couldn't help but wonder how it was the bruises were still visible two weeks after the attack. She had seen the pictures the sheriff's office had taken the night of the incident. They were graphic and disturbing but not incontrovertible evidence that Geoff Tate had tried to kill his wife. The prosecutor could argue that Geoff Tate was trying to defend himself from Jewel when she shot and killed him.

"There's an old saying when it comes to grand juries," Maggie explained.

"What's that?"

"That a grand jury would indict a ham sandwich if that's what you wanted."

Jewel only shrugged.

Maggie gently steered the conversation in another direction. "There are a few things I'd like to clear up, if I could."

Jewel slid her sunglasses off her head and perched them on the tip of her nose, peering over the tops at Maggie. "G'on."

"Was your husband a violent man?"

"No, he hardly ever raised his voice, let alone laid a hand on me. Sometimes, he'd curse and yell at Toby." Jewel leaned in and kissed the top of the dog's head.

"Do you think he was having an affair?"

"No way. I would have smelled it on him."

"And you, were you seeing anyone?"

"How can you ask that? I loved Geoff."

"I had to ask," Maggie said and noted on her yellow pad that Jewel dodged the question. She didn't pursue it.

"Okay, then, why do you think he attacked you?"

Jewel nudged the glasses back up on the bridge of her nose with her left index finger. Maggie noticed she was still wearing her wedding band and engagement ring. The ring was fitted with a diamond as big as a lug nut and as dazzling as a sparkler.

"I can't for the life of me figure it out," Jewel said and started quietly weeping.

Maggie stood and retrieved a box of tissues from the credenza and handed it to Jewel before sitting back down.

"No idea whatsoever?"

"None," she said. "Unless it has to do with that damn prenup."

"What about the prenup?"

Jewel gulped the last of the vodka in her glass. She was crying noticeably now, shoulders heaving, voice quivering, tears spilling out from under the sunglasses, two rivulets of clear liquid cascading from her nose. The dog woke and started licking her face. Jewel took a moment to compose herself, dry her eyes, and blow her nose.

"I heard Geoff on the phone discussing it with his attorney," she said, whimpering. "He was upset."

Jewel shifted the dog in her lap and fingered an ice cube from the glass and put it in her mouth. "When I asked him about it," she said, crunching the ice loudly between her teeth, "he pretended like he didn't know what I was talking about. I could tell he was lying."

"Did you hear anything else?"

"Yes. He screamed at his attorney, called him incompetent. Said it was malpractice. Said it could ruin him, interfere with his plans."

Maggie stiffened, reached across the table, and punched the intercom button on the phone again.

"Rose?"

"We're all out of vodka," came the tart reply.

"Cancel all my appointments for today and order lunch for two. Then bring a big pot of strong coffee to the conference room ASAP."

Turning back to Jewel, Maggie said, "Let's start over. From the beginning, shall we?"

CHAPTER 10

April 4

Samantha Whyte surveyed the sun-covered hillside with the lush grass and unobstructed view and decided that's where she'd set up camp. She spread out a blanket, set down a small cooler filled with iced bottles of sparkling water and veggie snacks, and withdrew a book from her handbag. She could have chosen to sit anywhere she liked in the small baseball stadium since there were fewer than two dozen fans in attendance. She recognized several of the spectators, new girlfriends mostly and young wives with toddlers. She caught Nik's eye and waved. He tipped his cap in return.

Sam felt guilty taking time off work in the middle of an ongoing criminal investigation to watch an intermural baseball game, but she told herself that she and Nik had seen so little of each other the past month that she was willing to make the sacrifice. If she had to work until midnight again, so be it. It's not like that would be a new experience for her.

That, and she was desperately horny.

She tried to recall the last time she and Nik had slept

together. *Seems like ages ago. A month? Could it be that long?* She was pretty sure it was at Nik's condo because she left her favorite red blazer with the gold crest embroidered on the breast pocket hanging on the bedpost when she tiptoed out well before dawn.

Sam stretched out on the blanket, uncorked a bottle of water, slipped on a pair of tortoiseshell sunglasses, opened her book, and started reading.

She noticed one of the young mothers pushing a baby stroller up the pathway that led to the top of the hill where she was sunning herself. The woman stopped about three-quarters of the way up and turned around to look back over the field and catch her breath. Sam didn't know her name, but she had seen her at other games with one of the players. Nik told Sam that the woman's husband, the team's shortstop, had played baseball in college for an Ivy League school. *Cornell,* Sam thought Nik had said, *or maybe it was Dartmouth.* She wasn't certain.

Nik contended shortstops were generally the best athletes on the team, followed by center fielders. Second basemen, like Nik, were farther down the pecking order. "But way, way above pitchers," he assured her.

Sam could hear the baby start to cry, and the woman set a foot brake on the stroller and lifted the infant out. The child was wrapped in a robin's-egg-blue blanket, and Sam guessed it was a boy. The mother started humming softly and swaying side to side and then started singing a song—"I Think about a Lullaby." Sam recognized the tune. It was one of Merle Haggard's.

The woman placed the baby's head on her shoulder and began to dance in small circles as she continued to sing. The mother lifted her eyes and saw Sam and smiled. Sam waved and smiled back. "You have a beautiful baby."

"Thank you," the woman mouthed.

And just as quickly as the baby had started crying, he stopped. The woman placed him in the stroller, turned back down the hill, and made her way toward the grandstand.

Sam watched her and sighed. She wanted children of her own, wanted a family, actually, but the tide was starting to run against her. Even if she got married this year or early the next, it'd still be months before she could conceive, if then. It had taken more than two years for some of her friends to get pregnant, and that was when they were still in their late twenties. She was now thirty-four, staring down thirty-five. When Nik moved in with her to convalesce after he was released from the hospital earlier in the year, they talked casually about marriage and children, but he hadn't mentioned anything since he'd moved out and into his new condo.

She pushed the thought out of her mind and returned to her book.

"That was touching," a voice from behind her said.

Sam spun around. It was Chase Hurley, a columnist for the *Washington Post* who Sam had once had a fling with.

"How long have you been standing there, Chase?" Sam demanded, rattled.

"Long enough."

"That's rude, sneaking up on people like that. What are you doing here?"

"Can't you tell?" he said, and pointed to his uniform. He was wearing stirrup baseball pants, maroon tube socks, and a Washington Supremes jersey. "We have the field next. I pitch for the Supremes. Nik didn't mention it?"

"No, why would he?" she lied.

Chase dropped his baseball bag on the ground, metal bats clanging inside, and lowered himself onto the blanket. Sam was wearing one of Nik's blue oxford cloth shirts knotted at the waist, exposing a stomach as flat as an iron; white shorts that accentuated her long legs; and sandals. It was a sexy outfit without being too revealing, but now she wished she had dressed in jeans, a hoodie, and sneakers.

"Make yourself comfortable," she said and scooted away.

"I dropped by your office a time or two to invite you to lunch when I've been by the courthouse," Chase said, "but you were never around. Pity."

"What's a feature writer doing at the courthouse?"

"Maybe I got an angle on a hot Yukon story."

"Ha, that's a laugh. You're a good writer, Chase, but you wouldn't know a news story if it landed on your head."

Chase chose to ignore the slight. "I heard you cooing at that baby," he said. "You know, I always said we'd have beautiful children if we procreated."

"Puh-leze." Sam snorted and inched even farther away. Chase had a high, wide forehead covered in wavy chestnut hair as dense as steel wool; half-moon dimples that flared when he smiled; and a squared-off chin. There was no question he was attractive, Sam had to admit.

The pair had dated for several months while both worked for a newspaper in Annapolis before Sam landed a job at the *Post* in DC. When the *Post* also hired Chase nine months later, they agreed it would be best for their careers not to rekindle the relationship.

"Come on, you have to admit there's still a little spark there."

"As if." Sam laughed. "No. No spark, not even a cinder."

Chase gazed down the hill at the game underway, a blade of grass stuck between his teeth, and sipped on the Red Bull he was holding.

When Sam had arrived, the game was already in the bottom of the seventh inning, with the Washington Cannons trailing 4–1 against the Potomac Admirals. It was now the ninth inning and the score was tied 4–4. Nik was standing on third base, and she had no idea how he'd gotten there.

The batter hit a sharp line drive to right field, and Nik tagged up before breaking for home. The right fielder made a one-hop pinpoint throw to the catcher, who had moved a half step down the first-base line. In one fluid motion, the catcher caught the ball in his gloved left hand and whipped violently around to make a tag as Nik went into a headfirst slide, arms fully extended. The catcher's mitt caught Nik on the side of the head, and the force of the blow knocked Nik out of the base path and slightly behind home plate.

Sam scrambled to her feet, her hand at her mouth.

"Aw, he'll be okay," Chase said.

When Nik didn't move, Sam raced down the hill. By the time she got to the backstop, Nik's teammates had crowded around him. He still hadn't moved.

———

"How's that feel?"

Nik grimaced. "Ouch! Cold."

Sam had wrapped ice cubes in a washcloth and was holding it against a doorknob-size knot on the left side of Nik's temple.

"I shouldn't have listened to you. We really should have gone to the emergency room."

Nik insisted he was only stunned by the catcher's tag, and not knocked unconscious as his teammates had told Sam.

"It's nothing. I've had worse headaches from hangovers."

"You could have a concussion."

Nik was in Sam's bed under the covers, propped up against the headboard, feet elevated on pillows, his uniform lying in a clump on the floor next to the bed, a tall glass of ice water with a straw on the nightstand. Sam dimmed the lights just in case Nik was concussed.

"Was that Chase Hurley I saw talking to you on the hill-side?" Nik asked, taking a sip of the water.

"Yeah, that was Chase, all right. Get this, he told me he had a lead on the Yukon story he was pursuing, if you can believe that."

"Well, that might explain why I've seen him hanging around the courthouse lately. Either that, or he's stalking you."

"Ha."

"Kinda looked like you guys were flirting?"

Sam dismissed it with an eye roll. "Chase may have been flirting, but I can promise you he didn't even make it to first base."

Nik laughed, and a sharp pain shot through his skull. He pinched his eyes shut to make the throbbing go away. He reached out and pulled Sam closer. "You know, I scored that run before the catcher made the tag."

"Yeah. So?"

"It was the winning run," Nik said and started to untie Sam's knotted shirttails.

"Lucky you."

Nik opened the front of Sam's shirt and ran his hands up her sides and slid them under her bra.

"I feel lucky," he said. "You know what else?"

"No. What?" Sam said, slipping lower on the bed, her face now over Nik's chest, hair dangling in his eyes.

"I got the feeling I'm going to score again."

"You might," Sam said as she pulled the covers back and straddled Nik's hips. "You just might."

CHAPTER 11

April 8

Nik racked his memory, trying to place the woman who was now seated alongside his *Newshound* desk furiously kneading her lap with what looked like a pair of chopsticks. From across the office, he judged her to be in her fifties, fit, a tassel of silver shot through a head of otherwise rich blue-black hair, leopard-spotted reading glasses perched on the end of her nose, her head bowed.

Nik approached unnoticed and hovered for an instant. "May I help you?"

The woman didn't look up but instead raised her index finger and said, "One minute." Nik waited patiently. "There," she said finally. "That was a particularly delicate pattern, and if I dropped a stitch, I'd have to go back and do the row all over again." She held up what appeared to be one-quarter of a cream-colored cable-knit sweater. "Knitting's yoga for the fingers," she said.

"Nice" was all he could think to say.

The woman tucked the unfinished sweater and knitting

needles into a bag at her feet and removed the reading glasses and stuffed them in a leather pouch before looking up at Nik. "Well, that's that," she said.

"Indeed," Nik said, a perplexed look on his face, wondering, *Did a street person slip past security again?*

"You're not much of an early bird, are you, Mr. Byron?" she said. "I've been here since eight o'clock. That's a nasty-looking bruise you have there."

Nik reached up reflexively and touched the bump on the side of his head from the collision on the baseball diamond. It still ached. Then it struck him. He remembered her.

"Mrs. Tate?"

"Marianne," she said with a warm smile. "Mrs. Tate is my late brother's widow, the no-good trailer-park slut."

"I've been looking everywhere for you, Marianne," Nik said, shoving the clutter on his desk to one side and clearing a space to sit down.

"That's what I understand. Well, here I am," she said and extended a hand toward Nik. He took it. She had a strong grip, fingers like tiny clamps. *Must be from the knitting,* he figured.

Across town, Yukon's ten directors—seven men, three women—were locked in a marathon board meeting. It had been weeks since Geoff Tate's death, and they still hadn't named his successor. Several directors favored installing a temporary figurehead, but there was no consensus on who that person should be, and besides, after stabilizing the company's stock price, they wanted to project strength, not more uncertainty.

Around and around they went, for hours on end, until finally, Rupert Olen, an activist investor and the largest shareholder in Yukon outside of Geoff Tate, put forth his candidate.

He had been waiting for just the right moment to spring his man on an exhausted board.

Olen had known Geoff Tate from Yukon's early days when the company consisted of Tate, a whiteboard, six baby-faced developers, a refrigerator with a sawed-off broomstick for a handle, and Sasha, an alley cat that had adopted the misfits. They all fit snugly in the garage of Tate's ranch-style rented house in Northeast DC.

Later, when Yukon was teetering on bankruptcy, Olen's firm stepped in and wired a $10 million payment to Tate in exchange for 20 percent ownership in Yukon. It was extortion, but Tate had run out of money and options and had no choice but to accept the terms of the deal. Tate had resented Olen ever since and tried to buy him out over the years, but Olen hung on and refused to sell.

"I believe the answer to our problem has been staring us in the face all along, but we've been too shook up by Geoff's death to see it," Olen said as he walked to the front of the ballroom in the Willard hotel, a giant crystal chandelier suspended overhead. Hotel staff had partitioned off the space to make it seem more intimate, but it was still cavernous, and Olen's voice echoed around the room.

The bleary-eyed directors were exhausted and desperate for a viable solution.

"I think we can all agree that Yukon needs, above all else, to preserve our relationship with the Department of Defense and protect the five-hundred-billion-dollar Bullwhip contract." Olen scanned the gathering, and all heads bobbed approvingly.

"And there is only one individual," Olen said, thumping his forefinger on the table for emphasis, "who was there every step of the way at Geoff's side negotiating the deal with the Pentagon, knows all the ins and outs, the important players. In fact, you could argue it was his deal as much as it was Geoff's."

Heads stopped nodding, brows furrowed, several directors coughed nervously.

"You can't seriously be suggesting . . ."

"Yes, Sheldon, I am. I nominate Dwayne Mack to replace Geoff as CEO."

"But he's a goddamned slimy lobbyist," Sheldon erupted, eyes flaring, the pate of his bald head reddening.

"Yes, that's true, but he's *our* goddamned slimy lobbyist," Olen countered. "And to state the obvious, none of that seemed to bother you or anyone else at this table when we hired him, Sheldon."

"I'll admit, he did a good job greasing the palms of politicians and military brass. But the man's like something you stepped in and want to scrape off the bottom of your shoe, not the face of a global company like Yukon."

"Fact is, Sheldon, without him, Yukon might just as well kiss the Bullwhip contract goodbye. Is that what you want?"

Pandemonium ensued. Three hours later, the board voted, 6–4, to install Dwayne Mack as the new CEO.

Mack was in Blue Sky Consulting's DC office strategizing with the Saudi Arabian ambassador to the United States about how to acquire Pentagon technology for his country when Rupert Olen called. Mack asked to be excused and walked into an adjoining office, his sneakers squeaking on the floor, to take the call.

"It's done," Olen told him. "I held up my end of the bargain. Now the rest is up to you."

Mack returned to his office and checked his watch. It was nearly six p.m. He had selected the Paul Newman–inspired chronometer that morning, his favorite and most expensive Rolex. "Please inform His Royal Highness for me that I feel confident we'll be able to reach an accommodation on the Bullwhip technology," he said. "And now, if you'll excuse me, something has come up that needs my immediate attention."

CHAPTER 12

April 19

Nik's iPhone alarm buzzed at five thirty a.m., an ungodly hour for an avowed night owl, but he wanted to make sure he was at the Northern Virginia County Courthouse in plenty of time when doors opened at seven. He was tipped to a possible major development in the Geoffrey Tate case, and he assumed it had to do with the grand jury, which had been meeting secretly ever since the district court, as expected, promptly referred the case for consideration.

Nik hurriedly showered, brushed his teeth, towel-dried his hair and combed it in place with his fingers. He pulled on a pair of charcoal-gray slacks, an oxford cloth blue button-down shirt, black loafers, and checked the weather app on his phone. It predicted showers, and he made a mental note to grab his Brooks Brothers raincoat from the hall closet on the way out the door. Gyp raised his head from his spot on the floor of Nik's bedroom and watched him with sorrowful eyes.

"Don't give me that look, Gyp. Your favorite dog walker, Sara, will be here at seven, and I promise you and I will go for a long run when I get back home later this afternoon. I need it as much, if not more, than you do," Nik said, patting his stomach. "No more Sugar Shack donuts for me until I drop five pounds." He grabbed his satchel off the kitchen counter, paused at the closet to get the rain jacket, and then dashed out the door.

He arrived at the Northern Virginia County Courthouse in a light drizzle and was surprised, but not shocked, to find Elizabeth Blake from Channel 13 already there, a large cup of coffee tucked in the crook of her elbow and pressed against her body, a notebook in one hand, her phone held pinned to her ear by her shoulder as she scribbled notes on the pad. Wind whipped her hair across her face.

Blake clicked off the call when she saw Nik approaching, stuffed the phone in the pocket of her fawn-colored trench coat, and brushed the strands of hair away from her eyes.

"Lizzy." Nik nodded as he drew near. "You look a little beat. Must not have gotten much sleep after closing the bars down last night, huh?"

"Nik," Lizzy scoffed. "I *thought* that was your nasally Midwestern whine I heard coming from the back of the room at St. Mary's press conference the night of the shooting."

He scratched his chin and looked around. The Channel 13 van with its telescoping satellite mast was parked out front next to a homeless guy asleep on a sidewalk grate, a sheet of plastic for a cover. The Metro's Orange Line ran below the courthouse, and warm air funneled out the opening. The historic courthouse had had its façade scrubbed recently, and its red bricks looked as new as the day they were first laid in 1799.

"Don't worry, Lizzy, I'm not going to scoop you."

"In your dreams, paperboy."

"I'm working on a long-range reporting assignment," Nik assured her.

"Oh, that's right, I forgot. You're Mr. Podcast now. How fucking precious. I downloaded one of your shows the other night when I had a touch of insomnia. After about two minutes of listening to you drone on, it was lights out. Better than Ambien, and I can guarantee you're nowhere near as addicting."

"Sends a chill down my leg just to know we were in the same bed together, Lizzy. I can die a happy man now."

Lizzy's phone burred in her coat pocket. Other members of the media and spectators started to stagger up the courthouse steps to get a place in the queue. Nik saw Mo's car parked down the street and scanned the crowd for his *Newshound* colleague but didn't see him. It seemed every news organization in town had gotten the same "anonymous tip" Nik had received.

Lizzy answered her phone and held her finger up to Nik. "I've got to take this," she said, "but remember I'm first in line when I get back." She walked off barking at the caller, demanding a story she was working on be offered to the national network for its evening news program.

Nik continued to search the crowd for Mo with no luck before turning back toward the entrance. He noticed movement inside the courthouse and pressed his nose to the window of the door to see what was happening. It was dark inside, but he could make out a small knot of people standing between two large marble columns that framed the entryway to the courtrooms.

He cupped his hands on either side of his face to block the glare from the outside, and after a moment, his eyes adjusted to the light imbalance and he was able to identify some members of the small group.

Northern Virginia County Commonwealth Attorney Lance St. Mary, with his back to Nik, was standing in the middle of a semicircle, gesturing and forcefully chopping his hand into his open palm to drive home some point he was trying to make. On his far left was Sheriff Korum; next to him, Sam; then a man and woman Nik didn't recognize; and finally, on

St. Mary's far right, Maggie, Nik's ex-wife and Jewel Tate's attorney.

When St. Mary finished talking, he pivoted 180 degrees and was now facing Nik. He placed one hand on his hip and ran his other hand through his hair, an exasperated look on his face. St. Mary took several deep breaths before turning back to face his audience once again.

The unidentified woman picked up the conversation and jabbed her finger at St. Mary, who crossed his arms in front of his chest and rocked back on his heels as if he were about to pitch over backward. This went on for several minutes before St. Mary stormed off. When he returned, the whole group walked down the hallway and filed through a door marked "Judge's Chambers."

"Whaddya looking at?" It was Lizzy.

"Nothing," Nik said, startled.

"Didn't look like nothing," she said and shouldered her way past Nik to peer through the window. She stared into a vacant corridor. "You're up to something, Byron. I know it."

"No, I'm not," Nik defended himself. "I was just looking to see if the judge's bailiff might let us in early," he said, pointing and shrugging at the doors. "I don't see anything stirring, so I guess not."

"Uh-huh."

"That coffee looks good," Nik said, motioning to the Starbucks cup Lizzy was holding. "I need to get a mug before I nod off. Now, it's your turn to hold my place in line until I get back."

Lizzy watched Nik disappear around the corner. He pulled out his phone and texted Sam: I'm outside the courthouse. What the hell is going on in there?

Seconds later, he got a reply. Hang on. I may have something for you to listen to shortly. Stand by. No guarantees.

As was his habit, Northern Virginia County Circuit Court Judge Roy Pickett was in his chambers at six thirty when there was a knock on the door. He opened it to find Lance St. Mary and a small band of followers on the other side.

"Lance." The judge acknowledged the attorney, craning his neck to see who else he knew. He nodded to Sheriff Korum and Sam. He didn't recognize the others.

"Judge, I'm sorry to bother you, but we need to clear the air about a matter, and it can't wait," Lance said.

"I'm assuming this is related to the Tate case."

"It is."

The judge waved them through and took a seat behind his desk while the others found chairs. Sheriff Korum and Sam remained standing in the back.

The judge's chambers were homey, with pictures of grandkids arranged on his desk, large black-and-white photos of the Virginia landscape on the walls, a small fly-tying table in one corner with a vise and magnifying glass clamped to its side, pheasant feathers and colorful yarn scattered everywhere. Directly behind his desk on shelves crammed with case studies and law books was an eight-by-ten portrait of a striking dark-haired woman in her twenties. It was Judge Pickett's late wife, Sophia.

"Lance, perhaps you should introduce the folks I don't know," the judge suggested after they had settled.

"Right. This is Margaret Stone, counsel for Jewel Tate," St. Mary said, gesturing to Maggie.

"I'm familiar with your work, Ms. Stone," Pickett said with an approving nod, "from your days in the US attorney's office, but weren't you Margaret Byron then?"

"Thank you, Judge. Stone's my maiden name, and it's Maggie."

The judge acknowledged Maggie with a nod.

"This lady and gentleman," St. Mary continued and gestured to the pair seated to his right, "are from the attorney general's office in Richmond, and, in my opinion, they have wasted a trip up here for absolutely no good reason."

"Hold on a second, Lance," the judge intoned and held up his hand. "Before we go any further, I'd like to point out there is no court reporter present and this is an informal proceeding, not in camera. And if everyone is comfortable with that, I'll hear what you have to say and see where it goes from there."

"Yes, Your Honor," they replied in unison.

"Okay, continue," the judge said.

"Judge, if I may. My name is Lisa Cranwell, state's chief deputy attorney general, and this is my associate Kenneth Larsen, assistant attorney general." Larsen dipped his head to acknowledge the judge. "We're here today because of statute 19.2-155 of the Code of Virginia Law," Cranwell continued.

"Ah, I see," Judge Pickett said, adjusting a patch he wore over his left eye, the result of an old college rugby injury. He reached across his desk and picked up an antique gold pocket watch. He fingered a hasp on the side of the watch, releasing its casing. He set the dials, wound the stem, and closed the case before replacing it back on his desk. "A wedding gift from my wife," he explained.

Cranwell was sturdily built and wore her auburn hair cropped close with bangs. She was dressed in a tan pantsuit and pumps, and her delivery was precise. Larsen was gangly with bony wrists and an Adam's apple the size of an avocado pit. His dark hair was long and stringy and hung limply over his shirt collar and the tops of his ears. The shoulders of his gray suit were covered in dandruff flakes as if seasoned with salt.

"As you no doubt are aware, Judge Pickett, that section speaks to the disqualification of commonwealth attorneys in the event of a conflict of interest . . ."

St. Mary bolted out of his chair. "I need to stop them right there, Judge."

". . . or a perceived conflict of interest."

"I have not acknowledged a conflict in this case because there isn't one."

"And therein lies the problem, Your Honor." It was Larsen now, tag-teaming with Cranwell, his Adam's apple yo-yoing up and down. "Whether Commonwealth Attorney St. Mary acknowledges it or not, he has both a real and a perceived conflict."

St. Mary paced around the office and, when Larsen paused momentarily, fired back, "Geoff Tate made a piddling donation to my campaign one time. I barely knew the man, and, besides, he's dead now. This is politics, all this is, Judge. Their boss sent them up here to torpedo me because she knows the case is going to receive national attention and she doesn't want me getting any exposure before next fall's election."

"Your Honor," Larsen continued, "it has only recently come to the attention of our office that the prosecutor was involved in the potential cover-up of an alleged crime involving Mrs. Tate."

"Now just one minute," St. Mary protested.

"Please sit down, Lance," Judge Pickett said in a grandfatherly tone. "So this explains why all the press is out front this morning. I wondered. Proceed."

"It appears that some time back, Mrs. Tate left a young man who had overdosed on drugs at the emergency room of a local hospital and then drove away. The young man later died."

"It was her car, Judge. We could never establish she was driving it. She claimed it was stolen."

"The campaign donation Mr. St. Mary just now referenced came after his office declined to press charges," Larsen said.

Judge Pickett looked at Sheriff Korum with arched eyebrows. "It was before I was in office, Your Honor."

"Ms. Stone, were you aware of this, and do you have an opinion on the matter?"

"Yes, Your Honor, my client informed me about the incident and swore she had no involvement, and I strenuously object to the assistant attorney general's characterization of Mrs. Tate and a cover-up. As to your second point, no, I do not have an opinion on whether the prosecutor should recuse himself."

"Very sensible of you," the judge said with a wink from his one good eye. "Depending on the outcome of this case, it might offer you an issue to latch onto in appeal if need be."

Maggie cocked her head to one side, a thin smile on her lips, but did not reply.

Judge Pickett sat quietly, smoothing his mustache with the thumb and forefinger of his left hand. "For what it's worth, Lance," he said after a pause, "I happen to agree with you."

"Thank you, Your Honor. That's a relief to know."

"It does seem political, but there's no denying you do have a perceived conflict. Perceptions matter, and I'm afraid it would be negligent of the court to look the other way, especially in a case with this much notoriety. If you refuse to recuse yourself, you will leave me no option but to disqualify you if an official petition is placed before the court, which seems likely."

"But, Judge," St. Mary pleaded, "this is the biggest case of my career."

"Your choice, Counselor."

St. Mary sank silently into his chair.

"Don't take it so hard, son," the judge said. "Look at it this way. There's a mob of reporters standing outside this courthouse this very moment dying to hear something. You can call a press conference and say you have major news to announce. They will be hanging on your every word, and you can claim that you're stepping aside for the good of the commonwealth."

St. Mary brightened. "Hey, that's not a bad idea."

Judge Pickett continued. "As for the rest of you, I'm not

going to impose a gag order. You are free to describe this discussion as you see fit, if asked. It's going to take a couple days to sort everything out and name the prosecutor's replacement. Lance, in the meantime, one of your assistants, as long as they played no role in the prior investigation, will handle the grand jury inquiry as it pertains to this case."

"Your Honor, the state's attorney general believes our office is in the best position to step in and take over the case, no matter the eventual disposition. She asked that I convey that message to you."

"No doubt she does, and please thank the madam attorney general for her offer. I will take it under advisement."

The group shuffled out of the judge's chambers and into the hallway. Sam ducked into the ladies' restroom and texted Nik. Just sent you a file.

Got it, Nik replied.

Not entirely comfortable with this and don't expect a repeat, Sam hurriedly typed out.

I appreciate it, Nik responded. He had turned the corner back to the courthouse when he saw St. Mary emerge from the front doors, the crowd out front surging toward him.

CHAPTER 13

April 19

Nik spied Mo forcing his way through the crowd like a runaway Humvee, jostling reporters and onlookers as he rammed them aside with beefy shoulders. Mo was nearly at the front of the pack when Nik caught his eye and motioned him with a flick of the head back toward the street. Mo reversed course, but this time, the onlookers saw him coming, and a seam opened before him in the throng.

"I swear, you're a one-man wrecking crew, Mo," Nik greeted him when he broke from the mob. Mo responded with an embarrassed grin. For all his physical attributes, Mo was a gentle giant and much more likely to break into an Irish ballad than he was to break someone's jaw.

Nik and Mo had first met in the newsroom of the *Michigan Daily*, the University of Michigan's campus newspaper. They were part of a small group of all-too-serious journalism students who bonded over beer, coeds, jazz, baseball, and late-night discussions about their favorite authors.

Mo came from working-class stock on the East Coast,

and his old man was an itinerant bricklayer, abusive husband, chain-smoker, and hard drinker; the latter two habits Mo inherited and, without much success, tried to kick about every six months after a bad bender. It was just serendipity that Mo and Nik had wound up working for the same news organization, but Nik was glad they had.

Mo had wispy sandy hair, fair skin, and pockets of bird's-eye-size freckles scattered over his forehead, arms, and hands. Although he sang in a haunting high tenor, he had a raspy speaking voice, made only more pronounced by the Lucky Strikes and Irish whiskey he favored. After he was elevated to deputy editor, Mo turned in his ratty Gold's Gym T-shirts, old Converse high-tops, and cutoffs for khakis, short-sleeve dress shirts, ill-fitting sport coats, and traditional Hush Puppies he found at a thrift shop.

"This better be important, I'm missing the press conference, brah," Mo said, glancing back over his shoulder at Lance St. Mary, who was standing at the top of the courthouse steps, the crowd squeezed in below him.

"Forget St. Mary's press conference. It's all bullshit. He's telling them he's stepping away from the Tate case in the name of justice when, in fact, he's been tossed from the case by Judge Pickett. I got the whole conversation recorded, and I'm going to give it to you, Mo."

"Fucking A."

"But you can't quote from the recording, only paraphrase, and you have to attribute it to anonymous sources. Understood?"

"Sure. You gonna tell me how you got it?"

"Nope."

"Li'l Dick might want to know."

"Screw him."

"Heh-heh. My pleasure."

"But you gotta do a favor for me in return."

"Shoulda figured."

"I need you to get into Whetstone's office."

"Why, what for?"

"To look for clues to the whereabouts of the Bullwhip files. They've gone missing, and since Whetstone has been trying to sabotage my career ever since I arrived, he's my number-one suspect."

"I dunno, Nik."

"Look, I'm not asking you to remove anything. Just have a look around," Nik said.

Mo stared down at the tops of his shoes. "You like Hush Puppies?"

"What?"

"My shoes," Mo said and stuck out a foot.

"Don't really have a feeling about them one way or the other, Mo, but what's that got to do with anything?"

"Whetstone told me when I got promoted to deputy editor I had to start dressing better. Said I looked like a slob."

"Well, now you look like a high school gym teacher."

"Yeah, that's about right," Mo agreed, then paused for a moment. "What the fuck, I'll do it."

CHAPTER 14

April 26

When Nik finally looked up at the clock in his home office, it was well past midnight. He had worked late into the evening putting the finishing touches on the first draft of a script for the podcast with Marianne Tate. He knew it was far from perfect, but he wanted to get it recorded while the conversation was still relatively fresh in his mind. He promised Mia she'd have it when she arrived at work the next morning, now just a little over four hours away. As usual, Nik slaved over the story, worrying about every word, sentence, and paragraph.

Nik's dithering with the writing wasn't the only thing that slowed his progress. He stopped work frequently to check Signal, the encryption app that allowed sources to share information with him anonymously.

Mo had told Nik he planned to access Dick Whetstone's *Newshound* office that evening when he was scheduled to work the graveyard shift. It was now two a.m. and there was still no word from Mo. It worried Nik that he hadn't heard from him, and he was unsure what to make of the radio silence. *Was Mo too busy with work and not able to carry out his plan? Did he get caught? Were there other people in the office, making an attempt too risky?*

Nik had intentionally neglected to tell Mia about his arrangement with Mo. He figured that gave Mia an out in case Whetstone uncovered the plan, and he knew she would never have endorsed it in the first place. Truthfully, he now had his own reservations. It was selfish of him to place Mo's career in jeopardy, and not for the first time.

Nik checked Signal once more before he began to record the podcast. Still no word.

He poured himself a fresh cup of coffee, placed a printout of the script on his reading stand, cued the audio on his laptop, checked Gyp to make sure the dog was sleeping soundly, put in his earbuds, hit Record on his iPhone, and began narrating.

Producer's introduction: This is the third installment of *The Front Page* podcast exploring the life and death of Geoffrey Tate and Yukon Inc., the company he founded. The podcast is narrated by *Newshound* reporter Nik Byron. His guest is Geoffrey Tate's sister, Marianne Tate.

Fool's Gold

Nik Byron: The late Geoffrey Tate, a three-time loser in the entrepreneurial lottery, was determined to make one last stab at creating a successful company. He decided to name his new venture Yukon after the vast northwest territory where the Klondike Gold Rush started in 1896 and ended, more or less, three years later in 1899.

Today, most people assume Tate chose that name

because he had a premonition that he would stake his claim in artificial intelligence, strike it rich, and become one of the world's wealthiest individuals.

In fact, the exact opposite is true.

A history buff with advanced degrees in engineering and computer science, Tate was aware that of the hundred thousand miners who streamed into Canada and Alaska in search of their fortunes in the goldfields, only a small handful actually became wealthy. Conditions being so harsh and inhospitable, the vast majority of prospectors quit and turned back for home, financially and emotionally impoverished, even before sinking a single pickax blade into the frozen tundra or panning for ingots in Bonanza Creek where gold was first discovered.

Tate's previous companies were all based on a singular goal: to create a multibillion-dollar enterprise. Now penniless and in deep debt, Tate had told family and friends Yukon would be his last start-up and he was determined not to repeat the same mistakes. His mission this time, he proclaimed, would be to create a company that would have a positive and lasting impact on the world, not be the next unicorn.

Through it all, there was one person Geoff Tate consistently turned to for guidance and counseling during most of his adult life and business career—his sole sibling, Marianne Tate.

Born eight years apart, the brother and sister were not close growing up. Marianne left for Swarthmore when Geoff was only ten years old, and, when she graduated four years later with a degree in English literature, she didn't share her brother's geeky passions for technology, science fiction, and space exploration. But that her brother was a prodigy, she never doubted. He finished high school at age fifteen and enrolled in college four months later.

Two years after that, he graduated and went to work getting dual master's degrees in engineering and computer science from Johns Hopkins University.

Over the years, Marianne Tate lent her sibling moral, emotional, and financial support when she could afford it and watched in agony as his business dreams, one after another, crashed and burned. But she never stopped believing in her little brother, and when he turned to her after another business failure, she told him to follow his heart, not his head. He heeded the advice.

Marianne Tate: By the time Geoff started Yukon, he was done chasing fame and fortune. I told him it was fool's gold and he saw where that had gotten him. He was determined to improve people's lives, and that's why Yukon's first product was a machine-learning wheelchair for quadriplegics.

Nik Byron: Marianne Tate joined Yukon as an unofficial adviser to the company three years after it was up and running, but slowly, over time, took on more and more responsibilities as the business grew and her brother was pulled in different directions. Her official title was changed to executive vice president, but for all intents and purposes, she functioned as chief of staff, overseeing her brother's schedule, shielding him from distractions, and keeping ambitious corporate climbers at bay.

Outside the office, it was a different story altogether. Try as she might, she could not protect her brother from his own wayward carnal impulses, especially after his separation and subsequent divorce. Socially awkward, Geoff Tate always had a hard time connecting with members of the opposite sex, and Marianne knew he spent a great deal of time and money in the back rooms of Las Vegas casinos where female escorts were discreetly delivered by the train-car load to high rollers. She would also come to discover that her brother had an extensive and indiscriminate secret online life and was active on multiple internet dating sites.

Marianne Tate: He's what my mother called a troubled soul.

Nik Byron: In its formative years, Yukon rolled out a succession of well-received products—an AI project that predicted and plotted dangerous virus outbreaks before they happened; a program that could identify and catalogue giraffes and other endangered species by their markings, to thwart poachers; and machine-learning applications to help developing nations avoid dire food shortages.

But critical acclaim did not necessarily translate into profits, and once again, Tate found himself facing financial ruin, only to be bailed out at the last minute by deep-pocketed investors who insisted the company turn its attention to working with the US government, primarily the military, NASA, and the national clandestine operations and their massive budgets.

Marianne Tate: What's ironic is my brother always considered himself a true patriot and was happy to use Yukon's technology to keep our country's servicemen and -women out of harm's way. No one had to twist his arm, but he never thought it would lead to the tremendous financial success that it did. Not in his wildest dreams.

Nik Byron: Yukon's work for the government initially focused primarily on reconnaissance hardware, code-breaking capabilities, and force-multiplier operations, but as time went on, it gravitated toward big-budget programs: un-crewed mini attack submarines; drone gunships; heavy armor equipment for combat zones; and the granddaddy of all projects, Bullwhip, the Pentagon's $500 billion unmanned and autonomous flying war armada. Marianne

Tate contends her brother began to have second thoughts about Yukon's work for the military.

Marianne Tate: Unfortunately, over time, my brother and I grew apart, our relationship strained by his marriage to Jewel. I never quite understood it, but he was spellbound by her, and he pushed me out of his life. One of the last conversations I had with him before he died, though, he hinted at two things that I believe may have had a direct bearing on what happened to him. He said he planned to reinsert himself in the day-to-day operations of Yukon and sever the company's ties to the military after the first phase of the Bullwhip project was completed. He didn't explain why he had a change of heart. He just said he had found out some things about the project that made him uneasy. The other thing he said is that he had come to a major decision about his personal wealth. Again, he wasn't specific, but he told me he planned to make an announcement after some legal issues got resolved with his estate and that it was going to be big news.

Nik Byron: When pressed, Marianne Tate concedes she lacks any documentation to back up either claim, and she freely admits she doesn't know what happened on the night Geoff Tate was shot and killed by his wife.

Marianne Tate: I don't know, but this I can promise you: I intend to find out, or die trying.

———

Nik hit the Pause button on the recording just as his cell phone started chirping loudly. It was Mo. Finally. He had sent Nik a message on the Signal app: Didn't find what you're looking for exactly, but found hints where it might be stashed. Don't contact me. I'll be in touch.

It was three forty-five a.m. Nik knew the podcast needed

additional material and polishing, but he was too tired to continue. He pushed the Send button and shot the "Fool's Gold" audio file to Mia's inbox. He stumbled to his bedroom, where he found Gyp sprawled across the covers. He shoved the dog over and collapsed diagonally on the mattress, facedown, feet dangling over the side. He fell asleep instantly, Gyp's head resting on his shoulder.

CHAPTER 15

April 30

Nik spotted his ex-wife as Maggie emerged from the Farragut North Metro station and turned onto K Street, heading toward her office at a fast clip. At first, he almost didn't recognize her. She had changed her hair color yet again. Over the years, Maggie's hairstyle and color fluctuated with the seasons. She predominantly favored hues that ran the color spectrum from light charcoal to brown sugar. She was now sporting an ash-blonde bob.

It was her walk that gave her away. Maggie was slightly pigeon-toed, and she had a distinctive gait that Nik would recognize anywhere. He fell in behind her and followed her for half a block before pulling alongside.

"Hi, Maggs," he said, matching her pace while looking straight ahead.

Maggie had earbuds in and didn't hear Nik, but when he continued abreast of her, she looked over and stopped in midstride.

"Nik?" she said, a confused look on her face, and removed the earbuds.

"Like what you've done with your hair, Maggs. Makes you look glamorous."

"What are you doing here?"

"Pure coincidence. I just happened to be passing by when I saw you, so I thought I'd say hello," Nik said, and gave her a quick smile.

"That's bullshit, Nik."

"That stings, Maggs. Honest, I wanted to say hello," he said.

"Okay, you've said it."

"But since we're here, there is something I've been meaning to talk to you about."

"Thought so. What is it?" Maggie said and looked at the smartwatch she wore on her left wrist. It was eight forty-five a.m. "And hurry up. I have a very important meeting and I can't afford to be late."

"This will only take a minute. Promise."

"Uh-huh."

"It's about Jewel Tate."

"Are you out of your fucking mind? I can't talk to you about my client. This conversation is over," she said and started walking away.

Nik hustled to catch up with her. "I think you'll want to hear this."

She stopped, and both she and Nik glanced around. The street was crowded with office employees, lobbyists, and bureaucrats scurrying to work or early-morning meetings and, nearly as Nik could tell, all lost in their own thoughts, headphones and earbuds walling off the outside world, and not paying one bit of attention to the pair.

Maggie stared up at Nik and bit down on the inside of her lip, nostrils flaring, her dark eyes boring into him like ice picks.

Nik was familiar with the look. He had seen it often during the course of their stormy marriage.

"I don't have time for this now, Nik. Meet me at the Old Ebbitt at seven thirty, and maybe, just maybe, I'll listen to what you have to say. If I'm not there, don't wait for me. It means I'm not coming."

———

Nik had been at the Old Ebbitt for nearly half an hour, and there was still no sign of Maggie. The after-work crowd had thinned out, and Nik was certain he hadn't missed her. He called and left her a voice mail and sent her two text messages.

Nik's first text read, I'm in Grant's Bar, referring to the bar named after the late Civil War general and US president, one of four bars in the restaurant. His second message said, I've ordered a dozen and a half Blue Point oysters. They were the Old Ebbitt's specialty and one of Maggie's favorite dishes. He received no reply to either message. Maybe she wasn't coming after all.

The inside of the clubby bar was illuminated by scores of leaded stained-glass lamps, revealing a forest of dark walnut-paneled walls and a sea of dining tables sheathed in white linen. A famous picture of Grant taken after a devastating defeat at Cold Harbor hung behind the bar. In the portrait, Grant leans against a tree, dressed in his Union blues, a broad-brimmed hat tilted back on his head, a grim, anxious look on his face.

Nik turned his back to the bar and doused an oyster in Tabasco sauce and slurped it down, keeping one eye on the door. When he spun back around in his chair to order another beer, Maggie was seated on the stool next to him. She had come in the back entrance.

"I thought I said not to wait for me if I wasn't here by

seven thirty," she commented by way of a greeting. She had changed out of her office attire and was wearing jeans, a white polo shirt, expensive-looking blue neoprene sneakers, her hair tucked behind her ears. She was carrying a leather satchel and had a gold blazer draped over her arm.

"You did, but you've never been on time in your life. Why should tonight be any different?" Nik patted his lips dry with a cloth napkin and leaned in and gave her a peck on the cheek. She smelled of soap and her skin was flushed. Nik could see small beads of perspiration on her upper lip.

"You been working out?"

"Peloton class."

"Ah. I've got friends taking those. Seems awful intense."

"That's the whole idea, Nik."

Of the two, Maggie was always the more competitive and ambitious, whereas Nik tended to move at a more casual pace, letting fate, more or less, dictate his life's journey. Having opposing personalities might not have doomed their marriage from the beginning, but it certainly hadn't helped.

Nik slid the iced platter of oysters toward Maggie and caught the bartender's eye. She ordered an IPA while Nik asked for another Budweiser.

"How'd your important meeting go this morning?" he asked.

"Not good, but I can't talk about it."

"Okay. I'll take it that means it had to do with the Tate case."

Maggie replied with a noncommittal shrug. "So, how you doing, Nik?" she asked, squeezing a lemon slice over an oyster before scooping it out of its shell with a miniature trident.

It'd been months since the two had last seen each other, Maggie having announced that she was removing herself from Nik's life—and Sam's hair—after Nik had fully recovered from the broken ribs, punctured lung, and busted teeth he had received at the hands of a mercenary.

"Good. Sometimes, if I lie wrong, I get a sharp stab of pain in my chest and have a little trouble breathing, but other than that, no complaints."

"Glad to hear it, and Gyp?"

"Hasn't changed."

"He's not the only one. Look at you. Still refusing to shave, and you dress in the same style of khakis, oxford button-down shirts, wire-rimmed glasses, and scuffed-up loafers that you wore when we first met," Maggie said. "And it's not like you can't afford to update your wardrobe after the windfall from the *Newshound* IPO. I assume you're still cutting your own hair?"

"I only did that a couple times," Nik protested. Maggie looked at him skeptically. "Awright, maybe more than once."

"So, what is it you wanted to talk to me about, Nik?"

"It's something Marianne Tate told me."

"Oh, please, not her. You do realize she hates my client and thinks Jewel stole her brother away from her. She had a weird mommy complex with her kid brother. Did she tell you they used to sleep in the same bedroom together?"

"What of it? Lot of kids do that."

"When they were adults."

"She told me Geoff temporarily moved into her studio apartment, if that's what you're referring to, when he had financial troubles. I wouldn't call that sleeping in the same bedroom."

"Believe what you want." Maggie sniffed. "So, what did she tell you?"

"That Jewel Tate's not to be trusted."

"What's that supposed to mean?"

"Do you know Jewel was married before?"

"Yes, just long enough to have a cup of coffee. Her husband left her after a couple of months and went into hiding. Apparently he had some outstanding warrants for identity theft that he failed to mention to her before they tied the knot."

"He disappeared, Maggs. They've never been able to find him."

"He didn't want to be found, Nik. That's the whole point of hiding. He fled to Mexico with another woman. The marriage was annulled."

"Well, that's the story everyone was told, but Marianne hired two private security agencies, one here and one in Mexico, to track him down. They were never able to find a trace of him. No digital fingerprints, no ATM or credit card transactions, no work history, and no sign of the woman he allegedly left with, either."

"The woman's unstable. Marianne mentioned she was institutionalized, did she?"

"She told me she had a nervous breakdown years ago, yes."

"And what do you make of her sewing circle?"

"It's not a sewing circle. It's a knitting group. She started it with women she met while she was in therapy. But hang on. This isn't about Marianne. It's about Jewel. It's about you. Jewel killed one husband, that's a fact, and her first husband vanished without a trace."

"She was defending herself. It's called justifiable homicide. She was just lucky to get to the gun before Geoff did."

"I'm just telling you, you need to be careful."

"And I'm just telling you, you need to stop listening to the kooky sister. And while you're at it, you might want to give me a little credit. I successfully prosecuted drug lords and mob bosses on behalf of the US government. I think I can handle whatever Jewel Tate throws at me."

Nik tossed up his hands in surrender. "Have it your way, Maggs. Maybe you're right. Maybe I am overreacting," he said and paused to take a swig of his beer.

"You've always been a worrier, Nik. It's in your DNA,"

Maggie said and speared another oyster. "I appreciate your concern, though. I really do. It's sweet. And since you're trying to watch out for me, however misguided, I'm going to give you a bit of advice as well." She stopped and sprinkled hot sauce on the oyster before gulping it down.

"Oh, yeah. What might that be?"

"Get to bed early tonight."

"Why? I look tired to you?"

"Not particularly, but I just got word before coming over here that the grand jury is going to report to Judge Pickett first thing in the morning. You might want to be there."

CHAPTER 16

May 1

The Northern Virginia County Grand Jury handed up a one-count indictment of second-degree murder against Jewel Tate, and Circuit Court Judge Roy Pickett wasted no time fast-tracking the trial despite objections from Special Prosecutor and Virginia Chief Deputy Attorney General Lisa Cranwell. After entering a plea of not guilty on behalf of her client, Maggie argued that the case should move as swiftly as possible to resolution in order for her client to clear her name and establish control of her late husband's estate and business affairs, which, she contended, were in limbo because of the investigation and impending trial.

The courtroom's gallery was packed with media and spectators, every seat filled, the walls lined with onlookers standing shoulder to shoulder. Sheriff Korum, Sam, and Lance St. Mary, as well as various other county employees, looked down from the second-floor balcony. Nik was seated in the front row, directly behind the prosecutor's table.

"Geoff Tate was Yukon's largest shareholder, and Jewel

Tate, as his widow, has a fiduciary responsibility to the company, its shareholders, and thousands of employees to remove this cloud of uncertainty that hangs over her head as expeditiously as possible," Maggie told the court.

Cranwell pushed back. "With all due respect, Your Honor, Mrs. Tate is a one-time yoga instructor with no formal business experience running a multinational company. It is our understanding that her title at Yukon is director of employee wellness, a job her late husband reportedly created so she'd have something to do at the office. It's hardly what one would call an essential position. In addition, the firm has appointed a new CEO who is capable of operating the company. There is no urgency here. We propose commencing trial three months from now."

"My client," Maggie rebutted, "has not gone into Yukon's offices since the tragedy, Judge, and she believes, with good reason, that every day that passes without her presence, the more the business suffers."

Judge Pickett adjusted the patch over his eye and peered down skeptically at both lawyers from his perch.

Turning to Maggie, he said, "That's debatable, but I will afford you the benefit of the doubt."

"Thank you, Judge."

"As for you, Ms. Cranwell, if I didn't know better, I'd say you were stalling in hopes the trial drags out until the fall when the election campaign for the attorney general's office is in full swing so your boss can get free publicity. No, there'll be no politics in my courtroom. You've had plenty of time to marshal evidence during the grand jury phase. Be prepared to go to trial in four weeks."

"But, Your Honor—"

"Four weeks, Ms. Cranwell, and please don't make me regret my decision to appoint you special prosecutor against my better judgment."

"Of course, Your Honor," Cranwell said and slouched back in her chair, leaning her head in to talk to her co-counsel, the bony-limbed Kenneth Larsen.

Maggie then made one additional request. "My client wishes to wave a jury trial and instead asks to be tried by Your Honor."

Judge Pickett looked over where Jewel was seated. She was dressed in a slim lavender skirt suit, belted at the waist with a slit that ran from her knee to midthigh on her left leg. Her hair was up, a string of jade around her neck, cheeks rouged, a fresh coat of fuchsia gloss on her lips. Maggie had suggested Jewel wear a loose-fitting below-the-knee dark-navy skirt and matching top, no jewelry, light makeup.

"And your client is comfortable with that?" Judge Pickett asked, eyebrows raised. "It's highly unusual. In fact, I can't recall it ever happening in a murder trial before. As I'm sure you are aware, most criminal defendants ask to be tried by a jury of their peers, if for no other reason than a single holdout juror can force a mistrial."

"I've explained all that to my client, Your Honor. She understands the trade-offs that are involved."

Judge Pickett flashed back to Jewel. She winked. "Well," he said, sounding flustered, "it will speed matters if we don't have to impanel a jury."

Jewel had instructed Maggie beforehand about her decision. "I'm not having a bunch of jealous old hags sittin' in judgment of my life. I'll take my chances with the judge. I've seen the way he looks at me."

When they exited the courthouse, Maggie and Jewel were swarmed by a herd of reporters. Elizabeth Blake from Channel 13 shoved a microphone in Jewel's face.

"Did you intentionally kill your husband?" Lizzy shouted.

Maggie swatted the microphone away and steered her client into the back seat of a waiting limo and walked around to

the other side. Jewel buzzed down the window, cocked her finger at Lizzy, and motioned the reporter over. Lizzy bent down
and leaned her head into the car, and when she did, Jewel said,
"Wouldn't you like to know, you fucking cunt."

CHAPTER 17

May 1

Mo waited until most of the media had cleared out of the courthouse before approaching Nik and Mia, who were tucked away in a small alcove off the main corridor, arguing, fragments of their heated words ricocheting off the marble walls and floors.

He was stepping cautiously toward the pair when Mia saw him and rounded on him.

"And you," she seethed, jabbing an accusatory finger at Mo, eyes snapping, cheeks as fiery as a sunset, "should be ashamed of yourself. Breaking into Whetstone's office like a thief in the night. Are you brain dead?"

Mo started to defend himself, but Mia interrupted him. "I should report the both of you. If this gets out, they will shut down the podcasts division and fire all of us. We'll all be painted with the same brush."

"I'll take the blame and make sure everyone knows it was my idea, if that happens," Nik offered.

"And what about him?" she said, cocking her head toward

Mo. "You didn't stick a gun in his back and march him into Whetstone's office. He did it voluntarily."

"If you'd just give me a minute to explain, Mia," Nik pleaded.

"Please, don't insult my intelligence. I know what breaking and entering is. It's a felony."

Mo dropped his head and looked at the floor and shuffled his feet. "It wasn't technically a B and E. As deputy editor, I have the authority to access all areas of the newsroom."

"Not to ransack your boss's office, you don't."

Mo shrugged his massive shoulders. It was a matter of interpretation. "I know where the missing Bullwhip files are," he said finally. Mia and Nik, who had gone back to arguing, both twisted around and studied him. "And these," Mo said and dug in his pocket and pulled out a ring with a half-dozen bronze keys attached, "will get us into the building where they're stored. We won't be breaking any laws. It's all perfectly legal, I swear."

———

It took the trio a couple hours to move the material out of a musty office in Northeast DC and into a spare bedroom in Nik's apartment. In all, there were a dozen security boxes crammed full of Pentagon documents related to the Bullwhip contract. In addition to the Pentagon files, there were also several boxes from various congressional oversight committees that held public hearings on the request for proposal and the final letting of the contract.

Mo and Mia helped Nik stack and arrange the boxes by date before leaving. They all agreed to meet for lunch in a few days when their schedules allowed and try to piece together how the material had ended up in the abandoned warehouse and what Whetstone's role was in the affair.

Nik estimated each box held roughly 300 documents, or

somewhere in the neighborhood of 3,300 pages total. Nik loved nothing more than to spend countless hours poring over records in search of a story, but he had never faced a challenge of this enormity. The chore of tackling the columns of boxes stacked against the wall was beyond daunting. It was paralyzing.

He cut the seal on the first box and was stunned to discover a typed note with a zip drive taped to the inside cover. The note read, "Brass insisted we stall and drown you in worthless documents. I pulled rank and sent you everything I could lay my hands on, including confidential memos you did not request and digital files. The Bullwhip contract reeks to high heaven. Good luck." It was signed "A Patriot."

Somewhere in the bowels of the Pentagon there was a whistleblower who was trying to point him in the right direction. Problem was, the Pentagon, at 3,700,000 square feet, is the world's largest office building, with more than twenty-five thousand workers. It would be nearly impossible to find the person if they didn't want to be found, and who knew if that person still worked there since the files had been sitting unopened for months.

Nik ripped the tops off the other boxes also to find zip drives affixed to the inside of all the lids. The digitalized material would help streamline the job of cataloguing the documents. He'd ask *Newshound*'s developers to write a computer program he could use to build a searchable database.

Still, Nik's task would be made far easier if he knew what he was looking for, but he didn't.

What he hoped was that somewhere buried in the documents were clues that would point to Geoff Tate's change of heart about the Bullwhip project and possibly even hints about his untimely death.

The only way to find out was to review every file. Nik reached in the first box and pulled a file folder, flipped it open, and began reading.

CHAPTER 18

May 6

Mia texted Nik and told him she was running late for their lunch date with Mo and would he go ahead and order for her. She wanted the chestnut soup, a half BLT, iced tea, and, if they had it on the menu, the lemon tart. She said she'd be there as soon as she wrapped up a meeting with Teo.

Nik had hoped Mia would be delayed. He wanted to have a private conversation with Mo to apologize for involving him in his scheme in the first place and, just in case Whetstone discovered his office had been rifled, to get their story straight. He knew Mo couldn't afford to lose his job, and Nik wanted to do everything possible to make sure that didn't happen.

Months earlier, Mo had agreed to be a kidney donor for their longtime colleague Frank Rath, who, like Mo and Mia, had followed Nik to DC to work in *Newshound*'s Washington office when everyone still thought Nik was going to be running the show. However, no sooner had Nik set foot in the nation's capital than he learned the dispiriting news that he had been demoted to deputy editor and Whetstone would become chief editor.

The abrupt career detour unmoored Nik emotionally and mentally, while his three transplanted colleagues seemed to not only effortlessly adjust to the unfamiliar surroundings but actually thrive. Mia shined as host of *Dateline Washington*, a new podcast covering the singles scene in DC; Frank, a veteran journalist who had covered wars, coups, and presidential campaigns, quickly established himself as the dean of the newsroom; Mo was widely admired for his unmatched professional and personal work ethic.

Nik drifted aimlessly for several months after the demotion, and it was only after he latched onto the OmniSoft story that he eventually found his footing once again. He and his three officemates had pooled their talents to pursue the story and formed a tight-knit working partnership.

But Frank's illness and subsequent medical leave, along with Nik's own long absences from *Newshound* during his rehab, had altered the group dynamic. With Frank out of the picture, the cement that bound the group together was weakening, and Nik blamed himself for not doing more to sustain their bond as they were pulled in different directions professionally and personally. It was clear that both Mia and Mo, once Nik's protégés, were on a management career track, while Nik's role was ill-defined. Maybe it was inevitable.

Nik was musing about all the unforeseen events that had transpired since he'd arrived in DC when Mo lumbered through the door of the restaurant, waiters loaded down with serving trays nimbly parting before him to avoid being plowed underfoot.

One would never know it to look at Mo now, but he had come within minutes of dying on the operating table during the kidney transplant procedure. His heart had temporarily stopped and his blood pressure plummeted before doctors revived him. Miraculously, within days of the operation, he was up on his feet and, in weeks, back at the gym doing weight training. He was as big and strong now, if not bigger and stronger than before the operation, and he was shy one kidney.

"I took the liberty of ordering lunch for you," Nik said when Mo slid onto the seat next to Nik. Mo's beefy body spread out in the narrow booth, squeezing Nik over to the outside, where he barely clung to the edge of his seat.

"How did you know what I wanted?"

"Because you've been ordering the same healthy option since the beginning of time—cheeseburger, fries, beer, and chocolate ice cream for dessert."

"That was the old me. I've changed."

"Here's our waiter now," Nik said, and waved him over.

"I'd like to change my order," Mo said. "Instead of ice cream, I'll have the pecan pie."

Nik smiled. "You're in luck. I saw it on the menu."

"Cool."

After their waiter delivered their drinks, Nik turned to his companion. "Mia's running a few minutes late, which is good because there's something I need to talk to you about."

Mo cocked an eyebrow and shook his head from side to side like a dog shedding water. "I know what you're going to say, and you can save it, chief," he said, waving Nik off with a hand the size of a bear's paw.

"No, you don't."

"Yeah, I do, and I ain't interested. I knew exactly what I was doing by going into Whetstone's office, and if he finds out, I'll deal with it." Mo took a long pull on his beer and wiped his mouth on his shirtsleeve. "And besides, you and Mia got a much bigger problem on your hands."

"What's that supposed to mean?"

"Here's Mia now," Mo said and stood to let her take his

seat in the booth while he pulled up a chair. "Let's get our food first, and I'll fill the two of you in while we eat."

"I miss anything?" Mia asked as she shrugged off her coat.

"Appears we're just getting started," Nik told her.

At Nik's request, Mo recounted the night he entered Whetstone's office. Nik said he was too preoccupied removing the files from storage to give full attention to the story the first time. Mo told the pair that he waited until the janitors had finished their nightly rounds before he retrieved the keys from the receptionist's area to unlock the office. By that time, he was the only one in the newsroom, other than a sports clerk who was at the other end of the building and was too busy handling late basketball scores coming in from the West Coast to pay any attention to Mo.

Mo said he was in Whetstone's office for about ten minutes and was just about to give up his search when he saw the corner of a slip of paper sticking out from under Whetstone's keyboard. Scrawled across the top of the page were the words "Tate/Bullwhip/Yukon files" and on the bottom "warehouse."

"That was it. There were no physical files in his office, and I couldn't find anything on his computer. I figured 'warehouse' referred to *Newshound*'s old offices in the Warehouse District. I went over the first chance I got, and there were all the cardboard security boxes covered under a tarp. You pretty much know the rest."

"Far as I could tell," Mia said as she bit into her sandwich, "Li'l Dick has no idea that his office was searched or that the files have been removed from our old offices. He was his normal self when I dropped in on him a few days ago."

"You mean he was a prick," Mo said.

"Pretty much, but no more prickish than what you'd expect, I guess is how I'd put it."

Nik shook his head. "I can't understand it. Why would Whetstone go to all the trouble to take the files if he didn't intend to use them, and how'd he even know we had them? They were shipped directly to storage when we decided not to pursue the Yukon story months ago. I hadn't even bothered to look at them."

"Maybe he didn't," Mo said.

"Maybe he didn't what?" Nik said, looking puzzled.

"Maybe he didn't know you had the files, and maybe he didn't take them. Maybe someone else is out to kill the project. Maybe that slip of paper I found is a note he made of a phone call. Maybe someone called him and told him about the files and where they were hidden, and he simply wrote down the information."

They then started batting around names of enemies they had in the newsroom who also knew about the existence of the files.

"My guess, it was Lauren DuCovy. She still holds a grudge against me because I kicked her off the podcast team," Mia said.

Mo dismissed DuCovy as the culprit and instead fingered an assistant editor on the news desk who coordinated all of *Newshound*'s Freedom of Information requests to the government. "Guy's a real snake and ass-kisser. He'd've seen Nik's paperwork and the Pentagon's reply."

The trio fell silent, heads down, absorbed in their own thoughts and desserts. Mo asked, "You got any ideas, Nik?"

"Just one, and you'll probably think it's crazy."

CHAPTER 19

May 6

Teofilo Mezos wasn't a journalist by trade, but rather a hip-hop DJ. Mia had met the twenty-two-year-old at a DC nightclub where he was then working and told him she was looking for someone to help produce her new podcast program—*Dateline Washington*—a show covering the singles scene in the nation's capital that had become an overnight sensation.

Teo was an unconventional choice for the position, but that made him all the more intriguing, and besides, many of Mia's female colleagues in the newsroom encouraged her to hire the artistic, moody Cuban American with the dreadlocks and tobacco-colored eyes.

Mia never once regretted the decision.

Teo was a maestro in the control booth. By expertly mixing sounds, inserting mood-setting music at just the right intervals, and pushing the narrators to paint more vivid descriptions with their words for listeners, he turned even the most mundane story into an enchanting audio journey.

Mia knew that for all of Teo's shortcomings—he was often

tyrannical and bristled at what he perceived to be even the slightest incursion on his turf by others—he, more than anyone else, was responsible for making the podcast division a success.

She pushed back hard when Nik asserted that it might be Teo who was trying to undermine them. She reminded her colleagues of all the countless hours Teo had spent working nights and weekends to produce and polish their stories when others had given up and gone home. It was Teo who often slept overnight on the office couch. It was Teo, she said, who, on more than one occasion, had caught what would have been embarrassing mistakes in their stories. It was Teo who constantly suggested ways to improve their pieces.

Mia told all of this and more to Nik until she finally convinced him he was wrong.

"Forget it. I said it was just a crazy hunch."

But what Mia didn't tell Nik and Mo that afternoon was the time she had recently encountered Teo in downtown DC.

Mia had just finished an interview with a congressional aide and was walking south along Fourteenth Street NW, and turned east on Constitution Avenue, when she looked up and caught sight of Teo entering a French bistro. Mia was going to call out to him, but she was too far away, so she doubled her pace, hoping to catch him just inside the restaurant's door.

She looked through the door before stepping inside the bistro and saw Teo being led to a table by the hostess. Seated at the table, with her back to Mia, was a thin blonde woman that Mia couldn't identify and a man she immediately recognized, Richard Whetstone. Whetstone stood and clapped Teo on the shoulder and introduced him to his companion.

PART II

TRIAL

CHAPTER 20

June 3

Judge Roy Pickett had been a Northern Virginia County circuit court judge for as long as anyone could remember. A
University of Virginia law school graduate, Pickett started his
career in the public defender's office, jumped to private practice after nearly starving to death on the paltry salary, hated
corporate law, did a quick U-turn, and joined the commonwealth attorney's office as an assistant prosecutor. Two years
later, he ran for the prosecutor's top job and won by twenty-six
votes, knocking off his old boss's handpicked successor.

He had served as the county's prosecutor for seven years
when he was selected for the circuit court by the state's general
assembly for the first of what would be an uninterrupted succession of eight-year-term reappointments.

Now approaching seventy, physically fit with a full head
of wiry steel-gray hair, a natty pencil mustache, and a patch
over his left eye, Pickett was the senior judge on the circuit
court and commanded attention on the bench. He was well
liked but, more importantly, respected by lawyers. Because

of the county's proximity to the District of Columbia, he had handled a number of high-profile criminal and civil cases over the years, but none as attention grabbing as the Geoffrey Tate murder trial.

If there was a knock against Judge Pickett, it was that he was a bit of a showboat. He not only liked the media spotlight, he courted it, which annoyed his fellow jurists to no end because he was so good at drawing positive reviews. "Judge Pickett: Constitutional Scholar," blared the Virginia Bar Association magazine's cover story. "First-rate legal mind, brilliant opinions," the *LegalBeagle Blog* proclaimed.

His colleagues had tired of the fawning coverage and were looking forward to the day when he'd be forced to retire at age seventy, but Judge Pickett managed to dodge that bullet when the general assembly pushed mandatory retirement to seventy-three.

He was as surprised as anyone when Jewel Tate's attorney requested he preside over the trial without impaneling a jury. He was also secretly thrilled. The process of selecting a jury, known as voir dire, could be tedious and time-consuming.

The full media attention would now rest on how he conducted the trial, and, to that end, Judge Pickett had his own surprise to spring on the two sides.

On the opening day of the trial, the judge called the prosecution and defense teams into his chambers to announce he had decided to allow television cameras in the courtroom to broadcast the proceedings live. His decision stunned the attorneys and delayed the start of the hearing for hours as the three sides argued over guidelines.

While it was not entirely unheard-of to have cameras in Virginia courtrooms, it nonetheless was a blow to judicial decorum, and Maggie was particularly uneasy with the decision. The trial promised to be sensational enough as it was without having around-the-clock television coverage. And there was also her belief that witnesses could be intimidated by having cameras in the courtroom recording their testimony.

After the sides ironed out their differences, Judge Pickett entered the courtroom from his chambers with a flourish, black robes billowing behind him like a ship's sails as he mounted the bench. He made a show of welcoming the media to his courtroom but warned them not to disrupt the proceedings. "You must remain as unobtrusive as the clock on the wall," he proclaimed from the bench. "If you are able to do that, I believe this will be a grand lesson in civics for the citizens of the great commonwealth of Virginia. They will see justice in action and realize it's much more than stuffy old law libraries and impenetrable legal opinions."

The judge's ruling was a victory for Elizabeth Blake and Channel 13 News, which had petitioned the court for the order. Lizzy was seated in the front row of spectators and beamed up at the judge as he delivered his remarks. She scribbled an inspired image in the notebook resting on her lap: "Judge Pickett, with a patch affixed over his left eye, slicked-back hair, and towering presence, appeared to the outside world like a swashbuckler athwart his sloop. He was only missing a parrot on his shoulder and a peg leg to complete the appearance." She had to know it was over the top, but it was how she would lead off her news segment for the evening's broadcast.

Jewel also seemingly loved the announcement. As a former beauty pageant contestant, she knew how to play to an audience.

Lead prosecutor Lisa Cranwell chose a stylish off-white pantsuit, and her co-counsel, Kenneth Larsen, donned the same frayed gray two-piece suit he had worn at the preliminary hearing. His white shirt was a good two sizes too big in the neck, and his head floated above his shoulders like a giant soap bubble. They were joined at the prosecutor's table by Rory Adams, a young assistant prosecutor in Lance St. Mary's office who had few duties other than to keep St. Mary informed of all the inner workings of the trial.

Since there was no jury to sway, Cranwell kept her opening statement short and confined it to the bare-bones facts of the case. Maggie had informed Judge Pickett in chambers before the opening of the trial that she intended to reserve her opening statement until the prosecution finished presenting its case.

"As is your prerogative," Judge Pickett replied.

Cranwell pushed back her chair and stood alongside the prosecutor's table. She glanced down at a yellow legal pad where she had outlined just a few key points she wanted to make.

"If you'll permit me, Your Honor, on the night in question, the state intends to demonstrate that Jewel Tate shot and killed her husband, Geoffrey Tate, not out of self-defense but out of pure selfishness. Despite her efforts to make it seem otherwise, Geoffrey Tate did not dress up like a cat burglar, break into his own home, and attack his wife. Quite the contrary. You'll hear testimony that Geoffrey Tate came home from a long business trip, tired and looking forward to sleeping in his own bed, when he was gunned down in cold blood by his young wife.

"Jewel Tate staged her husband's murder and planned it for months. Why she did this is fairly obvious. Greed. Pure and simple. She wanted to get her hands on his fortune, but to accomplish that, she had to get him out of the way. Why she thought she could get away with it is another matter entirely, but Jewel Tate has been getting away with things to do with men since an early age, when she seduced her high school math teacher to get passing grades. She simply figured, Why should this time be any different?

"The defense is asking the court to suspend disbelief and accept that Geoffrey Tate, a hundred-ninety-five-pound, muscled fitness fanatic, was overpowered by a wisp of a woman that he could easily pick up and toss across the room like a pillow. It defies logic."

Cranwell turned to face Jewel, who stared straight ahead, refusing to engage in eye contact. "I ask, is the picture you see sitting here today in the courtroom that of a grieving widow or an opportunist? Thank you, Your Honor, that is all," Cranwell said and retook her seat.

Once again, Jewel had rejected her attorney's advice to dress and act modestly. For the opening day, she had selected a hip-hugging cotton-candy-pink collarless Coco Chanel tweed skirt suit, gold bangle earrings, and open-toed shoes. Maggie had tried, unsuccessfully, to get Jewel to wear a trench coat over the outfit and forgo contact lenses for glasses.

"You worry about the legal and let me handle the wiggle," she had told Maggie before sashaying up the courthouse steps and into Judge Pickett's courtroom.

Judge Pickett fingered the gold pocket watch that he had propped up on the bench in front of him and studied it before addressing the courtroom. "Because of pretrial consultations, today's proceedings regrettably, but unavoidably, started later than anticipated. The court will recess until nine a.m. tomorrow morning. Madam Prosecutor, be prepared to call your first witness at that time."

In a town that can't keep secrets, the staff of the Four Seasons Hotel in Washington's Georgetown neighborhood is a study in discretion. Urbane, understated, and meticulous, employees are schooled in the old-world arts of service, diplomacy, and, above all else, ironclad guest confidentiality.

There is a private elevator staffed twenty-four hours a day in the parking garage that whisks valued guests directly to top-floor suites without ever having to set foot in the lobby or be forced to rub shoulders with others at a public entrance. To keep their comings and goings private, staff refer to long-time patrons by sobriquets, usually historical figures, instead of their actual names. There was a Mr. Jefferson and Mrs. Madison, for example. Of course, there was a Mr. Washington. Indeed, many staff didn't know the true identities of the guests at all, and that's how the guests preferred to keep it.

The gentleman who always requested the bridal suite was known as Mr. Nixon.

Even with these extra layers of security and precaution, Mr. Nixon thought it foolish and unnecessarily risky to meet at the hotel, but a rendezvous at his private residence was out of the question.

"This was not one of your better ideas," he said while lying splayed on the king-size bed in the bridal suite. "What if someone spotted you?"

"Stop worrying, no one saw me, and even if they did, they'd never recognize me in this getup," Jewel Tate said, and pulled a waist-length black wig from her scalp. She shook her head vigorously back and forth, sending a lush carpet of hair unfurling down her bare back and shoulders.

"But we agreed to wait until after the trial, or at least until things cooled down a bit. That was the plan," he said, unable to stop himself from staring at the diamond stud that pierced Jewel's marble-size nipple.

"Plans change. I got lonely in that big house all by myself, and I needed a little pick-me-up before the trial gets into full swing tomorrow morning."

Jewel sat astride his chest, leaning back against the hump that was his belly. "I got an itch and you need to scratch it."

"Okay, but just this one time. Things are really busy at work right now," he said, his arms spread wide, wrists clamped to the metal bed frame by handcuffs. "And did you have to bring the dog?" Toby was coiled like an armadillo on a chaise longue, his ears festooned with rainbow ribbons.

"Hush," Jewel whispered and covered his mouth with a length of gray duct tape.

Jewel exited the hotel after midnight, Toby tucked under one arm, asleep inside his carrier. She used the back stairwell and walked out the service entrance into an overcast nighttime sky that was spitting cold rain. The hotel's clock tower rang out at half past the hour. She had parked her car in an underground garage on Thirtieth Street, one block over, and cut through a courtyard to make the short trek in under five minutes. Jewel was in her vehicle, sailing down George Washington Memorial Parkway, her favorite playlist blaring through the radio's speakers in no time at all, having never noticed the man in the alleyway photographing her as she stepped out into the street from the hotel, or the car trailing fifty yards behind her.

CHAPTER 21

June 4–5

On the first day of witness testimony, Lisa Cranwell walked first responders, crime-scene investigators, and the county's pathologist through their official written reports. She also entered into the record five years of Geoffrey Tate's tax reports and a financial statement from his accountants showing his net worth to be in excess of $150 billion, most of that in Yukon stock.

With the exception of a small detail here or there, Maggie's objections were few and far between. The only heated exchange came when the state's chief crime lab technician testified that test results were inconclusive as to whether Geoffrey Tate's moccasin made the footprint on the second-story window seal. Try as she might, Maggie couldn't get the woman to concede the print came from Tate. "There was no tread on the moccasins to speak of, and the window had been left open, and rain washed away nearly all of the evidence," the woman said, holding fast to her official report.

Otherwise, Maggie's cross-examinations were routine, and the first day of testimony was uneventful.

On the second day, Cranwell called Whit Browne to the stand, the owner of Whit's World of Guns & Ammo in Middleburg, Virginia, forty-five miles west of DC in the heart of horse country where wealthy Washingtonians kept second homes and on the weekends dressed in scarlet five-button frock coats and white breeches, black boots with patent-leather tops, and funny-looking hunting derbies called billycocks to ride to the hounds, and where the Tates owned Rebel's Yell, a 250-acre estate and horse farm off Snickersville Turnpike.

Browne, a retired DC cop with a flattop haircut, bent nose, and chipped front teeth, testified that Jewel Tate was a frequent customer at his indoor shooting range and that he sold her a prepaid package of twenty target-practice lessons. According to his records, she had used twelve of the twenty sessions.

"Did you ever have occasion to see Mrs. Tate fire her weapon at your shooting range?" Cranwell asked.

"I did."

"And how would you describe her abilities?"

"Not an expert by any stretch, but good enough."

"And by 'good enough,' what do you mean?"

"At thirty yards, she could put four out of six rounds on the target."

"And the targets at your range, they are paper cutouts representing a human form. Is that correct?"

"That's right."

"So, in the cutout, what area exactly could Mrs. Tate hit?"

"Middle of the chest."

"So, would you say she was proficient with a handgun and knew how to handle the weapon?"

"I would."

"And do you know what kind of gun Mrs. Tate practiced with?"

"I do. It was a .38-caliber revolver."

"The same caliber of revolver she shot and killed her husband with, isn't that right?"

"Yes, appears so."

"Thank you. That is all."

"Defense, your witness," the judge said.

Maggie remained seated. "Mr. Browne, were you familiar with Geoffrey Tate?"

"I was."

"When did you meet him and under what circumstances?"

"Met him at the Whitehorse Pub in Middleburg about a year ago. We just happened to be in the bar at the same time one evening."

"And what did you and Mr. Tate discuss at the Whitehorse Pub that evening?"

"When he found out that I owned Whit's World, he said he wanted his wife to take shooting lessons. He said he worried about her on the occasions when she was alone by herself at Rebel's Yell so far out in the middle of nowhere."

"So, it was Geoff Tate's idea for his wife to learn how to use a gun?"

"As far as I know, yes."

"And it was sometime after your conversation with Mr. Tate in the Whitehorse that Jewel Tate came to your shooting range and started taking target practice. Is that correct?"

"I believe it was a few weeks later that she came by for her first lesson."

"Thank you, Mr. Browne. That's all, Judge."

"Sorry, Mr. Browne. A couple more questions," Cranwell said as Browne stood to leave the witness stand. He lowered himself back into the witness chair. "You said you witnessed Mrs. Tate taking target practice at your range. Did you ever talk to her?"

"I did."

"And what did you talk to her about?"

"Oh, the weather, this and that. You know."

"Did you ever talk to her about guns?"

"Sure."

"And what did she say to you about guns?"

"She said she liked the feel of a gun in her hand."

"Did she say anything else?"

"Yeah, she asked me if I ever shot anyone when I was a DC cop."

"What did you tell her?"

"That I had, and those were the worst days of my life."

"How did she respond to that?"

"She said she often wondered what it would be like to shoot someone. Said it must be thrilling. Said she wouldn't hesitate to pull the trigger."

"Objection," Maggie protested.

"Overruled."

"Thank you, Your Honor. No further questions."

"Defense?"

"No, Your Honor."

Judge Pickett rapped his gavel. "Court will adjourn until tomorrow morning. Madam Prosecutor, do you anticipate presenting final witnesses tomorrow?"

"We do, Your Honor. Barring any unforeseen circumstances, we hope to conclude our portion of the trial by tomorrow afternoon." Cranwell looked to Larsen for confirmation. He nodded his assent.

"Very well, nine a.m. tomorrow morning it is, then."

CHAPTER 22

June 5

Nik was about three-quarters of the way through a box of Pentagon documents related to Yukon's Bullwhip contract when he thought he heard a rap on his apartment door. Gyp's ears perked up ever so slightly, though the dog didn't otherwise stir. Absorbed in his task, Nik had completely lost track of time. He had reviewed nearly five hundred pages of material so far, and the only interesting artifact he had uncovered was that the Bullwhip project was initially code-named Warthog.

The nine-foot ceilings, plaster walls, and hardwood floors in Nik's condo distorted sounds, turning even crystal-clear voices into babble if you were only a few feet away. He thought maybe someone was at his neighbor's door. He listened more closely. Definitely a knock. Harder this time.

He boosted himself up off the floor, his knees stiff from sitting in the same position for hours, and limped from the rear bedroom to the front of the apartment.

"Nik, you there?"

He unlatched the lock and flung the door open. Sam stood on the other side of the threshold, arms loaded with takeout boxes from Wild Nectar, their favorite neighborhood restaurant. "Don't tell me you forgot about our date night?" she said, an exasperated look on her face.

"No, of course not. How could you even think that? I was just about to call you and see where you were," he fibbed. "Here, let me help you with that."

Gyp appeared, tail wagging, and rammed his snout between Sam's legs.

"Gyp, stop that," Sam scolded and handed the packages to Nik. The dog dropped his head and slunk off.

Nik carried the food into the kitchen and set it on the counter. "You're a sight for sore eyes. I've been staring at documents for the last"—he checked the time—"four hours."

"Wow, you really know how to charm a girl."

"Okay, you look beautiful. How's that?"

"Much better," Sam said and leaned in and kissed Nik. "Is the wine in the fridge?"

"Aaah . . ."

"I knew it. You did forget about our date. Luckily, I bought a couple bottles of chilled wine. They're in that bag," Sam said and nodded to a sack she had set on the floor.

Nik picked up the bag and removed the bottles. "Hmm, not bad," he said, examining the labels and choosing one. Truth was, he didn't know the first thing about wine. He opened a drawer, found a corkscrew, pulled the cork, and poured two glasses. "I have an excuse. Cheers."

"Cheers."

They both sipped their drinks.

"Okay, let's hear it. This oughta be good."

"Well, first there was the trial today."

"I'm aware. I popped in and out and saw you. You could barely take your eyes off Jewel Tate."

"What? That's silly. She just happened to be sitting directly in front of me."

"Uh-huh."

"Anyway, after the court session, I got into a blowup with Mia."

"About?"

"An issue having to do with Teo."

Sam leaned against the counter, legs crossed, drink cradled in her arms. She was wearing white straight-leg jeans, red cowboy boots with white stitching, and a yellow linen shirt, the top three buttons undone. Nik, as usual, was dressed in khakis, gray sweatshirt, and in stocking feet, his hair mussed, glasses slightly askew. He refilled both their glasses.

"Thankfully, things finally calmed down, but Mia's still not happy with me. I can tell you all about it if you'd like."

"Mmm, maybe later. Let's enjoy each other's company first, then eat. We can talk shop later," Sam said and stretched out her right leg and snaked it around Nik and pulled him closer.

"I like your plan a whole lot better than mine," Nik said, and removed his glasses and leaned in to kiss Sam. Within minutes, they were tugging at each other's tops and soon were sprawled on the kitchen floor, Nik fumbling with Sam's belt while she tried to kick off her cowboy boots. Finally, Sam said, "The hell with it. The boots stay on," as Nik unclasped the belt and she wiggled free of her jeans and panties, bunching them over the top of the cowboy boots.

Sam and Nik ate dinner propped up in Nik's bed, swapping gossip about the trial, flipping channels back and forth between a Netflix series and a spring training baseball game for the Washington Nationals. Gyp was curled up in a ball at their feet. Sam dug into a carton of mint chocolate chip ice cream she was holding on her lap and spooned it into her mouth. "Do we really have to watch preseason baseball? Isn't it enough that you insist on watching all hundred sixty-two regular-season games?"

"Hey, don't hog all the ice cream," Nik said and plunged his spoon into the container. With the Nationals down by seven runs, Nik had lost interest in the game and switched over to Channel 13 just in time to catch the tail end of Lizzy Blake's nightly report.

"Confidential sources have told this reporter that Jewel Tate was in secret negotiations with the Northern Virginia County commonwealth attorney's office for a plea agreement of manslaughter in the death of her billionaire husband, Geoffrey Tate. Mrs. Tate, who would have received a light prison sentence in a minimum-security lockup under terms of the settlement, abruptly broke off negotiations before her trial for second-degree murder. Stay tuned right here for more developments on this ongoing story. This is Elizabeth Blake reporting for Channel 13 News from the historic Northern Virginia County Courthouse."

Nik shook his head. "I swear, I don't know how the woman does it. She's a scoop machine. Those plea discussions are inviolate, reporters never hear about them."

"I know how she does it," Sam said, polishing off the ice cream.

"Oh, yeah, how?"

"Yeah, she's sleeping with Lance St. Mary."

"Get outta here."

"Yup. Been a couple months now."

"That explains a lot. Lizzy's determined to land a job on one of the national networks, and Lance just might be her ticket if he can keep feeding her stories on the Tate case. She didn't say why Jewel backed out of the deal. That would be worth knowing."

"I have a theory about that. You familiar with the slayer rule?"

"You mean sleigh ruler?" Nik said and spelled it out: "S-L-E-I-G-H. I heard someone ask St. Mary about it at the briefing and have been meaning to follow up but haven't had time."

"No, slayer rule—S-L-A-Y-E-R—as in to kill."

"Oh, no wonder everyone I mentioned it to looked at me funny."

"It's a law that basically states if you kill someone, say a spouse or a relative, you cannot legally benefit from the deceased's estate and are disinherited. For the longest time, the state of Virginia had the most forgiving definition of the rule and allowed persons to claim inheritance even if they had a hand in a person's death. There were a number of high-profile cases in Virginia several years back."

"Sounds vaguely familiar."

"The most famous case involved a former US marshal from Loudoun County who shot and killed his wealthy wife during a domestic dispute. He was charged with first-degree murder but was convicted of the lesser crime of voluntary manslaughter and sent to prison. Initially, his claim on his wife's estate was denied, but he appealed, and the court ruled a conviction of manslaughter didn't justify barring him from her fortune."

"And you think Jewel Tate was familiar with the case?"

"Someone in the Tate household was, that's for certain. We confiscated a laptop from the home and we searched the browser's history. It contained numerous stories on the trial and the appeal."

"Whose laptop was it?"

"We could never determine ownership, and that's why the prosecution's unlikely to bring it up during the trial. Jewel claims it belonged to her husband and swears she didn't know the password, never touched it."

"Hold on, if it was Jewel who used the computer for

research to cover her tracks, why didn't she just take the plea agreement and walk away with the whole of the estate? Seems a couple years in a country club prison would be worth all the billions she'd rake in. Prison didn't seem that big of an inconvenience for Martha Stewart."

"Because it's no longer that simple. The Virginia state legislature finally got around to enacting tougher regulations. I'm guessing someone, probably your ex-wife, brought the new law to Jewel's attention before it was too late. Virginia went from having one of the most liberal interpretations of the slayer rule in the nation to one of the strictest. Now, if you're convicted of manslaughter, the chances of you getting even a dime are pretty remote—not impossible, but remote."

Nik was lying on his back, staring up at the ceiling, and recalled the important meeting that Maggie was rushing to when he ran into her outside the DC Metro station and wondered if it had to do with the plea bargain.

Just then, another thought occurred to him as well. He propped up on his elbows and twisted around to face Sam. "Back up a minute," he said. "You knew about all this and didn't mention it until now?"

"That's right, and I wouldn't have told you now had Lizzy not broken the story."

"Well, what about the recording in the judge's chambers?"

"I told you then, that was a one-time deal, and, strictly speaking, the judge said it wasn't an official hearing. Besides, it wasn't directly related to the sheriff's department's investigation."

"So that's how it's going to be."

"Listen, Nik, I said from the start I'd help where I could, but let's get something straight, it's not my job to do your job."

CHAPTER 23

June 6

"Prosecution calls Maria Santiago."

A slight, dark-haired woman with fierce eyes and thickly veined hands mounted the witness stand.

"Your Honor, I object. This person was not on the prosecution's list of possible witnesses," Maggie said.

"I can explain, Your Honor," Cranwell said. "It was only late last evening that we learned that Ms. Santiago would make an appearance. She was out of the country, and we have been desperately trying to locate her and get her back here to testify."

"I'll allow the witness," Pickett said. "But there's a limit to my patience with this type of conduct."

"Understood, Your Honor. It was unavoidable."

"Proceed."

"Who is she?" Maggie mouthed to Jewel.

"Former housekeeper," Jewel whispered.

"What does she know?"

"Nothing."

Maggie and Jewel put their heads together and started talking in low voices as Cranwell began her examination of the witness.

"Please state your full name for the court."

"Maria Catalina Santiago."

"Please tell the court who your employer has been for the past seven years, Ms. Santiago."

"Mr. Geoffrey Tate, God rest his soul."

"And what did you do for Mr. Tate?"

"I was his housekeeper."

"And were you employed by Mr. Tate on the night of his death?"

"I was."

"And where were you on the night in question?"

"I was in my cottage on the back of the Tate property in McLean."

"Did anything out of the ordinary happen that evening? And I'm not referring to Mr. Tate's death; I'm asking about your normal work routine."

"Yes."

"And what was that?"

"After I cleaned up after dinner, Mrs. Tate, she ask me to take her dog, Toby, for the evening."

"And why was that unusual?"

"'Cause she go nowhere without that dog. She don't take a crap without that dog in the bathroom."

"Objection, Your Honor."

"Sustained."

"Had she ever asked you to take the dog before?"

"No. That dog, he no like me. He no like anybody but her."

"Did he like Mr. Tate?"

"No. He hate Mr. Tate and bark like crazy, growl, and snap at him whenever he set foot in his own home. He didn't like Mr. Tate getting near her," she said and cocked her head toward Jewel. "You can ask anybody and they tell you same thing. The gardener, the pool boy, the repairman."

"So, in your opinion, could Mr. Tate have broken into his own home and snuck up behind Mrs. Tate as she claims if Toby had been in the house, without raising a storm?"

"Absolutely not."

"Objection. Calls for speculation on the part of the witness."

"Sustained."

"Ms. Santiago, is it fair to say that, in your experience, Mr. Tate never entered his house announced or unannounced without Toby barking wildly and sounding an alarm?"

"Yes. That is right."

"Did Mrs. Tate tell you why she wanted the dog out of the house that night?"

"No. She tell me nothing. She say she get him in the morning, is all."

"But she didn't get him in the morning, did she?"

"No. When I went outside to have a cigarette, he snuck out the door and ran back up to the main house."

"When was this, approximately?"

"Sometime around eleven o'clock. Just before all hell break loose."

"No further questions."

"May I approach the witness, Your Honor?" Maggie asked. Judge Pickett nodded.

Maggie was on her feet and in the witness's face in three quick strides.

"You're in this country illegally, aren't you, Maria?"

"I entered legally. My green card expired."

"It expired years ago, but you told the Tates it was valid, didn't you? You lied to them."

"Mr. Tate, he know my status. He try to help."

"You stole from the Tates, didn't you?"

"Never."

"Wasn't an expensive necklace belonging to Mrs. Tate found in your cottage?"

"I don't know how it got there."

"And Mrs. Tate told her husband that you were stealing money from her purse, hundreds of dollars, in fact."

"She say that, but no is true."

"You don't like Mrs. Tate, do you, Maria?"

"She not a nice lady. She not good enough for Mr. Tate."

"You didn't like her because she made you do your job, didn't she? She caught you sleeping in a guest bedroom one afternoon when you were supposed to be working. She caught you drinking on the job. Found drugs in your cottage."

"I nap once in seven years when I was sick. Those other things are lies."

"The only one who is a known liar here is you, Maria. No further questions."

"Maria," Cranwell said, picking back up her questioning of the witness, "why did you leave the country?"

"I didn't voluntarily leave. I was deported. The day after Mr. Tate was killed, ICE agents showed up at my door and took me away."

"Who do you suspect reported you to authorities, after all these years?"

"She did," Maria said angrily, pointing at Jewel. "She no want me around to tell what I know."

"Objection, speculative."

"Sustained."

"No further questions, Your Honor."

"Court will take a short recess," Judge Pickett said, banging his gavel.

———

When court resumed, Kenneth Larsen, Lisa Cranwell's gangly co-counsel, called Alan Koch to the stand. Koch was Geoffrey Tate's personal attorney, and he had a mop of black hair, unruly eyebrows, and, despite being dressed in an expensive Italian suit, a disheveled look about him.

"How long have you been Mr. Tate's attorney?" Larsen asked after Koch was sworn in and identified himself.

"Nearly fifteen years."

"And how would you describe your work for Mr. Tate?"

"I advised him on any number of legal matters—investments, real estate acquisitions, estate planning, company issues, personal liabilities. Pretty much anything with a legal aspect attached to it."

"A man such as Mr. Tate must have had a tremendous amount of legal work, I'm guessing."

"Indeed, he did. It was a full-time job, and then some, keeping up with everything."

"So, did your job require you to write contracts and draw up business agreements?"

"No, not normally, but occasionally. I didn't mean to imply that I did all the work myself. I would employ, on Mr. Tate's behalf, outside counsel, people with area-matter expertise, to draft the requisite legal documents. I would review their work. That was my role. That was the normal course of things."

"I see. Were you familiar with Geoffrey Tate's estate planning?"

"I was and I am."

"When was the last time Mr. Tate updated his will, if 'will' accurately describes what I'm sure must be a very complex estate with complicated trusts and tax ramifications?"

"We were discussing changes to Mr. Tate's will just weeks prior to his death for that very reason. He wanted to make his estate less complicated and simplify his bequests."

"And did he?"

"Well, he told me what he wanted to do, and I started making inquiries and drafting language to capture his desires."

"And what was it that Mr. Tate wished to do with his estate?"

"He had a change of heart. He intended to take the Giving Pledge. He wanted to give it all away, with the exception of a few modest bequeathals. He insisted he didn't want to pass down his money to individuals just to make others rich. He wanted it to go toward causes, to help solve the world's biggest, most pressing problems. It was very admirable."

"What is the Giving Pledge?"

"It is a concept put forward by billionaires and wealthy individuals to donate their fortunes to philanthropic causes, instead of transferring it to heirs. He planned to call a press conference to announce it after all the legal work was complete. Unfortunately, he died before the documents were executed."

"So, in the scenario you described, had Mr. Tate not been killed, the bulk of his fortune would have bypassed individuals—siblings, a spouse, children, if he had any—and gone directly to the causes that he designated?"

"Yes, that was his intention."

"So, when Jewel Tate shot and killed her husband, she cut those plans short, did she not?"

"I guess that's one way to look at it."

"Did he merely tell you his wishes, or did he put them in writing?"

"He sent me emails with very specific instructions outlining his plan."

Larsen handed Koch a stack of paper. "And are these copies of the emails you reference?"

Koch looked over them. "Yes, they are."

Larsen then entered the emails into the official court record.

"No further questions, Your Honor."

Maggie rose from her chair but stood rooted to her spot. She was dressed in navy pumps and a dark-blue pin-striped skirt suit that rested just above the knee.

"Mr. Koch, did Geoffrey Tate's will predate his marriage to Jewel?"

"It did."

"And the Tates had a prenuptial agreement, isn't that correct?"

"That's true."

"And that agreement was entered into just prior to their marriage in the Virgin Islands, isn't that also correct?"

"It is."

"What would Mrs. Tate have received upon her husband's death under the terms of the prenup?"

"She would have received a few million dollars. Mr. Tate said he wanted to leave her 'enough so she could do anything but not enough to do nothing.' I believe he was quoting Warren Buffett."

"Who drew up the prenup agreement for Mr. Tate to sign?"

"I did. It was pretty straightforward, and he needed it in a hurry."

"That seems reasonable, since it's my understanding the wedding came about rather quickly."

"Precisely."

"And who prepared Mrs. Tate's prenup agreement?"

Koch cleared his throat and answered in a barely audible voice.

"I'm sorry, Mr. Koch, I couldn't hear your answer. Could you repeat it, more loudly this time, so everyone in the court can hear? Perhaps water would help to clear your throat," Maggie said, pouring a glass from a pitcher on her table and offering it to the witness. "May I, Your Honor?"

Pickett nodded.

Koch took the glass of water from Maggie. "Thank you," he said and took a long drink. "My throat's parched."

Maggie smiled patiently before saying, "Should I repeat the question, Mr. Koch?"

"That's not necessary. I did. I drew up Mrs. Tate's agreement as well."

"You did?"

"That's right."

"At the time, was Mr. Tate or the soon-to-be Mrs. Tate aware of that fact?"

"They were not."

"In fact, you told them that you had another attorney prepare the agreement for Mrs. Tate, isn't that correct?"

"Yes."

"And why did you do that?"

"Because Geoff insisted on having the documents immediately. It was on a weekend, and there wasn't time to recruit another lawyer, and they would have just copied exactly what I had drafted anyhow."

"But by not allowing Mrs. Tate to have her own impartial legal representation, that invalidated the prenuptial agreement, didn't it, Mr. Koch?"

"Well . . ."

"Are you familiar with the 'omitted spouse clause' in Virginia estate law, Mr. Koch?"

"I've heard of it."

"Doesn't the clause stipulate that one hundred percent of an estate be granted to a surviving spouse if the will of the deceased spouse predates a marriage without a valid prenuptial agreement in place and where there are no children involved?"

"That's a very generous interpretation of the statute."

"Would you like me to read you the exact language, Mr. Koch?"

"No, that's not necessary."

"And when Mr. Tate discovered that you had drafted Mrs. Tate's prenuptial agreement as well as his, he became furious with you, didn't he? Screamed at you on a phone call, called you incompetent because he knew that, in your haste, you had jeopardized his fortune. That Mrs. Tate was no longer bound by the prenup. And, as his wife under the omitted spouse clause, she potentially could be entitled to the whole of the estate upon his death."

"He wasn't happy, that's true, but I told him it could be remedied."

"Oh, indeed, it could be remedied, all right. By killing Mrs. Tate, and that's exactly what Geoffrey Tate set out to do the night he broke into his own house . . ."

"No, that's not true."

"And it was only by the grace of God that Mrs. Tate got to the gun first, or she would have been the one who would have been killed."

"Nooooo . . ."

"Just a few more questions before I'm through with you, Mr. Koch. The bulk of Geoffrey Tate's fortune is tied up in Yukon stock, isn't that correct?"

"Yes. Geoff Tate was what you'd call cash poor. He sold Yukon stock from time to time for tax purposes, but it pained him to do so. When he wanted to make a large purchase, he'd simply get bank loans and collateralize the loans with company stock."

"So, it's not as if, upon Geoffrey Tate's death, the skies would open up and money would rain down upon Jewel Tate."

"No, she'd be entitled to some liquid assets and cash, but, truly, there are only a couple ways to unlock Geoffrey Tate's wealth at this point. One would be to sell shares, which is difficult because of restrictions and covenants placed on the stock by his lenders and the company."

"And the other way?"

"Sell the company outright, of course."

"No further questions, Your Honor."

CHAPTER 24

June 6

Geoffrey Tate's personal bodyguard, Shaka Wulf, was the final witness for the prosecution. An ex–Navy SEAL whose father was Samoan and mother African American, Wulf was an imposing figure on the stand, with his gleaming shaved head, thick chest, and ramrod posture. He was one of the last people to see Geoff Tate alive.

Wulf testified that Tate's most recent overseas business trip was particularly grueling, meetings in five European capitals in four days, filled with breakfast, lunch, and dinner working sessions each day with government officials, investors, and business partners.

"As his bodyguard, you spent a lot of time with Mr. Tate, isn't that right?" Cranwell asked.

"Pretty much sunup to sundown."

"And were you friends?"

"I'd like to think so. I was the best man at his wedding."

"So, you got to know Mr. Tate's moods, seeing him up close at his best and not so best?"

"You could say that."

"And on these trips, would he talk to you about his wife?"

"Quite often."

"And on the most recent trip, did he talk about Mrs. Tate?"

"He did, yes, when he wasn't in meetings and we were alone."

"Where would these discussions take place?"

"Driving back and forth to the hotel, on the plane, in the gym working out. That sort of thing."

"And how would you describe his mood when he was talking about Mrs. Tate?"

"Upbeat."

"Would you say happy?"

"I would. In fact, I've never seen Geoff so happy as when the plane's wheels touched back down in DC. It was a hard trip, but he was happy to be home," Wulf told Cranwell.

"And did he mention why he was especially happy?"

"He did."

"And what did he say?"

"He said Jewel told him she had a big surprise waiting for him at home."

"'A big surprise waiting for him at home.' Those were his exact words?"

"Yes."

"And did he speculate about what the 'big surprise' might be?"

"No, he only said he knew what it wasn't."

"And what was that?"

"He said it wasn't going to be a chocolate cake. Said Jewel was a disaster in the kitchen. Said she couldn't boil water."

"Thank you, Mr. Wulf. No further questions, Your Honor."

"Your witness, Ms. Stone," Judge Pickett intoned.

Maggie rose slowly to her feet. "Who hired you, Mr. Wulf?" she asked.

"I work for Mr. Tate."

"Please answer the question I asked."

"It was Mr. Tate's decision."

"It may have been his decision, but weren't you, in fact, recommended to Mr. Tate by his sister, Marianne? Didn't she specifically recruit you for the job?"

"The security firm I worked for at the time had conducted work for Ms. Tate in the past, and I met her through my employer, yes."

"How would you describe your relationship with Marianne Tate?"

"Businesslike."

"Wasn't it more than businesslike? Didn't you have a romantic involvement with Geoffrey Tate's sister?"

"We dated a couple times."

"I have documentation here that shows you and Marianne Tate took multiple trips together to Palm Beach, Aspen, La Jolla. I'd hardly call that a couple of dates, Mr. Wulf."

"That was before I went to work for Yukon. We broke it off shortly after I was hired."

"In all your talks with Geoff Tate about his wife, did he ever mention that his sister hated Jewel? That she was trying to destroy their marriage?"

"I knew they didn't like each other. I believe the feelings were mutual."

"Were you aware Geoff Tate cut off nearly all contact with his sister because of her obsession with Jewel?"

"I knew it was a sore subject."

"You don't like Jewel Tate, do you, Mr. Wulf?"

"She's not my favorite, if that's what you mean, but she was my boss's wife, so I tried to get along with her. In my experience, she could be volatile, unstable."

"Marianne Tate used her sway over you to pull you into her scheme to sabotage the marriage, didn't she, Mr. Wulf?"

"That's bullshit, lady," Wulf said with a sarcastic laugh. "Nobody pulls me into anything I don't want to be pulled into."

"Objection, argumentative," Cranwell called out.

"Overruled. I'll caution you to watch your language, Mr. Wulf. This proceeding is being broadcast live. Continue."

"You testified that you broke off your relationship with Marianne Tate, but isn't it true that the two of you were seen together recently in the restaurant at the Ritz hotel?"

"We met for coffee. She wanted to know what I thought about a private security firm she was considering hiring to beef up protection around her home."

"Wasn't the real reason the two of you met was to plot ways to get rid of Jewel Tate and that the discussion about a security firm was just cover?"

"Objection."

"Lady, you're as batshit crazy as she is," Wulf said and chinned toward Jewel.

"Overruled. I'm warning you, Mr. Wulf," the judge said.

"And didn't other diners overhear Marianne Tate say that she would like to—quote—'poison the bitch'?"

"Objection, hearsay."

"Sustained. The defense is treading on thin ice," Pickett admonished.

"My apologies to the court, Your Honor. No further questions."

"You may step down," the judge said to Wulf, who glared at Maggie as he stepped off the witness stand.

"The prosecution rests its case," Cranwell said.

"Very well," Judge Pickett said. "Tomorrow morning, we will hear opening statements from the defense. Court is recessed."

"I'll be ready, Your Honor," Maggie said.

Maggie was in her office late that night polishing her opening remarks for the following morning. She felt she had done a credible job of blunting the prosecution's case, but the fact remained that somehow, miraculously, a petite woman with no particular defense skills or expert training had managed to fight off a surprise attack by a physically superior opponent and not only escape but kill the assailant in the ensuing struggle.

She wrestled with putting Jewel on the stand. If she didn't, the judge would no doubt wonder how Jewel had fended off the attack, and if she did, Cranwell would tear into her like a Rottweiler, delving into Jewel's sex life, scrapes with the law, drug use. Maggie might not have any choice, depending on how the next couple days went.

Maggie wrote out her opening comments longhand on a yellow legal pad with a Montblanc pen, wadded discarded attempts littering the floor and looking like a lemon tree that had shed its fruit. She was working on her umpteenth draft—the first several all felt too passive and small for the seriousness of the moment—when the cell phone on her desk chirped. The screen display read: N. VA Sheriff's Dept. She answered it.

"Hello."

"Maggie?"

"Yes."

"It's Samantha Whyte at the Northern Virginia County Sheriff's Department. How are you?"

Sam and Maggie had a rocky first encounter months earlier when Maggie had tried to persuade Sam to get Nik to drop an investigative story he was pursuing. Over time, they became better acquainted while Sam nursed Nik back to health. Maggie came to admire Sam, and even thought they could be good friends, if not for the awkward Nik component.

"It's awful late, Sam," Maggie said, glancing at the clock on her phone. It said 1:20 a.m. "Everything okay with Nik?"

"Nik's fine, or, at least, he was when I last saw him several hours ago. Sorry about the lateness of the call, but it couldn't be helped. We believe we've discovered some new evidence related to the Tate case at the estate, and we're asking everyone— including Judge Pickett—to meet there tomorrow morning at seven a.m. to view it."

"What? That's strange, to say the least. What is it you think you uncovered?"

"I agree, it's highly unusual, and I'd rather not say what the evidence is at this point. We need to confirm it first. We have a team of investigators there now. In the meantime, Sheriff Korum has dispatched several units to make sure the estate is secured and locked down."

"Well, can you at least tell me if what you believe you have discovered could change the outcome of the trial?"

"If it is what we think it is, yes, there's a very good chance of that."

"For or against?"

"That's all I can say right now, I'm sorry. We'll all know more in a few hours. Good night, Maggie."

"It won't be now. There's no way I'm going to be able to sleep a wink after this news."

"That makes two of us, then."

CHAPTER 25

June 7

Nik and Elizabeth Blake from Channel 13 were stationed outside the twelve-foot wrought-iron gate at the Tate estate, shivering in the early-morning dampness. Looking through the gate's bars, they could see police cruisers, black sedans, and a white paneled cargo van with lettering etched on the side that read, in part, "Sure Shot. Shoot to . . ." parked along the drive that led to the main house.

Nik had called Sam three times and sent her five text messages trying to find out what was going on. "Stop it, Nik. I don't have time for this now. It's starting to piss me off," Sam replied angrily to his last text. He called Maggie and got a message saying her voice-mail box was full. She, too, ignored his multiple text messages.

"Why don't you call Lance," Nik suggested to Lizzy, referring to the county's prosecuting attorney who had been removed from the case. "I hear the two of you are close."

"Fuck off," Lizzy said and walked over to her cameraman,

who was setting up his equipment to get a shot of the parade of vehicles when they exited the compound.

The cargo van parked in the drive intrigued Nik. Given the writing on the side, he assumed it belonged to a company specializing in ballistic investigations, and he started searching the web for "Sure Shot gun experts" on his mobile phone. The only result he got was for a company in Baltimore with a disconnected phone and a website that had not been updated in four years.

Lizzy wandered back over toward him. "They've been in there for more than an hour," Nik said when she drew near. Other media started arriving, having first gone to the courthouse only to learn the judge, prosecution, and defense all were at the Tate estate. "You don't think something happened to Jewel, do you? She wouldn't have tried to hurt herself, would she?"

Lizzy looked at Nik as if he'd lost his mind. "Are you kidding? That gold digger? No way."

She had no sooner finished her sentence than Samantha Whyte and Sheriff Korum appeared at the top of the drive and began to amble toward the knot of reporters. Korum held his Stetson in his hand, and he fitted the hat back on his head when he reached the gate, Sam taking a position behind him.

"Y'all listen up. I have a brief statement. Last evening, investigators from my office discovered what we believe to be a crucial piece of evidence that was overlooked in the initial search of the Tate estate. We have confirmed the evidence to be authentic and not planted after the fact. The evidence will be transported back to the Northern Virginia County Courthouse, where it will be examined in Judge Pickett's chambers with prosecution and defense teams in attendance. After that, a determination will be made on whether to enter it into the trial. Now clear a path so we can depart."

Reporters could hear the whine of car engines turning over as the iron gate started to silently glide open.

"Sheriff," Lizzy called out as Sam and Korum turned and headed back up the driveway, "how do you explain that your investigators overlooked such a potentially important piece of information in the first place? Are you saying your department dropped the ball on one of the biggest cases this county has ever seen?" It was an intended swipe at both Korum and Sam, and everyone in earshot knew it.

Korum stopped, turned back around, and slid the toothpick he was sucking on to one side of his mouth. "Easy," he said. "It was camouflaged."

CHAPTER 26

June 7

The trial resumed with a packed courtroom in the early afternoon. Maggie and Jewel were deep in conversation while Lisa Cranwell and Kenneth Larsen sat frozen like icebergs, glumly staring straight ahead. Nik scanned the gallery for Sam but didn't see her.

The door to Judge Pickett's chambers flew open, and the judge stepped through. He stopped momentarily to take in the crowd and then bounded up the stairs to his bench with the energy of a man half his age and settled into his chair.

"I think it only appropriate that I say a few words before this trial gets underway today," the judge said, turning his attention to the television cameras. "In an extraordinary turn of events, new evidence has come to the court's attention that may cast these proceedings in a different light. I will not attempt to characterize the evidence, as we are all about to see it momentarily, but I will say that the court has every reason to believe it is genuine and has not been tampered with in any way. With that, Ms. Stone, I yield the floor to you."

"Thank you, Your Honor," Maggie said, pushing back her chair while standing. She placed one hand on Jewel Tate's shoulder and said, "If you please, the defense will forgo an opening statement and call Samantha Whyte to the stand."

Nik whipped his head around, a stunned look on his face, and watched as Sam entered the courtroom from the rear and glided, in several long strides, up the center aisle, not once glancing in his direction.

"State your full name and occupation for the court," Maggie said after Sam was sworn in.

"Samantha Whyte, chief investigator and spokesperson for the Northern Virginia County Sheriff's Department."

"Ms. Whyte, last evening, your team of investigators recovered a piece of evidence at the Tate compound that, until that point, had remained unearthed. Could you please describe to the court what your investigators discovered?"

"It was a trail cam."

"And what exactly is a trail cam, and what is it used for?"

"It's a portable, motion-activated camera used primarily by outdoor enthusiasts and hunters to capture images and video of wildlife. Many of the cameras, like the one we found, are outfitted with infrared lenses, solar-powered batteries, and memory cards."

"And where did your investigators find this trail cam?"

"It was located about thirty feet off the ground in a tree on the Tate property."

"This tree where you discovered the trail cam is on the backside of the Tate residence and near a second-story window that leads to the Tates' primary bedroom, is that right?"

"Yes, that's correct."

"And the camera was positioned in a way that allowed it to record, when it was activated, the back portion of the home, is that also correct?"

"That appears to be the case, yes."

"And where did these cameras come from?"

"The Tates had them installed. The estate is in a heavily wooded area of the county, and there have been sightings of black bears and rumors of mountain lions out that way. They had several cameras stationed around the property by a local firm. The company's name is Sure Shot. Their motto is 'Shoot to Capture, Not Kill.'"

"And have you interviewed the owner of the firm, and what did you learn?"

"We did. He verified it was his equipment and that he placed the camera in the tree at Mrs. Tate's request. He said the camera was still functioning and had not been tampered with."

"But why did they need trail cams if they have an elaborate security system with its own cameras?"

"For a period of several weeks late last year, there were problems with the software that controlled the security system on the property. During that time, the main system's coverage was spotty, so they installed the trail cams as a temporary backup. When the main system got restored and working properly, they stopped monitoring the trail cams, and, over time, most stopped working."

"Your Honor, with your permission, I'd like to now play for the court a portion of the trail cam video from the night in question."

"Proceed."

Bailiffs wheeled three large flat-screen televisions to the front of the court and set them up so the judge, spectators, and the television crews that were positioned off to the side could view what was being displayed.

The courtroom lights dimmed, and a ghostly image floated onto the television monitors. At first, it looked like someone in a bad gorilla costume, but as the lens on the trail cam automatically adjusted its focus, it became clear the image was that of a man standing at the rear of the Tate residence, back to the camera. A date and time stamp appeared in the upper corner of the picture frame.

The man lifted his head and studied the roofline and a second-story window above the ground. He reached into his coat pocket and withdrew a piece of fabric that appeared to be a woman's stocking before slowly turning around to face a large tree next to the house. His neck was bent, and all the spectators could see was the crown of the man's head.

The man worked the fabric down over his head and ears, and, in several quick bounds, he was up the tree and out on a limb overhanging the roof. He dropped softly down, the soles of his moccasins skidding on the Spanish tiles before arresting his descent.

He bear-crawled up the slope of the roof to the window, peered inside, then placed gloved hands on either side and slid the window open. He stepped through, first the left leg, then, as he twisted his body to pull his right leg through, he turned and faced the trail camera head-on. The last image viewers saw was of the man yanking the stocking down over his face and disappearing into the darkened room.

The lights came back up and Maggie addressed Sam.

"Ms. Whyte, the sheriff's department technicians reviewed the video the court just saw. Is it their opinion it is authentic and taken the night of Mrs. Tate's assault just prior to when Geoffrey Tate was shot and killed?"

"It is."

"And did they conclusively establish the identity of the man in the video?"

"Yes, they did."

"And what methods did they use to make that determination?"

"Facial-recognition software, enhanced video screening, and the naked eye."

"And who is the man we see in the video?"

"Geoffrey Tate."

A loud gasp rose from the courtroom.

"You're one hundred percent certain?"

"One hundred percent."

"So Geoffrey Tate did, indeed, break into his own home and assault his wife with the intention of doing her mortal harm, as my client has contended all along."

"Mr. Tate entered his home from a rear, second-story window on the night in question. That much is clear from the video. As to his intentions, I could only speculate."

Turning to face Judge Pickett, Maggie said, "Your Honor, at this point, based on the evidence we've just seen, I request a summary judgment from the court dismissing all charges against my client and a finding of not guilty."

Pickett adjusted his eye patch with one hand while drumming his fingers on his armchair with the other. He looked out over the courtroom as if searching a far horizon for an answer before settling his gaze on Lisa Cranwell at the prosecutor's table.

He dabbed at his mustache with his thumb and forefinger. "You did an admirable job, Ms. Cranwell, but . . . ," Pickett said, shrugging and showing her the upturned palms of his hands.

The judge turned toward Jewel Tate, who once again appeared to bat her eyelashes at him. Pickett cleared his throat. "Ahem, Ms. Stone, your request is granted. The defendant, Jewel Tate, is found not guilty of all charges and released from bond."

Pickett hammered his gavel authoritatively. "Case dismissed."

As the courtroom crowd erupted, Jewel plucked her cell phone out of her purse and began typing a message, not the slightest hint of emotion showing.

CHAPTER 27

June 7

Marianne Tate sat quietly in the back row of the courtroom, a baseball cap pulled low over her head, her face obscured behind a pair of oversized mirrored aviator sunglasses, and listened as the judge issued his ruling. She remained motionless for a moment, absorbing what she had just heard, and closely monitored Jewel, who was applying a coat of fuchsia gloss to her lips from a compact she held in her hand while Jewel's lawyer chatted nearby with opposing counsel. Marianne shook her head, discouraged. She slipped out of the courtroom unnoticed, past security, down the front steps, and out onto the street.

She turned right and walked briskly down Courthouse Boulevard, crossing the street to the other side when she saw a phalanx of reporters heading her way. She needn't have bothered. No one recognized her. Instead, the journalists were converging on Jewel and her lawyer, who were exiting the courthouse.

Marianne pivoted, cemented to the spot, and watched as the horde descended on the pair and thought:

That slut is much craftier than I gave her credit for. She pulled the wool over my brother's eyes, but, on a certain level, that's understandable, if not forgivable. He was just a man, after all. How hard could that be? She flashed Geoff that waxed snatch of hers and fake tits, and his brain went haywire.

But that's not what's bothering me. What worries me most is she fooled the sheriff's investigator, a sharp woman, with that trail cam bullshit, and she fooled her attorney, another supposedly smart woman. She even fooled the judge, for crying out loud, but there again, he's a man. Impartial, my ass.

If they think I'm going to stand by and let them loot my brother's company, well, they don't know me, then. I told that reporter I'd get to the bottom of this or die trying, and that's exactly what I intend to do.

I got a plan. It's messy, for sure, but it's coming together. Who said, "Everybody's got a plan until they get punched in the mouth?" Some boxer, I think, maybe Rocky, and he was right. I got me a list, and I'm checking off names. It won't be complete until I cross off that bitch's name. Save the best for last.

Shaka's gonna be a big help. That man is money. Couldn't do it without him, and it doesn't hurt he's great in the sack. I'd never let getting laid interfere with my business judgment, though. That right there, in a nutshell, is the biggest difference between a man and a woman, if you're looking for one. There're lots of others, but that's numero uno.

Time's running out. Word is Mack is looking for a buyer for Yukon. That'd be a disaster. Geoff borrowed a lot of money against Yukon stock, and banks are now clamoring to get repaid with the stock price depressed. I told the bankers not to panic, the stock will rebound, they'll get their money. But that's what bankers do, panic. That's about all they do.

Once Mack sells the company, it's all over, and Geoff's dreams will be as dead as he is. They'll scatter to the wind.

Jewel will grab the cash and run, and good luck trying to find her then.

Shaka says tracking Jewel and Mack is as easy as following a funeral procession. He strung StingRay eavesdropping devices near their homes and offices and has followed them every step of the way.

Wonder what that reporter Nik Byron is up to? I should check in on him, see if Jewel got him fooled, too. Wouldn't surprise me one bit. Men.

Well, she ain't fooling me, I guaran-fuckin'-tee you that.

A town car pulled up alongside Marianne as she studied the crowd that now ringed Jewel and her attorney. The window buzzed down.

"You coming?" Shaka asked, and Marianne pulled open the passenger's door and climbed inside.

PART III

FALLOUT

CHAPTER 28

June 15

Working off-hours and nights, it took Nik nearly three weeks to plow through the thousands of pages of Bullwhip documents that were sitting in his condo's spare bedroom. The task was staggering, even with the zip drives the anonymous Pentagon source had hidden in the files. Discarded pizza boxes, sandwich wrappers, and empty cans of Dr Pepper covered the bedroom floor by the time he finished.

Fortunately, Nik had some alone time on his hands after he and Sam had a heated exchange at a DC bar following her surprise courtroom testimony. Nik was furious she had not tipped him off about her appearance and the discovery of the trail cam, while Sam was unsympathetic and contemptuous that Nik felt entitled to the information.

"Maybe I'm old-school, but no one ever handed me stories when I was a reporter. I had to dig and fight for every one I got," Sam had castigated Nik.

"That's not fair, Sam. It'd be different if we weren't seeing each other. Don't you get that?"

"Grow up, Nik. We're not in junior high."

"I looked like an ass, with no help from you."

"You don't need my help, Nik. You manage well enough on your own," Sam said belittlingly.

"If that's the way you feel, Sam, maybe this thing between us ain't such a good idea."

"You'll get no argument here," she said dismissively and took a sip of wine.

Nik tossed two twenties on the bar. "Screw this," he said and walked out.

Now, sitting in his condo, Nik regretted the row and blamed himself. He sighed, picked up another file from the endless pile, and started reading again.

Mia had offered to help Nik sort through the mounds of paper, but he had declined. Over the years, Nik had developed his own particular method for surveying and cataloguing records, and he didn't have the time or patience to explain the labor-intensive process to others.

When working on an investigation that involved extensive documentation, it was Nik's practice to begin by constructing a series of concentric circles that placed the subjects—in this instance, Geoffrey Tate and Yukon—at the center of the bull's-eye. Each circle that emanated from the middle contained additional names that represented potential sources and avenues. The lines were color coded to reflect the number of times a person, company, or record was mentioned, and the closer the line was to the center, the more relevant the lead.

When he was done, Nik had no fewer than eighty-three potentially promising targets—not an insignificant number, but manageable, especially if past was prologue. Nik had found that the first 25 percent of the names on a list produced 99 percent of the material he needed for a story. If that experience held true this time, he'd only have to track down twenty or so sources.

The process, though tedious, had the added benefit of allowing Nik to see interlocking relationships he might otherwise overlook. Three such connections here jumped out at him immediately.

One was Thomas Polk, the former CEO of a Silicon Valley company who now co-chaired the National Security Commission on Artificial Intelligence, a congressional advisory committee; the second, Alexander Hiatt, a retired lieutenant general who once oversaw the military's technology budget; and the third was Allan Trumbo, former chief of staff to the vice president of the United States.

The men had one thing in common: Blue Sky Consulting, Washington, DC's premier lobbying firm and the most recent home of Dwayne Mack, Yukon's former chief lobbyist and the company's newly installed CEO. All three individuals, at one time or another, had office space in the same K Street building that housed Blue Sky.

Happy coincidence? Maybe. Nik didn't know. Maybe not. He intended to find out.

But first, he owed Mia a script on the military's artificial intelligence program.

CHAPTER 29

June 21

Dwayne Mack shuffled into his kitchen, head down, deep in thought, the skies outside his window a brackish hue. It was barely daybreak, but it was already hot and muggy and it promised to be another sticky, blistering Washington, DC, day, a carbon copy of the day before, and the day before that, and the week before that. Mack retrieved a bag of French roast coffee beans from a cabinet and poured them into a $1,200 Italian espresso machine that ground the beans, heated water, and brewed a perfect cup of coffee.

The first few months on the job had not been kind to Yukon's new CEO. The company's initial phase of the Pentagon's Bullwhip contract was behind schedule and over budget, a congressional armed services committee was threatening to hold hearings on the project; the Saudis were demanding access to Yukon's military technology that they had paid handsomely, and secretly, for; and Nik Byron, a reporter from *Newshound*, was badgering him for an interview. Mack's hair was falling out in clumps, and he had packed on an extra eight pounds.

But those problems were not weighing on him this morning. Instead, Jewel Tate occupied his thoughts.

After a self-imposed hiatus following her courtroom victory, Jewel had publicly resurfaced at Yukon's annual shareholders' meeting, and then, several days later, at the company's offices, and then at Mack's apartment building late one evening.

Standing in the hallway outside his apartment, Toby clutched under one arm, Jewel wore a waist-length flaming-red wig, mid-thigh overcoat, and black stiletto heels. When Mack cracked open the door, she unzipped the front of the coat, exposing a skimpy mauve negligee no larger than an embroidered doily.

"I think you look better in the black wig," Mack said, sticking his head out the door and craning his neck side to side to make sure the hallway was clear before ushering her into his apartment.

The sex was, as always was the case with Jewel, rough, and for a moment, Mack was convinced Jewel had dislocated his shoulder when she wrenched his right arm behind his back. When he screamed in pain, her only reaction was to twist the arm even harder.

When they were through, Jewel said, "Now we can get down to business."

"What do you mean?" an exhausted Mack said, massaging his shoulder and worrying she intended to torture him further.

"Company business. I want that skank of a sister-in-law gone from Yukon's office. Like, yesterday."

"I'm not sure that's such a good idea, Jewel."

"And I want access to the company jet, like you promised. I'm so over flying commercial."

"All in good time. We had a plan, and we need to stick to it."

"And where are you on negotiating the sale of the company? I'm sitting on all this fuckin' Yukon stock that's absolutely no good to me since Geoff had it tied up six ways to Sunday. The only way I hit pay dirt is when the company's sold. So far, all I got out of this deal is a mortgage on a big house, a horse farm out in the middle of Bumfuck, and a yacht, and I get seasick if I'm in a body of water any larger than a swimming pool."

Mack got up and waddled over to a liquor cabinet in his bedroom, ass cheeks flapping, and poured himself a tumbler of Scotch. "Well, there's a small problem there, Jewel," he said and took a sip.

"You gonna offer a lady a drink?" Jewel asked, spread-eagle on the bed.

"Sure, whaddya have?"

"Vodka. Rocks. What's this small problem?"

"Rupert Olen," Mack said, referring to Yukon's second-largest shareholder, who had orchestrated Mack's hiring at Yukon. Mack filled Jewel's glass with Russian vodka he had gotten from a Moscow oligarch as a gift. "He doesn't want to sell so close to Geoff's, ahhhh, passing with the stock price still soft."

"Rupert?" Jewel spat. "When did he start calling the shots? I thought you were in charge."

"Rupert's the chairman of the board now. Believe me, he wants to cash out as much as we do, but he says the timing's not right. It's gonna be a while longer, but I'm working on him."

"How much longer?"

"Rupert says six months, maybe a year, and besides that, I got these politicians and the Saudis breathing down my fuckin' neck that I need to take care of first."

"Now, you listen to me, Dwayne," Jewel said, reaching for her drink, "because I'm only gonna say this one time. I don't give a rat's ass about the board, the politicians, or the A-rabs.

You better find a buyer right quick or people might just learn how you fixed it to land that Bullwhip contract in the first place."

"What about Rupert?"

"Don't you worry about Rupert. You just worry about a buyer, you hear me."

"Awright, awright. I said I'm working on it."

"We understand each other?"

Mack nodded.

"Good. Now get back over here. I ain't finished with you yet."

Mack gulped his drink, grimaced, and edged back toward the bed.

———

Jewel's words were still rolling around in Dwayne Mack's head days later when he swung his canary-yellow Mustang into Yukon's parking garage a little before six a.m. He guided the car into the slot marked "Yukon CEO. Reserved 24 hours daily. Violators will be towed," lost in his musings. The more he thought about Jewel's threats, the more it pissed him off.

Who the hell does she think she is, talking to me like that? She really thinks she can intimidate me and Rupert. Stupid fuckin' cracker. Mack gathered up his belongings from the passenger's seat and stepped out of his car.

He congratulated himself again for making sure he had a rock-solid alibi the night Geoff Tate was killed. *No way they can put me anywhere near the scene of that crime,* he told himself.

Mack fumbled in his coat for his Yukon identity badge and keys, and that's when he noticed Rupert Olen's black Range Rover on the other side of the garage, its parking lights on. He thought, *That's odd,* and made his way over to the vehicle.

He approached from the back and looked through the rear

window, but he couldn't make out much through the smoked glass and high seat backs. He circled around toward the front and could see Olen's head resting against the driver's side window. Mack didn't want to startle the sleeping Olen, so he walked in a wide arc to the front of the Rover and peered in through the windshield.

He was staring at Olen, lips peeled back, capped teeth glistening under the garage lights, his skin tawny, channels of dried blood running down his face and neck, a handheld pickax plunged into his right eye socket.

Mack puked on his shoes and passed out.

CHAPTER 30

June 22

Nik was alone in *Newshound*'s darkened recording studio, editing sound bites and finalizing the script he had promised Mia. He preferred to work deep into the night, when there were fewer distractions. Once, as punishment, *Newshound*'s chief editor assigned Nik the graveyard shift for a couple of months. Nik had embraced the solitude and flourished. It turned out to be one of the most productive periods of his career.

Nik booted up the recording equipment, ran a quick sound check, and laid the completed script out in front of him. It wasn't exactly the story that Mia was expecting. In fact, he thought it was much better.

The story idea had evolved as Nik dug into the military's artificial intelligence program and the Bullwhip contract. He had also managed to get Tanner Black, one of the few military critics of the program at the time the contract was awarded, to go on the record. Black, a former Pentagon official, now worked for one of DC's leading military think tanks.

Nik adjusted his headset, began to narrate, and selectively dropped in audio quotes from Black.

Producer's introduction: This is the fourth install-ment of *The Front Page* podcast exploring the life and death of Geoffrey Tate and his company, Yukon Inc. The podcast is narrated by *Newshound* reporter Nik Byron. His guest is Tanner Black, a military expert.

Bullwhip

Nik Byron: When people hear the word "Mars," they gen-erally think of the fourth planet in the solar system, or the candy bar company.

There is another MARS, and it is the backbone of the US military's battlefield analytics strategy for the twenty-first century.

This MARS stands for Machine-Assisted Analytic Rapid-Repository System.

The brainchild of the Defense Intelligence Agency, MARS aims to harness the power of artificial intelligence, cloud computing, big data, and machine learning to pro-duce dynamic information for fighting forces in real time to counter and thwart enemy aggression, according to Tanner Black, a former Pentagon official and military expert.

Tanner Black: If warfare was conducted on a chess-board, MARS theoretically would enable the US to know its adversaries' moves ten steps in advance and neutralize them.

Nik Byron: But as ambitious and promising as MARS sounds, it is ultimately one-handed clapping. The Pentagon concluded that in order to create a truly lethal deterrent, it had to develop MARS in parallel with AI-inspired armament: autonomous drones, helicopters, fixed-winged planes, tanks, ships, and all manner of offensive weapons systems.

That insight gave birth to the single largest military AI procurement in the history of the Pentagon, otherwise known as Project Bullwhip—the US government's $500 billion bet to build an unmanned and autonomous war armada powered by artificial intelligence.

Tanner Black: As far as the brass at the Pentagon and US politicians were concerned, there was only one company on the face of the earth that could pull off Bullwhip—Yukon Corporation.

Nik Byron: For the US military, Bullwhip represented the dawn of a new era in warfare, and for Yukon, the project cemented its reputation as the most advanced artificial intelligence company in the world.

The Bullwhip project eventually received bipartisan support in Congress, but not before fierce battles over the price tag and the moral ambiguity of building machines that could indiscriminately slaughter thousands without human intervention, according to Black, who objected to the program's cost and questioned Yukon's ability to deliver on its promises.

Tanner Black: Ironically, Bullwhip might never have gotten off the drawing board had it not received an assist from an unexpected quarter.

Nik Byron: That help came in the form of America's top adversary—Russia. The country's Advanced Research Foundation, the equivalent of DARPA in the United States, unveiled Marker, an autonomous, unmanned ground vehicle with the goal of eventually weaponizing swarms of the tanklike machines for war zone conflicts. Subsequently, Russia also suggested it was conducting trials with robots

to take the place of combat troops. The United States decided it could no longer wait to launch its own unmanned
autonomous program, and Bullwhip was officially born.

Critics of the Bullwhip program did come away with
a partial victory. The Department of Defense formally adopted the Five Principles of Artificial Intelligence recommended by the Defense Innovation Board to govern the
"ethical design, development, deployment, and use of AI"
by the military.

The Bullwhip project celebrated its second anniver-
sary last month. It is $157 million over budget and ten
months behind schedule.

CHAPTER 31

June 24

"Investigators are refusing to comment on potentially new explosive information surrounding the gruesome murder of Yukon Corporation's chairman of the board and second-largest shareholder, Rupert Olen," Elizabeth Blake's voice blared from the television set while Nik stood in Samantha Whyte's bathroom toweling himself off after a shower.

"You hear that?" Nik called to Sam, who was in the kitchen making coffee and scrambling eggs for breakfast. Nik and Sam had only just reconciled after falling out over Sam's surprise courtroom testimony, and the relationship, while still on shaky ground, was slowly returning to normal.

"Yeah, I heard," Sam replied.

"Could you turn it up?"

"However, this reporter has learned that DC Detectives Yvette Jenks and Jason Goetz suspect that Olen was killed elsewhere and that his body was moved to Yukon's parking garage, where it was discovered by company CEO Dwayne Mack," Lizzy continued.

"Did I hear that right?" Nik shouted.

"Yup."

Nik cinched the towel around his waist and walked hurriedly into the living room, where he stood in front of the TV, a puddle of water forming on the hardwood floor at his feet. Sam joined him and handed Nik a cup of black coffee and a slice of buttered toast with strawberry jam spread on top.

"Thanks," he said, and took a bite of toast and began to chew.

"What time's your baseball game?" Sam asked, pulling her phone out of the pocket of the cotton robe she was wearing and checking its clock.

"Early. I gotta get a move on, but I want to hear this first."

"Based on information harvested from heart rate and GPS apps on the smartwatch Olen was wearing, investigators were able to pinpoint the time and location of his death when his heart stopped beating. Sources tell this reporter that the evidence indicates that the crime took place outside of the District of Columbia in an unincorporated area of rural Northern Virginia County."

"Wait," Nik said, perplexed. "Did she just say unincorporated Northern Virginia?"

"Hush. Listen."

"This is Elizabeth Blake . . ."

"Sam?"

"For Channel 13 News reporting."

"Olen was killed in Northern Virginia County. That's your jurisdiction, Sam."

Sam picked up the TV remote from a coffee table in front of the television and hit the Mute button. She could feel another storm brewing between them, and she wanted to head it off.

"Look, Nik, we've been down this road. I don't want to fight again. We're just getting over our last argument."

"Tell me, did you know about this information beforehand?"

"Maybe."

"And is there more to it?"

"Possibly."

"Who's Lizzy's source?"

"How should I know?"

"Sure it's not you?"

"Don't go there, Nik. I told you she was sleeping with the county prosecutor."

"You don't trust me, Sam. That's a problem," Nik said angrily. Blood rushed into Sam's cheeks, turning them a sunburned red. "The problem here is you, Nik. You don't respect me or what I do."

"Whaddya expect, Sam, you're a flack," Nik snapped and regretted it the moment it left his mouth.

"You need to go," Sam said coldly.

"Don't worry, I plan to."

"I mean now."

She spun around and stormed back into the kitchen, and Nik headed to the bedroom. Over her shoulder, Sam added, "And wipe up that water on the floor before you do, and make sure you leave the house key on the hallway table on your way out. You're not going to need it."

———

The baseball game was a travesty. Nik's fight with Sam had rattled him, and he had a hard time concentrating. He booted two easy ground balls, flubbed a relay at second base, and had a throwing error. Worse still, it was against Chase Hurley's Washington Supremes team, and the whole time Nik could hear Hurley hectoring him from the dugout. After the game when the teams lined up to shake hands, Nik was tempted to punch Hurley in the mouth.

Nik called Sam at least a half-dozen times to apologize, but she didn't answer her phone. He decided against sending her a text and thought about driving over to her house with flowers following the game, but he remembered he had agreed to take Maggie out for a drink to celebrate her courtroom victory. He briefly considered canceling on Maggie but wanted to find out if she knew anything about the Bullwhip contract. He had a vague recollection that the Justice Department had looked into the project at one time when Maggie still worked for the US attorney's office.

Nik dashed home, took a quick shower, and fed Gyp before rushing back out to meet Maggie. When he opened his apartment door to leave, though, Gyp bolted out and tore down the hallway.

"Gyp, whoa," Nik commanded, but the dog bounded away, and, not for the first time, Nik felt the money he had spent on obedience training was a complete waste. He found Gyp in the lobby sitting quietly next to an attractive woman in running shorts, shoes, and a T-shirt who was stroking the top of the dog's head.

"Sorry," Nik said and grabbed Gyp's collar. "Bad dog."

"That's okay, I like dogs."

"You might have a different opinion if you knew him better."

"He's got a beautiful coat. What is he?"

"A vizsla. Thanks for corralling him for me."

"Don't mention it. Name's Reese, by the way. Moved in recently. I'm subletting from a woman who's on assignment for the World Bank in Vietnam," she said and extended her hand.

He grasped it and said, "Nik, nice to meet you. This is Gyp. Headed out for a run?"

"Yeah. Still trying to get my bearings and figure out the best routes around here," she said, bouncing on the balls of her feet. Reese had an angular face; developed shoulders; and long, lean arms and legs. Nik wondered if she might be a competitive swimmer or rock climber.

"Try Kalorama. That's where I usually run. Take a right out of the building on Connecticut Avenue, then a left on Kalorama Road, and that will take you right into the heart of the Kalorama neighborhood and past all the embassies. The Obamas have a house there."

"I'll give it a shot."

"I think you'll like it."

"Thanks, and nice to meet you. Nice to meet you, too, Gyp," Reese said and bent down and patted the dog's head. Gyp responded by lifting a paw for a shake. Reese wrinkled her nose, laughed, and grasped his paw. "I do love dogs. If you ever need anybody to watch him, I'd be happy to help. I work from home."

"Really? If you're serious, I'll drop off a key to my place. The pet sitter isn't always available, and it would save me a trip running home from the office during the day to give him a walk or feed him."

"Happy to," Reese said, gave Nik and Gyp a quick wave, and headed for the door.

"I got to hand it to you," Nik said, tugging at Gyp's collar as they walked back up the staircase. "You always seem to find the good-looking ones to take you in."

CHAPTER 32

June 24

Maggie was fifteen minutes late for her drink with Nik, and when she arrived, she told him she couldn't stay long. "Got a firm function with clients," she explained. Nik suspected she had a date but didn't want to tell him.

They met downstairs in the Churchill Club in the Chevy Chase neighborhood of DC, where Maggie had recently moved. The club featured a billiards room; library; dining room; two bars, one on the fourth floor and one on the ground floor; and a walk-in humidor where members stored their cigars. The building was originally a hotel where, legend had it, Winston Churchill stayed when he visited Washington.

There were about a dozen customers in the bar talking softly when Maggie and Nik found a booth near the back and ordered champagne. After the waiter served them their drinks, they toasted Maggie's courtroom triumph.

"I gotta say, Maggs, that trail cam video was devastating," Nik said.

"Well, Sam and her team of investigators deserve most of

the credit. You know, the damn thing was concealed in the crook of the trunk covered in camouflage webbing. No wonder they didn't see it the first time."

"Sam said they would never have found it had an arborist not been on the property pruning that tree. She said it was just coincidence the tree doctor had been called to cut back some dead limbs when investigators revisited the estate."

"Hmmm," Maggie said and took a sip of her drink. "How is Sam anyway?"

"Couldn't tell you. She's not speaking to me."

Nik quickly filled Maggie in on their argument. When he was done explaining what had happened, Maggie said, "Apologize, Nik. You're a fool if you let her get away. And this isn't about Sam's career, or, at least, it's not *just* about that."

"What makes you say that?"

"Well, it's kind of obvious, isn't it, Nik?" Maggie added and looked down at her phone to read an incoming text message.

"What is?"

"That Sam wants to get married and have a family," she said and typed a quick reply to the text.

"Tried that once," Nik said with a frown, "and if you recall, I sucked at it."

"Wasn't entirely your fault, but if that's the way you feel, you need to tell Sam and let her get on with her life."

Nik took a handful of nuts from a bowl on the table. He wasn't sure what he felt, either about Sam or having this conversation with Maggie. He and Maggie had been good friends before they got married, and now they got along ten times better than they did when they were married. It was only when they were married that they hated each other. He didn't want the same thing to happen with Sam.

"One more drink?" he asked.

"I really do need to be going, Nik."

"Come on, just one more."

"Okay, but it's gotta be quick."

Nik flagged down their waiter and ordered Maggie another glass of champagne while he switched to a Budweiser. "There's been something I've been meaning to ask," he said when the drinks arrived.

"I can't talk to you about the case, Nik. Client confidentiality, you know that."

"It's not about the case, exactly, but Yukon. When you were at Justice, did you open an investigation into the Bullwhip contract?"

"I didn't personally, but our office did. Why?"

"What became of the investigation?"

"Nothing, as far as I recall. It just kinda quietly went away."

"Was that normal?"

"Not abnormal. What are you getting at?" Maggie's phone chirped again, and she reached for it and batted out another text. "I really am running late. You got two minutes, Nik."

Nik told Maggie about uncovering the overlapping connections he had come across while researching the Bullwhip documents. "All these people—former vice presidential aide, retired army general, former Silicon Valley CEO—had ties to Blue Sky Consulting, and now Blue Sky's top lobbyist, Dwayne Mack, is running Yukon. And, oh, by the way, Yukon's chairman of the board had a small pickax buried in his skull."

Maggie stood to leave. She was wearing a flattering black dress with a scooped back. It didn't look like the type of outfit she'd select for an office function. When she leaned in to give Nik a goodbye kiss on the cheek, he could detect the unmistakable scent of Shalimar perfume, her favorite. "All right, give me a couple days. I'll make a few calls."

"Great, Maggs. I appreciate it, and I got this," he said, reaching for the bill.

"And you can do something for me."

Nik cocked his head and looked over at her.

"Sort things out with Sam, for your own sake."

CHAPTER 33

June 26

Closing time was seven p.m., less than thirty minutes away, and the crowd at the panda exhibit at the National Zoo had finally begun to thin out. The only people remaining were a young couple and two families with little kids, all eating ice cream. A zoo caretaker appeared and reminded the observers they needed to start heading for the exits before the park closed and locked its gates.

Teo Mezos was sitting on a wooden bench under a shade tree watching the attendant coax the visitors to leave. The stultifying heat that had gripped the region for days on end was finally showing signs of lifting. Teo got up and strolled over to the exhibit after the last of the onlookers departed. He was standing there when Elizabeth Blake walked up behind him.

"Thought they were never going to leave," she said and lit a cigarette.

Teo glanced at the television reporter, her upper lip sprinkled with perspiration. She looked different on camera. For one, she seemed more effervescent, and for another, the makeup she wore made her skin appear as smooth as polished marble. Up close, she looked tired, her complexion pale, her lips encircled by a spiderweb of microscopic wrinkles.

"You're not supposed to smoke in the zoo," Teo chided and turned to see if the attendant was still nearby.

"Look at you, Mr. Boy Scout," Blake said with a sneer. "No one's gonna know, Teo. Place is nearly deserted."

Teo first met Elizabeth Blake at a lunch in DC arranged by Dick Whetstone, *Newshound*'s chief editor. He didn't particularly like her then. She flirted with him during lunch, pawed his arm, and wanted to touch his dreadlocks. He liked her even less now, he decided, but Whetstone assured him he could work with her.

"Next time, let's meet somewhere else. Makes me sad to see these animals in cages."

"Sure, whatever, Teo. What do you got for me?"

Teo reached into his pants pocket and produced a flash drive and passed it to Blake. She dropped the drive into her purse.

"What's on it?"

"Unreleased Yukon podcasts, Byron's notes on the Bullwhip contract, list of sources and contact information. That sorta thing."

Elizabeth paused to take a deep drag on the cigarette. "Thanks, but why, exactly, are you doing this?" she said and blew out a cloud of smoke that encircled Teo. "Don't misunderstand me. I'm happy to get the information. I just can't figure out what's in it for you."

Teo had his reasons, but he wasn't inclined to share them with a television reporter, of all people. He hadn't left his job as a nightclub DJ just to produce news podcasts. He had much larger ambitions. He cared deeply about current affairs—culture, politics, race, sports—and believed there was a huge podcast audience and business opportunity for these topics told from a young person's perspective, if done right. He thought it a waste of time and resources to chase the Yukon story when there were much more important issues to pursue.

To Elizabeth Blake, he said, "I don't care about rich white people killing one another. Let 'em have at it."

"Charming," she said, bored, and then paused. "I want to get a look at all of Byron's Yukon scripts and stories."

"Shouldn't be a problem."

"I also want access to everything the team is working on, not just Yukon."

"No. I told you when we first met, Yukon material only. All the other podcast stories are off-limits."

"You know, Teo," she said, resting a hand on his back and gently rubbing it, "you don't have a lot of bargaining power. They find out that you moved those Bullwhip files and that you've been furnishing me information, you'll be fired. Might even get prosecuted."

Teo glared at Blake. "That's bullshit. You wouldn't do that. We had a deal."

"You and Whetstone had a deal, and don't think for a moment he'll back you up. He hates Byron, and he'd like nothing more than to see the whole podcast operation go up in flames."

"Hey," a voice called out. It was the zoo employee Teo had seen earlier. "You need to leave. Gate closes in five minutes. And no smoking in the zoo."

"I told her," Teo said.

"Leaving now. We were hoping to see the pandas one more time. We just love them," Blake said.

She dropped the smoldering cigarette on the walking path and ground it into the dirt with her toe. "Remember, Teo, next time I want everything," she said before spinning around and walking off.

CHAPTER 34

July 1

Allan Trumbo prided himself on being unshakeable. As the former chief of staff to the vice president of the United States, Trumbo glided from one crisis to the next like an Olympic figure skater, head held high, chest out, always racing forward, never losing his composure. He even looked like an Olympian—tall, fit, dashing, Brylcreemed hair. His peers took to calling him Never Stumble Trumbo. The bigger the stage, the greater the performance. He was never so good as when his boss was backed into a corner by political scandal or personal indiscretions. He managed to convince the religious right to support his candidate for the veep position even after audio recordings surfaced revealing the man took indecent liberties with a female intern.

"The sounds you hear on that tape are two incredibly driven individuals working out in the gym together, side by side, pushing each other to excel, and for anyone to suggest anything untoward is, honestly, just disgusting and beneath contempt," Trumbo, with a straight face, told an incredulous

press gathering, an event that salvaged the vice president's political career and cemented Trumbo as a world-class fixer.

Political watchers were shocked when Trumbo left his job
with the vice president to enter the private sector, but assumed
he would return to public service when the right ambassador-
ship or agency head position came along.

Trumbo had no such ambitions. He was tired of seeing
half-wits with nowhere near his abilities raking in piles of
money from their government connections, and he was bound
and determined to cash in while his party still held power.

His plan was working flawlessly, too, right up until the moment Rupert Olen was found with a pickax buried in his eye
socket. For the first time he could remember, Allan Trumbo
did something out of character.

He panicked.

———

"So best guess it was the Saudis," Trumbo informed the small
group sitting around an enormous oak table laden with bottles
of single-malt Scotch and cigars in Dwayne Mack's rustic fishing lodge on Chincoteague Island on Virginia's Eastern Shore.
The wind was howling off the Atlantic Ocean, and they could
hear powerful waves crashing against the dock outside.

Trumbo and Mack had arrived a day earlier on a small
charter plane. The other two members of the group, retired
three-star army Lieutenant General Alexander Hiatt and
Silicon Valley entrepreneur Thomas Polk, drove separately and
took the Chesapeake Bay Bridge to the island. They had shown
up at the lodge only hours before.

"This better be important," the general had growled, removing the rain slicker he was wearing. The general hadn't set
a boot on a battlefield in more than a decade and had grown

soft around the middle and was slightly stooped from years sitting behind a desk at the Pentagon. "It's risky as hell."

"It's gonna be awright, Al," Polk assured him. "We're out in the middle of nowhere with a nor'easter stewing offshore. Ain't nobody moving about in this weather."

Mack nodded.

The last time this group—which Mack had dubbed his X-Team—met was more than two years before at the same location to secretly hatch a plan to rig the $500 billion Bullwhip contract and steer it to Yukon. After that, they dispersed and pledged never, under any circumstances, to meet again as a group unless it was an absolute emergency.

They had honored that commitment until a rattled Allan Trumbo sent an encrypted message and insisted they reconvene.

Trumbo's role in the rigged Bullwhip contract was to author documents lauding Yukon that the vice president's office circulated to the White House and on Capitol Hill; General Hiatt, who oversaw the military's technology budget before retiring, used his influence to bribe Pentagon contacts with promises of future employment, luxury vacations, and payoffs; Mack ginned up phony bid sheets and extorted key senators and Congress members into voting for the bill authorizing Bullwhip; and Polk strong-armed members of the National Security Commission on Artificial Intelligence, a congressional advisory committee that he co-chaired, to publicly endorse the program.

The only member of the group who was absent was moneyman Rupert Olen, who had bankrolled the kickback scheme and stood to gain untold riches.

"To Rupert," they said in unison and hoisted a drink in his memory, each quietly calculating the extra share they now stood to gain with Olen out of the picture.

"It's gotta be the Saudis," Mack agreed with Trumbo. "They paid a couple hundred million for Bullwhip's AI technology, and so far, we haven't held up our end of the bargain. As far as they're concerned, we've given them dick."

The general lit a cigar and asked, "What about the broad?"

"What, Jewel?" Mack said.

"Yeah, her, the little strumpet. She plugged Tate and got away with it, didn't she? Wouldn't surprise me at all that Rupert was dipping into her honeypot as well."

"Naw," Mack said dismissively, avoiding any mention of his private late-night sessions with Jewel at his apartment and her threats to expose him and Rupert. "Definitely the Saudis."

"Fucking towelheads," the general said. "Up to me, I'da nuked the whole motherfuckin' nest of 'em after nine/eleven."

Polk got up and strutted to a window. "Anybody else hear that?" he asked just before the lights in the cabin flickered before going out. Polk was staring into an island-wide blackout.

"It's the storm, Tom," Mack said. "It's knocked out the transformer. Give it a minute."

Moments later, they heard the twin diesel engines on Mack's generator cough, then kick in, restoring the lodge's power. "One of us needs to parlay with the Saudis," Mack said when the lights came back up, "and it can't be me. I'm already under a microscope as it is."

All eyes shifted to Trumbo.

"You called this meeting, Allan, so I'm hoping you got some ideas," Polk said.

"I do."

Mack picked up a bottle of twenty-five-year-old Macallan from the table and refilled everyone's glasses. "Okay, let's hear 'em."

They all nodded when Trumbo had finished his presentation. His plan just might work.

"We should turn in," the general said after he polished off

his Scotch, "if we want to be out of here by zero-dark-thirty. And, remember, we leave separately and by different routes."

"I'll go first," Trumbo said, "and drop Mack's vehicle at the ferry terminal. I'll catch the early-morning boat back to the mainland and get a flight to DC from there. I'll reach out to the Saudis and arrange a meeting. Look for an encrypted update from me in a day or two."

Outside, the waves battered a skiff as it clawed its way toward the lodge's swaying dock, a lone figure debarking when it finally edged alongside. The pilot handed up a small dry bag before shoving off. The boat cleared the dock and the pilot gunned the motor. The craft struggled against the chop, the engine's whine muffled by the building storm.

CHAPTER 35

July 2

The storm that was threatening landfall had moved back out to sea overnight, and the air was quiet and heavy when Allan Trumbo stepped out of the lodge early the next morning, the island plunged into nearly universal darkness by the power outage, tens of thousands of stars winking overhead like popping flashbulbs at a rock concert. Trumbo tossed his overnight bag into the trunk of the cream-colored Chevy Caprice that was sitting in the carport and went back inside to get a cup of coffee and send an encrypted message to his Saudi contact before departing for the ferry terminal. Dwayne Mack had gotten up early to make coffee and clean up, and Trumbo could hear the others stirring as he headed back out the door to the car. It was three forty-five a.m.

Trumbo wrestled open the door on the late-model Chevy and slid behind the wheel. It reminded him of his grandfather's car—a land yacht, steering wheel the size of a Hula-Hoop, back seat like a separate country, AM radio with push buttons, crank-down windows. The engine sputtered to life, and he shifted into drive and slowly weaved his way back to the main highway.

The road was deserted, and he made the ferry landing in forty-five minutes and parked the car in the long-term lot, knowing Mack would send one of his workmen to fetch it in a few days.

He tuned the radio to an easy-listening station, tilted his head back against the seat, closed his eyes, and waited for the boat. The ferry slid silently into its slip, moored at the dock, lowered its gangplank for walk-on passengers, and gave a short blast of its horn, announcing its arrival.

There were only a handful of cars in the lot, and people staggered forward in darkness, rubbing their eyes and slowly feeling their way along the uneven gravel path. Trumbo popped the car's trunk, removed his luggage, and fell in line with the other zombie passengers as they made their way toward the terminal.

Trumbo climbed the stairs to the boat's upper deck, which, unlike belowdecks, was more exposed to the elements and therefore deserted. He scouted out a booth in the back of the boat and rolled his bag across the linoleum floor. Once the boat got underway, the crew dimmed the lights to allow passengers to get some sleep during the hour-plus journey. Trumbo rested his head against his bag, closed his eyes, and fell fast asleep to the vessel's gentle rocking.

When the ferry docked, an attendant made a sweep of the decks. He was used to rousting sleeping passengers who nodded off during the predawn cruise. In the dimness, he could make out the shape of a passenger in a back booth shrouded in darkness. He called out as he approached. When there was no response, he said, louder this time, "All ashore." There was still no movement. "Probably had a little too much to drink last night," he muttered to himself and reached over the bench to shake the figure.

"Hey," he said, jostling the body, "we've arrived. It's time to debark."

That's when Allan Trumbo's body pitched backward, head lolling to the side. The attendant gagged, staggered, got his feet entangled, and slammed into a table. If he lived to be one hundred, he'd never forget what he saw: the man's throat splayed open like a gutted fish, chest drenched in syrupy beet-red blood, the liquid pooling on the seat and floor.

CHAPTER 36

July 3

Nik was driving across the Key Bridge from Virginia back to the District, headed to Sam's house, when he got the call from Maggie. "Jed Doyle is the guy you want to talk to," she said when Nik answered. "He led the investigation into the Bullwhip contract."

Nik pulled the top off a ballpoint pen with his teeth and scribbled Doyle's name down in a notebook he retrieved from his satchel. "You got a number?"

"Yeah. It's a 206 area code," Maggie said and rattled off a number.

"Where's that?"

"Washington State, Seattle area, I think. He abruptly resigned and moved out there after higher-ups in the Justice Department pulled the plug on the investigation."

"Did you know Doyle?"

"Knew of him. Good reputation. Career DOJ attorney. That's why everyone was surprised when he resigned."

"Can I mention your name?"

"Rather you not. I'm still in good standing with folks at Justice, and I'd like to keep it that way. They find out I'm feeding stuff to a reporter, that wouldn't look so good."

Maggie told Nik she wasn't sure if the phone number she had was Doyle's private or office number and that she heard he had formed a law firm with a couple of other ex–Justice Department attorneys who were already living in the Pacific Northwest. Before she hung up, she asked, "You straighten things out with Sam yet?"

It'd been more than a week since their last argument, and Sam still had not returned Nik's calls or responded to his stream of text messages. "Matter of fact, I'm pulling up outside her house this very minute. I went by her office but she wasn't there. I plan to surprise her when she comes home."

"I don't know, Nik. You think that's a good idea? You don't want Sam to feel like you're ambushing her," Maggie said.

"Ambush? Nonsense," Nik said dismissively. "Hey, there's her car now. I gotta go. Wish me luck, and thanks for the info, Maggs."

Sam swung her Mini Cooper into the driveway and parked. Nik scooped up a bouquet of flowers and a bottle of her favorite chardonnay from the passenger's seat and stepped out into the road. He was approaching Sam's house when she exited her car, her back to him, talking on her phone.

He heard her say, "Yes, that's right, take a left at the intersection," before she hung up. Nik called out to Sam, and she spun around, a look of confusion on her face. She said something just as a dump truck rumbled past, and he couldn't make it out.

A car door slammed behind him, and Sam looked past Nik's shoulder, her expression shifting from confusion to apprehension. Nik followed Sam's gaze and slowly turned his head and saw Chase Hurley crossing the street.

CHAPTER 37

July 5

Teo opened his eyes wide, leaned back in his chair, interlaced his fingers behind his head, and stared at the control booth's ceiling with one overriding thought: *I'm seriously fucked.*

What had started out as a simple, if naïve, idea to undercut the Yukon story and redirect Mia's and Nik's attention back to what Teo considered more relevant topics had spiraled out of control, and now Elizabeth Blake was threatening to blackmail him.

He was convinced that removing the Bullwhip files and soliciting *Newshound*'s chief editor to help execute his scheme was justifiable. Actually the best thing for the team, in fact. *Let the sixth floor chase ambulances. We have a much higher calling,* he had told himself.

But handing over all of their story files, scripts, podcasts, and notes to the television reporter would be a clear betrayal. Yet if he refused, he was certain Blake would fulfill her threat and get him fired, maybe even prosecuted, and he'd be black-balled from ever working in media again.

He leaned forward and dropped his head into his hands, unable to see any way out.

"Two raw eggs in a glass of cold milk sprinkled with Tabasco. It's a surefire cure. Got it from Frank Rath, and he knows a thing or two about hangovers."

Teo looked up, his face drained, to see Patrick "Mo" Morgan standing in the doorway of the production booth, his wide body filling the frame and blocking out light like an eclipse.

"But you have to drink it in one swallow," Mo said with a grin and stepped inside. "If you try to sip it, you'll throw up."

Teo emitted a soft chuckle. "Wish it were that simple."

"Looking for Mia, have you seen her?"

"She hasn't come in yet."

Mo pulled up a chair and sat down. He folded his thick arms, heavily veined and knotty with muscles like the roots of an old tree, across his chest. "Just as well. Been meaning to have a chat with you anyhow, give you a little piece of free advice."

Teo looked skeptically at Mo. He had always considered *Newshound*'s deputy editor a somewhat buffoonish cartoon character with his lumbering walk, massive chest, and bulging biceps. They'd probably had fewer than a half-dozen conversations in the time they'd known one another, none longer than a couple of minutes.

"Oh, yeah, don't recall asking you for any."

"I like you, Teo," Mo started out, uncrossed his arms, and pointed at Teo's chest, nodding agreeably. "You've got a lot of talent."

"Uh-huh."

Mo dropped his hands to his knees and drew closer to Teo, looking him directly in the eyes. "But you're just a kid, and you got a lot to learn about this business . . ."

"I don't need a lecture from . . ."

"And who to trust and, more importantly, who not to trust," Mo said, speaking over the interruption. "One person who you absolutely should never put your trust in is Dick Whetstone. That's a fool's errand."

Mo then told Teo about the scribbled note he had found in Whetstone's office concerning the Bullwhip files.

"Told Mia and Nik about the note. It's okay, we got the files back. But what I didn't mention to them was what else was on the slip of paper. Didn't seem important at the time." Mo paused. "Care to guess what it was?"

"Not really."

"Two lowercase letters—*tm*—circled in the corner of the note. I figured it was an abbreviation for 'tomorrow.' Later, after I thought about it, it occurred to me they were actually initials. Your initials. Teofilo Mezos. You moved those files and then told Whetstone where you hid them."

"You don't know—"

"Save it," Mo said and stood up. "You don't owe me an explanation."

"You said something about advice?"

"Yeah, talk to Mia and Nik. Maybe you can work this out—whatever this is—before it's too late."

———

Mia looked at Nik as if she were pondering an utterly impenetrable mathematical equation and just shook her head.

It was late afternoon, and the pair was at an outdoor café on the backside of Dupont Circle just off Twenty-First and P Street NW, waiting for Teo, who had asked to meet with them. Mia had ridden the Red Line from her apartment, while Nik had made the short walk over from his condo with Gyp, who was lying on a patch of grass in the shade, tethered to a small tree, a bowl of water alongside. The storms in the Atlantic

Ocean had pushed cool air into the nation's capital, and people were milling about, enjoying the break in the heat wave and being outdoors.

"That was really, really stupid, Nik," Mia finally said.

"Tell me about it," Nik replied sheepishly and took a sip of his beer. "Not like I planned it."

Nik had explained to Mia what transpired outside of Sam's house after Chase had walked across the street and sneered, "You shouldn't have," and then lunged for the flowers and wine.

"That's when I drove a shoulder into him. Our momentum carried us off the sidewalk and into the road. Next, I hear a sickening crack followed by a primordial scream. I look down, and Chase's right foot is bent at a ninety-degree angle, a splintered bone sticking through his pant leg. It was gruesome," Nik recounted. "His ankle was broken in two places."

"Oh, God," Mia gasped.

"They operated and put in a steel plate and five titanium screws to hold the ankle in place. He'll be in a cast for six weeks. Gotta give credit to Chase, though. He joked with the attendees about having two left feet after they loaded him up with painkillers."

"I'll bet Sam didn't think it was funny," Mia said.

"She's refusing to speak to me."

Mia glanced up. "Here's Teo now," she said as the young producer zipped around the corner on his electric scooter.

Nik watched Teo skim down the street. "What did he want to talk to us about anyway?" he asked.

"Didn't say," Mia said and gave the unsmiling Teo a wave of her hand.

CHAPTER 38

July 8

Faud Asma took a table in the back of his uncle's restaurant-slash-bodega in Adams Morgan and ordered a Turkish coffee and waited, fingering a string of worry beads. He gave an order in Arabic to a jumpy-looking waiter, who served him his coffee before the boy hurriedly disappeared behind lace curtains, returning a few minutes later with a plate of dolmas, dip, pita, and olives that he placed on the table.

Asma had a slight build with dark, close-cropped hair, the tips dyed silver, and a dense, scruffy beard. He wore his shirt collar open, exposing a thick patch of bristly chest hair and a roped gold chain.

He preferred to meet at his uncle's restaurant. It was out of the way and didn't draw attention. The boy placed a "Closed" sign in the window and drew the shades after the small lunch crowd had dispersed.

Since there were no other customers to complain, Asma lit a Marlboro, opened a sports app on his smartphone, and started skimming professional soccer news.

He was reading a story about Manchester United when Thomas Polk, co-chair of the National Security Commission on Artificial Intelligence, walked through the door, looking nervous and sweaty.

Asma stood and embraced Polk with a perfunctory hug and then stepped behind the small counter in the restaurant and turned up the volume on the Middle Eastern music streaming from speakers set around the room. The boy had reappeared when he heard the bell above the door ring. Asma told him to bolt the door and chased him away after Polk declined an offer of coffee.

"What is going on, Thomas?" Asma asked in a soft voice. "I get an urgent message from Allan Trumbo about a meeting, and when I show up, he's not there, and then I get another urgent message from you."

"Trumbo is dead," Polk said.

"Allah maeah," Asma offered his condolences. "God be with him."

"Throat ripped open, head nearly severed. Fucking barbaric."

"That's unfortunate. America has become a very violent society."

"Cut the bullshit, Faud. First Rupert and now Trumbo."

Asma stubbed out his cigarette in a saucer on the table and thought, *Spilled blood always focuses the mind. It's the same the world over.* "You think I did this?"

"Yes, who else?"

Asma finished the bitter coffee and set the cup back down. He tapped another Marlboro from the pack and offered one to Polk, who shook him off. He lit the cigarette and inhaled deeply.

"We are not happy with our arrangement, Thomas, this is true, but I know nothing about this. Perhaps you've made one too many enemies," Asma said flatly and blew smoke rings out into the empty dining room.

"We understand the prince is frustrated with the lack of progress of the program. It's not what we expected, either. There've been some hiccups since Geoff Tate's death, but we're back on track and it's going to get better, much better."

"It is shit."

"We're dealing with some setbacks."

"We think you are trying to fuck with us. We think you are keeping us in the dark purposely."

"No, I swear, we're not, and we'll prove it, but you have to assure me no more killings. It's bad for business."

Faud shrugged. "I repeat, this is not my work."

"Please tell His Highness we are working as hard as we can."

"I will let him know. In the meantime, the prince asked me to convey a message to you, Thomas. Either begin delivering the AI military technology you promised or give us back our two hundred million. Makes no difference to the prince one way or the other. You have one month."

"Jesus Christ, Faud, that's an awful tight deadline. What if we can't deliver in a month?"

"In that case," Asma said and dug his hand into his coat pocket, "I have a gift for you." He withdrew the worry beads and laid them in front of Polk. "Take these. You will need them."

CHAPTER 39

July 9

Nik sat at his desk studiously examining the white envelope he had unearthed from a stack of mail he found waiting for him on his return to *Newshound*'s offices after having been away for the better part of a month covering the Jewel Tate trial and then at home plowing through the Bullwhip documents.

It was late on a weekday night, and the offices were virtually deserted. He figured few people would be around, and so he brought Gyp with him, and the dog was now curled up under his desk asleep. Nik had come into work to pick up some old notebooks that he hoped contained jottings related to the Yukon story, and, quite frankly, he was tired of working from home and thought a change of scenery might do him good.

Two words with a punctuation mark—"The Key?"—were typed on the front of the envelope. He peeled it open and gave it a shake. A baseball card fluttered out and landed facedown on his desk.

Nik craned his neck and hunched over to study the card. He could tell immediately from the statistics on the back that the ballplayer was a pitcher. He picked the card up and continued to examine the information and then turned it over.

He was looking at a smiling, shaggy-haired nineteen-year-old Dale "Butch" Colson in a Toronto Blue Jays uniform. Nik had been a baseball card fanatic when he was a teenager and had built an extensive and valuable collection. To Nik's everlasting regret, his mother had cleaned out his room one weekend when he was away at college and given the collection away. Even still, he was fairly certain he had never heard of Colson before.

He flipped the card back over to discover that Colson, a right-handed middle reliever, was drafted by the Toronto Blue Jays out of college and played professional ball for five seasons, including stints in St. Louis, Pittsburgh, Colorado, and Seattle.

Colson never spent a full year in the big leagues and bounced back and forth between the major and minor leagues his whole career before retiring with a shoulder injury.

Baffled, Nik had no idea of the meaning behind the card and shoved it into his satchel and made a mental note to look into it later. He picked up his desk phone and dialed Jed Doyle's number again. Doyle, the former Justice Department attorney, picked up on the fifth ring.

After a quick introduction, Nik said, "I apologize for calling so late."

"It's not that late. It's only nine o'clock here," Doyle said. "How can I help you?"

"Oh, right. You're on the West Coast. Just past midnight here. I'm calling because it's my understanding that you investigated Yukon Corporation at one point when you worked for the government."

"I'm awful busy right now, Mr. Byron," Doyle said, obviously trying to brush Nik off. "Besides, it's been a while since I worked at Justice. I'm not sure I could be of much help to you."

"This won't take but a few minutes," Nik pleaded.

"Perhaps if you tell me specifically the angle of your story, that might help."

"The Pentagon's Bullwhip contract," Nik started in, and then recapped what he had learned about Yukon's ties to Blue Sky Consulting, Dwayne Mack, the overlapping relationships with ex-government officials. "And on top of that, people connected to Yukon and the Bullwhip project are dropping dead."

"I saw the news about Allan Trumbo," Doyle said.

"I was hoping maybe you could shed some light on what's going on."

"Listen, Mr. Byron . . ."

"Nik."

"Okay, Nik. I'm wrapping up a very important trial and I don't have a second to spare."

"Okay, how about when the trial is over?"

"Can't promise anything, but if I do agree, it would have to be in person. I'm not doing this over the phone."

Nik sighed loudly. This was going to be tougher than he'd thought.

"You're in DC, right?" Doyle asked.

"Yes."

"Just so happens I have a three-hour layover at Dulles on my way to Barcelona to speak at an international criminal conference at the end of the week. Maybe we can meet then. I need to think about it."

"That would be fantastic."

"Call me Wednesday and I'll let you know my answer."

"It's a deal."

"And, Nik."

"Uh-huh."

"I worked with a Margaret Byron at Justice. She a relation, by any chance?"

Nik hesitated. That must have been before Maggie had

reclaimed her maiden name, he thought. "Yeah. I'm her ex-husband."

"Hmmm. I see," Doyle said and hung up.

Nik reserved a guest conference room at Dulles International Airport for the meeting with Doyle. It rented by the hour for $95, or $500 for the full day. He booked it for the full day. It was windowless with a whiteboard, speakerphone, an eight-foot table, lectern, and six flags: United States, state of Virginia, and four flags Nik didn't recognize. Airport catering had stocked the room with coffee, bottled water, tea, and light snacks that Nik had arranged on the conference-room table.

Doyle's flight from Seattle to Washington, DC, hit a violent thunderstorm over the Rockies and had to divert north to avoid the turbulence. His plane touched down an hour late, but his Iberia flight to Barcelona was delayed two hours, also because of weather.

"It was a white-knuckler nearly coast to coast," Doyle said, slipping off his jacket. He looked wrung out as if he had just finished a marathon, sweat-soaked hair pasted to his forehead, skin clammy, armpits stained by large rings of perspiration.

Doyle had a leathery face, sandy hair, and intense green eyes. "People praying and tossing lunch everywhere you looked. It was awful."

"Sorry to hear that," Nik said and offered Doyle something to drink.

Doyle took a bottle of water and collapsed in a chair. "I called Maggie, your ex, and asked her about you," he said, uncapping the bottle and draining it in one long swallow.

"Oh, yeah, what did she say?"

"Said I could trust you."

"She's right. You can."

"She better be."

Nik walked Doyle through everything he had learned about Yukon and Bullwhip from interviews and reviewing thousands of pages of Pentagon documents—Blue Sky Consulting's involvement in securing the $500 billion Pentagon contract; Marianne Tate's assertion that her brother intended to withdraw from the project; Geoff Tate's death; Dwayne Mack's installation as CEO; the murders of Rupert Olen and Allan Trumbo, the vice president's former chief of staff.

When he was finished, Doyle complimented Nik. "Congrats. You've done your homework."

"Yeah, but I don't know how any of it fits together," Nik said. "I have a lot of interesting facts but little connective tissue. For instance, why would Geoff Tate tell his sister he was going to withdraw from the Bullwhip contract after landing the biggest deal in the company's history? That doesn't make any sense."

"There were rumors," Doyle said and stood and started pacing around the room. He pumped his arms and legs vigorously, presumably to get the blood flowing back into his limbs after the long flight.

"Rumors?"

"Yeah, that the bidding process was rigged. You always get some of that backstabbing on big contracts and this was the biggest in the history of the Pentagon. The rumors were pretty persistent, and that's what I was investigating."

"But, if the contract was fixed, you'd have to assume Tate knew that, since his company won the bid, right?"

"Not necessarily. Dwayne Mack and Blue Sky Consulting handled most of the negotiations with Pentagon brass and politicians on Capitol Hill. Believe me, there're plenty of places to hide kickbacks in a half-trillion government project, and that doesn't even take into consideration all the cost overruns, add-ons, and software code that can be peddled out the back door to outside groups just dying to get their hands on state-of-the-art technology."

Nik was writing furiously in his notebook to keep up with Doyle. He was also recording the interview. It was Nik's practice to supplement the tape recordings with handwritten notes. He found the act of note-taking enhanced his ability to recall interviews in greater detail and surface nuances he might otherwise skim over.

"Who killed your investigation?"

"I never figured that out. God knows I tried. One day, the order came down to pull the plug."

"No one explained to you why?"

"Oh, sure, they did. I asked and got a dozen different answers. I was asking right up until the day I walked out of the office. At that point, I figured I'd never know the truth."

Doyle stopped pacing the cramped room and retook his seat, stretched his legs, and let out a long yawn. "Is the coffee fresh?"

Nik nodded and Doyle poured himself a cup.

"So that's it, then?" Nik said.

"That was it," Doyle said, "until about six months ago." Doyle reached down to retrieve his briefcase from the floor. He set it on the table, snapped it open, and twisted it away from Nik so the reporter couldn't look inside. Doyle shuffled some papers around and then said, "That's when I received this," and handed Nik a large envelope. "No clue who sent it."

Nik unclasped the envelope and withdrew the contents. It was a letter addressed to the attorney general of the United States of America. The seal at the top of the letter was from the Office of the Vice President of the United States. The subject was "Bullwhip Contract."

In a carefully worded letter, the vice president suggested the AG's investigation into the letting of the Bullwhip contract could jeopardize national security by unwittingly revealing highly classified military and technology secrets to the country's enemies.

"'While neither the president nor this office would ever deem to interfere with an independent investigation by the Department of Justice, we are nonetheless concerned that the DOJ, in general, and Assistant Attorney General Jed Doyle, in particular, are on a fishing expedition that could expose our country to great harm if this investigation into Yukon and Bullwhip should continue.

"'In closing, we trust you will do what you believe is right for your nation in this matter.'"

It was signed by "Matthew Pound, Vice President."

There was a postscript.

"P.S. The Second Lady and I need to have you and Betsy over for dinner again soon. —Matt."

Doyle was leaning back in his chair, tossing a rubber ball in the air that he had pulled from the pocket of his suit coat. "If I had to guess," he said, "that letter was the handiwork of the recently departed Allan Trumbo."

"Because?"

"Because Pound doesn't have enough sense to look both ways before crossing a street."

CHAPTER 40

July 12

The memorial service for Allan Trumbo was conducted under a large, open tent on the Georgetown University commons, his alma matter, followed by a light lunch at the Tombs restaurant, just a few steps from campus and one of Trumbo's favorite hangouts as a student.

An overnight rain had spawned swampy air, causing clothes to stick to the skin like sap. Women pawed at dresses to unseal their garments from damp arms and legs, while men tugged at the seats of their pants. Attendees grumbled that the event should have been moved indoors to the climate-controlled auditorium. Still, a large crowd turned out to pay its last respects and hear Matthew Pound, the vice president of the United States, deliver the eulogy.

"Allan Trumbo," the vice president, a former right-wing radio talk show host, said in his best broadcast voice, "was destined for greater things, but it was not to be. His Maker had other plans for 'Never Stumble Trumbo,' and the country has been denied a valuable public servant who always, and I mean always, put other people's needs above his own." Pound paused, a practiced catch in his throat, before continuing.

"Indeed, we all knew Allan had a higher calling, but it never occurred to his many admirers that it would not be of this world."

Nik arrived late for the service. Gyp had cut the pad on his right front paw when they were out for a walk that morning, and he had been reluctant to leave the dog by himself. Luckily, Reese, his new neighbor, was at home, and she had agreed to pop up to Nik's place on and off throughout the day to check in on Gyp.

Nik found an open spot in the last row of white plastic chairs inside the tent and took a seat. The ground was soggy from the rain, and when he sat down, the legs of the chair made a sucking sound as they sank into the turf.

Surveying the crowd, Nik recognized several attendees—junior congressmen and -women, the president's press secretary, one minor cabinet official, and two cable TV reporters, one from CNN, the other from MSNBC. In other words, a typical Washington, DC, gathering.

He saw several women quietly weeping, tissues pressed to their eyes, and young children pulling at their parents' arms, trying to break free and run off. Several rows in front of Nik, he noticed DC detectives Yvette Jenks, a veteran cop and ex-marine, and her young partner, Jason Goetz. He doubted they were social acquaintances of Trumbo's and were more than likely there on official business. No suspects had been publicly identified in either Trumbo's or Rupert Olen's murders.

He spotted Dwayne Mack about halfway up the middle aisle, on the right-hand side, head drooping. He appeared to be nodding off as Pound concluded his remarks.

"We may never know who the depraved individual was that took Allan Trumbo from us or why," Pound intoned, looking down, shaking his head, his hair the color of tinsel, "but in my heart, I know the Good Lord will smite that person and deliver justice. God bless Allan Trumbo, God bless America, and amen."

The gathering rumbled an "amen" in unison, and Dwayne Mack's chin snapped up off his chest as if he had been jabbed with a needle. The vice president made his way down the center aisle, Secret Service agents floating ahead of him, squinty-eyed, grim, serious expressions on their mugs. Pound stopped to offer a private word of sympathy to Trumbo's parents and partner and exchanged handshakes with other mourners, a sorrowful look flash frozen on an otherwise bland, pasty face.

When he reached Dwayne Mack, the vice president briefly paused, grasped Mack's elbow, and pulled him close, whispering in his ear, and just as quickly, he stepped back, patted the ashen-faced Mack on the shoulder, nodded solemnly, and continued on his way toward the exit.

***

"Well, well. Look who's here. Always turning up like a bad penny," Detective Jenks said when she saw Nik approach her and her partner at the Tombs restaurant following the service.

"Detectives Jenks, Goetz," Nik acknowledged. "I didn't know you were familiar with the deceased."

"Nik, good to see you again," said Goetz, a former middle school teacher turned cop, beaming and thrusting out his hand. If Jenks was a pit bull, Goetz was a golden retriever, always friendly, trusting. He wore a freshly pressed tan two-piece suit and heavy-soled black cop shoes. "Looks like you fully recovered from your injuries."

Goetz and Jenks had interviewed Nik in his hospital room shortly after he was attacked in Rock Creek Park while he was reporting on the OmniSoft story. His attacker had been killed by an expert archer who Nik swore he never saw. The shooter carved up Nik's assailant with the precision of a surgeon before delivering the fatal shot through the back of the neck and out the throat.

Jenks didn't believe Nik's story, while Goetz gave him the benefit of the doubt. Later, after Nik had recovered from his injuries, Sam invited Goetz and his partner, Daniel, to a get-well party.

"Shoulda known you'd show up sooner or later, Byron, gruesome killing like this," Jenks said bitterly.

"I don't know what I can do to convince you that I never saw the killer," Nik said.

"Not a damn thing. I don't believe a word that comes out of your mouth, Byron," Jenks spat and turned her back on Nik to survey the crowd. Jenks had a large Afro, turning gray, and wore a black pantsuit with padded shoulders and gold piping around the cuffs. Nik noticed the bulge from her service revolver on her hip. He had a hard time seeing around her and stepped to the side to keep an eye on Dwayne Mack, who was in an intense conversation with a dark-haired, slightly built man.

"Try the crab rolls before they're all gone," Goetz said and offered his plate to Nik. "They're very tasty."

"No, thanks." Nik waved him off. "You folks got any leads?"

"Well, we don't think it was a random act, if that's what you're asking," Goetz said and stuffed another crab roll into his mouth. "Secret Service is poking around to see if someone was trying to send a message to the vice president. Seems like a stretch."

"Goetz, stop your jawboning," Jenks barked over her shoulder. "Our guy's on the move."

"Nice seeing you again, Nik," Goetz said and wiped his mouth with a napkin. Jenks was already halfway across the room, and Goetz hurried to catch up with her. The pair fell several paces behind the man who had been talking to Mack and followed him out of the restaurant.

Nik spotted the reporters from CNN and MSNBC he had seen at the service huddled in a corner and drifted toward them. The murders of Rupert Olen and Allan Trumbo were receiving intensive, around-the-clock coverage from every media outlet in town, including *Newshound*, since it boosted ratings, and with Congress in summer recess, it was really the only game in town.

"Nik," the pair acknowledged him when he walked up. "We were just talking, and we think it's either some twisted, sex-infused motive or a drug deal gone bad. Where do you come down on the killings?" the CNN staffer, a pinched-faced, prematurely silver-haired man with large-framed glasses balanced on his forehead, asked.

"Yeah, love triangle," the MSNBC woman added.

"Sounds about right," Nik said impassively. "Who's the third side of the triangle?"

"Well, that's the question, isn't it? I'm not saying I have it nailed down, but I have it on pretty good authority that it's some very important French diplomat's wife," the woman said. The CNN reporter nodded his head aggressively.

"Well, you guys are miles ahead of me. Don't even know why I bother to compete." Both reporters gave Nik sad smiles as if to say they understood his plight and that he had correctly assessed his situation.

Nik's stomach stirred, and he excused himself and made his way to the buffet table.

"I hear the crab rolls are excellent," he suggested to the person ahead of him in the line.

"Thanks. I'll have to try them," the man said, stabbing a forkful.

"Terrible about Allan."

"Unspeakable. Can't imagine why anyone would want to harm him, let alone do what they did."

"I saw the man you were talking to a moment ago. He looked like an old college friend," Nik said conversationally.

"Faud Asma?" the man snorted. "I seriously doubt it. Don't believe he's ever set foot in a college classroom."

"Must have been mistaken," Nik said, continuing down the food line. "I couldn't help but notice that you looked very upset after the vice president stopped to chat briefly with you when he was leaving the memorial service. Was it something he said?"

The man in front of Nik stopped piling his plate with food, stepped back, and turned to face the reporter. "Excuse me, but do I know you?"

"Nik Byron," he said and shot out his hand. "I'm a reporter with *Newshound*. You're a hard man to get ahold of, Mr. Mack."

CHAPTER 41

July 12

Nik's encounter with Dwayne Mack was brief, prickly, and instructive.

After Nik had introduced himself, Mack had attempted to stiff-arm the reporter—"A memorial is no place to be talking business, Mr. Byron. Please show some respect for the deceased." But when Nik mentioned that he was in possession of documents that suggested that Allan Trumbo might have used his influence to get Vice President Pound to pressure the Justice Department to drop its investigation into Yukon and the Bullwhip contract, Mack seized his arm and steered him to a quiet table in the back of the room.

"Who told you that?" Mack demanded.

"Doesn't matter. Question is, is it true?" Nik said. "Seems plausible, given the timing."

"Fake news. It's not the first time our competitors have planted false material to discredit Yukon. You will have egg on your face, and your little media company will be in a world of pain if you publish that garbage."

Mack's voice was angry and growing louder. People were beginning to stare at the pair. Nik didn't take notice and pressed on. "I'm also told Geoff Tate was planning to terminate the Bullwhip contract."

"That's a crock of shit, mister," Mack growled. "I don't know who your so-called sources are, but they're dead wrong. Geoff put his heart and soul into winning that contract. He would never have walked away from it."

"Tell me, how is it that a lobbyist lands a job as CEO of the world's largest AI company?" Nik asked, snapping off a carrot stick and chewing it. "I mean, somehow you've managed to come out on top of all this, haven't you?"

"I don't like what you're implying, Byron. And as far as why and how it happened, you'd have to ask the board about that. They're the ones who voted me in."

"Just so you know, I submitted an FOIA request to the Pentagon. I have all of the military's Bullwhip documents. I also have the lobbyist registration forms from the US Senate and House of Representatives. Blue Sky, Allan Trumbo, General Hiatt, and Thomas Polk are all mentioned prominently."

"Well, la-de-fuckin'-da. You want a medal, or a chest to pin it on?"

Nik grinned. He hadn't heard that taunt since grade school.

"Side by side, the documents make for pretty interesting reading. All three men, when they were in public service, advocated for Yukon's bid, and when they left their government roles, they wound up renting offices next door to Blue Sky. Helluva coincidence, wouldn't you say?"

"I don't have the slightest idea what you're talking about. Now, if you'll excuse me, this conversation is over," Mack said and wheeled around and started walking away, then stopped and turned back to face Nik. "You did manage to get one fact right, Byron."

"That's good to know. What was it?"

"The crab rolls. They're excellent."

———————

What a galactic clusterfuck.

Serves me right getting in bed with a bunch of fucking amateurs. Bad enough that stupid fucking twat Jewel is turning out to be a huge pain in my ass, but now I got the vice president of the United States demanding a cut of Allan Trumbo's Bullwhip share. And on top of it, that greaseball Saudi is starting to breathe down our necks.

And where did that fucking reporter come from anyway? Can't believe I told him Faud's name. Goddamn it.

Wanted to slap those silly fucking glasses right off his smug face. Would have, too, had we not been in public. Giving me the third degree like that at Trumbo's memorial service. The nerve of that little prick, insinuating I benefited from Geoff's death.

Lost my cool with that dickhead. Wish I hadn't done that, but he got under my skin with his innuendos about a rigged contract, kickbacks, and Geoff's intentions to abandon Bullwhip.

Terminate Bullwhip, my ass, not with hundreds of millions in under-the-table payoffs changing hands. Should have known Geoff would go wobbly if he found out Yukon hadn't won Bullwhip fair and square and the contract was a scam. Jesus H. Christ. What a fuckin' altar boy.

Yeah, I bribed folks, doctored bid specs, paid for inside info, extorted, called in favors. So the fuck what. Who doesn't in this town? What did Geoff think he hired me to do, serve tea and treats to politicians and their mistresses? It's a mystery to me how that man ever got as far as he did. Maybe that ballbusting sister of his is really the brains of the outfit after all.

Well, I didn't get to be Washington's top lobbyist by letting others walk all over me. I got an escape hatch and a wad of Saudi money stashed in an offshore account.

You just wait. I'll show those fuckers who's who. Sons of bitches won't know what hit 'em, especially that douchebag reporter.

CHAPTER 42

July 15

Jewel Tate's presence at Yukon headquarters never needed to be announced. Instead, there were slamming doors, raised voices, harried assistants running blindly from office to office, Toby yapping and snapping at anyone in his path as the small dog patrolled the corridors. A day of this activity exhausted everyone. A week set teeth on edge. Any longer, and people were openly weeping. Jewel had been coming to Yukon's offices for two solid weeks now, and Dwayne Mack faced an open insurrection from employees.

"Jewel, you've got to step back and let me do my job. You being here every day is very disruptive, and people are already jumpy enough over Rupert's murder," Mack pleaded with her after one executive suffered a nervous breakdown and had to be removed from the building, while another had to be restrained from using a stapler to attack a colleague whose only provocation was not refilling the copy machine with paper.

It was two o'clock on a Monday afternoon, and Jewel was already on her second vodka martini. She had brought a cocktail-mixing kit from home and had placed it atop her desk, where she could easily reach it without getting up from her chair. She initially didn't start drinking until four p.m., but gradually, she shaved a couple hours off the schedule as she got bored with the office environment.

"I'm not going anywhere until I get my money, Dwayne. You've jerked me around enough. Drink?" She hiccupped, leaned back in the chair, and propped a pair of red Jimmy Choos up on the desk. Mack recognized the shoes. Jewel had once nearly punctured his lung with the spiky heels.

Mack shook his head no. He'd been drinking way too much lately as it was, his blood pressure and weight at all-time highs. "I've got some promising prospective buyers coming in next week, but they'll turn right around and flee if they walk in here and find the place in chaos. You'll only be hurting yourself."

"How promising?" Jewel asked and splashed more vodka into her glass.

"Real promising. Big Boston outfit with deep pockets," Mack lied. He was telling the truth about the company but not necessarily about its intentions. He knew the Boston company was bottom-fishing, hoping to steal Yukon for pennies on the dollar, but at this point, with both Geoff Tate and Rupert gone and the stock depressed, he was willing to cut a deal to unload Yukon.

Mack told Jewel, "You stand to make a killing."

"Is that supposed to be a joke"—Jewel sniffed—"because if it is, it ain't funny."

"No, no, no. I didn't mean to imply anything about what happened to Geoff," Mack stammered.

Jewel ignored him, picked up Toby, held the dog to her face, and started baby talking to it: "When Mommy found out about Daddy's plans to cancel the Bullwhip contract, Mommy told Dwayne and Uncle Rupert, didn't she, Tobykins, and they promised Mommy lots of money if she helped persuade Daddy not to go through with it. Mommy did her part, but now Dwayne is trying to take advantage of Mommy."

"It's not like that, Jewel," Mack protested.

Jewel hugged Toby and kissed the dog on the nose. "Mommy would hate to have anything bad happen to Dwayne, isn't that right, Tobykins?"

"Jewel, please."

Jewel stood and clipped a leash on Toby. "Don't fuck with me, Dwayne," she said, nostrils flaring, eyes boiling. "Sell the fucking company and get me my money, or they'll be digging lead out of your sorry ass next."

CHAPTER 43

July 16

For a big man, Shaka Wulf, Geoffrey Tate's former bodyguard, was lightning quick and silent as a mime. He attributed his quickness to his mother, Dorthea, a top-ranked collegiate fencer, and his stealth to his father, a Samoan, whose ancestors terrorized Japanese soldiers stationed on Pacific islands during World War II, slipping past their guard posts late at night and into their jungle camps, disemboweling them as they slept in their cots, before fading back into the bush undetected.

Shaka's Navy SEAL unit always elected him to lead assaults when lethal finesse, not firepower, was called for. He was an excellent marksman, for certain, but was particularly valued for his close-in work with garrotes, blades, and his bare hands.

Shaka seldom had to apply his warrior skills as Tate's personal bodyguard. His mere presence—he was six-foot-three, 220 pounds of lean muscle with a shaved head the color of cordovan that looked like a battering ram—was enough to keep most onlookers and potential troublemakers at bay. He was licensed to carry a sidearm but rarely felt the need to do so and preferred to use technology to monitor and assess potential threats.

On one occasion, a group of activists opposed to Yukon's AI work with the defense department managed to encircle Tate after he stepped down from the stage following his keynote address to software CEOs at Washington's Hilton hotel. The small band locked arms and started to move toward an exit as one, pushing Tate along like a piece of driftwood bobbing on the water.

Shaka penetrated the circle, wrenching one protestor's arm nearly out of its socket. He dislocated the left elbow of another, while a third suffered a broken wrist and a splintered shin. The whole affair was over in less than a minute. Wulf never even unbuttoned his sport coat.

After Tate was killed and Dwayne Mack was installed as Yukon's new CEO, Shaka was told his services were no longer needed, and he was given a stingy severance and shown the door.

Two days later, he formed Lone Wulf Protection, an intelligence-gathering and personal-security firm. Shortly after that, Lone Wulf signed its first client, Eureka Inc., whose registration papers on file with DC's Department of Consumer Regulatory Affairs office described its charter as a shareholders' rights organization aimed at restoring corporate governance in technology companies by all legal means possible.

The sole shareholder and founder of Eureka Inc. was listed as Marianne Tate.

Lone Wulf Protection's offices were tucked away in a nondescript strip shopping center down a backstreet in Tysons Corner and situated between a dry cleaner's and a pho restaurant. For years, the space had been rented to the owner of an exotic-pet store who'd lost his lease after he was accused of selling banned elephant ivory.

"Eeewww, smells like a women's barracks in here," the customer said when she entered the front door.

Shaka Wulf looked up from his desk where he was working in the back of the building to see a tall, solidly built Black woman and her white prep-school-looking companion eyeing the surveillance equipment on display and thought, *Cops.*

"Don't believe I'm familiar with that particular fragrance," Shaka said.

"Really, I figured you for military," the woman said. "Navy?"

"Women's quarters were off-limits. SEALs. You?"

"Corps."

"Semper fi."

"Oo-rah. Why the funky smell?"

"Used to be leased to a guy who ran an exotic-pet business."

"Might want to Febreze the place, freshen things up a bit."

"I'm nose blind to it by now. Didn't realize that was a verb."

"Absolutely. You can use it as a gerund, too: 'Febrezing.'"

"Interesting."

"What is?"

"Wouldn't have pegged you for a grammarian."

"Oh, yeah, why's that?"

"I dunno, you look more like an econ major to me."

"English major, econ minor."

"Ahhh, that explains it. Now, how can I help you, Officer . . . ?"

"Jenks, and it's 'Detective.' Tonto here," Jenks said and jerked a thumb toward her partner, "is Detective Goetz."

Goetz gave Shaka a friendly wave and a smile.

"Either I'm getting older or they're getting younger," Shaka said.

"Both," Jenks said with an eye roll.

"Good to see the Northern Virginia County Sheriff's Department has a farm system."

"We're DCPD, and we got a few questions for you, Mr. Wulf, if you don't mind."

"A little far afield for the District's finest, aren't we?"

"We're investigating the murders of Rupert Olen and Allan Trumbo."

"Sorry, but I didn't know Mr. Trumbo and only had a passing acquaintance with Mr. Olen. Seen him at meetings with Geoff Tate now and then. Spoke to him maybe a half-dozen times at most. Thought I read both murders took place outside DC, though."

"You believe everything you read?" Jenks said and picked up a pair of translucent eyeglasses with a miniature camera embedded in the frame from a display case and tried them on. She looked at herself in the mirror. "Whatcha think, Goetz?"

"Go for the red ones. Think the color better suits your complexion."

Jenks shook her head. "Don't even know why I bother," she said and placed the glasses back in the display. To Shaka, she said, "That's right. We have reason to believe the crimes were committed outside our jurisdiction, but we're being good neighbors and assisting in the investigation, following up on some DC leads."

"What would you like to know?"

"You know this man?" Jenks asked and nodded at Goetz, who produced a five-by-seven black-and-white photo from his inside coat pocket and held it up for Shaka to inspect. "Man's name is Faud Asma."

"I've seen him a time or two," Shaka said.

"And where was that, exactly?"

Shaka considered the question. He'd have to be careful how he answered. "We do surveillance work for clients. He's popped up on our radar."

"Which clients?"

"I'm sorry, Detective, but that's confidential. I'd need to see a court order to give you that information, you understand," Shaka said, figuring, rightly, that Jenks didn't have one in her purse and was unlikely to get a judge to issue one since DC was not the main investigatory agency.

"Back to my original question. Do you know him?"

"No. Like I said, we've crossed paths, but I've never spoken to the gentleman. Why, what's he done?"

"We know you've been following him," Jenks said, and Goetz pulled out another black-and-white photo, this one of Asma in a cab stopped at a traffic light with Shaka's vehicle several car lengths behind him.

"So that was you who had a tail on me. I was wondering," Shaka said.

"We weren't tailing you. We were tailing Asma when you got in the way."

"Sorry for stepping on your surveillance," he said, embarrassed he had gotten himself tangled up in DC's net.

"Whaddya know about him?"

"Not much. Works out of the Saudi embassy, part of their intelligence operation."

"What makes you say that?"

"His movements. You can tell he's a pro. He's always checking for shadows. Changes vehicles, doubles back, runs figure-eight patterns to confuse tails. That sorta thing."

"Yeah, we think he's trying to make us. Goes out but seldom with a destination. Leaves the embassy, does his little goose chase thing around the District, sometimes Northern Virginia or Maryland, for an hour or so, and then back to the roost," Jenks said.

"Is he somebody I should be worried about?" Shaka asked.

"You know about the Khashoggi murder?"

"Sure."

"Then, yeah, he's somebody you should be worried about."

Jenks picked up a brick-size device off a shelf and held it up for inspection. "What's this?"

"It's called a StingRay. It mimics a cell-phone tower to intercept mobile phone activity," Shaka explained.

"Is it legal?"

"Legal-ish."

Jenks returned the device to the shelf. "On a couple of occasions, Asma has been surveilled by a pair of characters from his own embassy, a swarthy-looking gentleman and a plump woman with raven hair. Any idea why they'd do that, spy on one of their own?"

"You're asking the wrong person, Detective," Shaka said, "but if I had to guess, I'd say he must have given them some reason not to trust him."

Jenks nodded her head. "Yeah, that's what I think, too. Anything else, Goetz?" she asked her partner.

"Think that about covers it," Goetz said and took out a business card with all his contact information, including his Twitter account, and handed it to Shaka, who looked at it before dropping it in his desk drawer.

"Let's go, Goetz," Detective Jenks said and chinned toward the door.

"Good meeting you, Detectives," Shaka said. "Sorry I couldn't be of more help."

"It was a pleasure meeting you, Mr. Wulf," Goetz replied enthusiastically.

Jenks stopped and looked back over her shoulder. "What kinda name is Shaka anyway?"

"Mother's family was from Kenya, father's from Samoa. It's a mash-up of two warrior names."

"No shit," Jenks said. "Well, I'm a warrior, too, Mr. Shaka Wulf. Best keep that in mind."

CHAPTER 44

July 17

Nik pushed open the door to his apartment, greeted by a blast of "I Put a Spell on You" by Creedence Clearwater Revival. "Gyp," Nik said sternly as he stepped across the threshold, "you're in big trouble. I've warned you for the last time about romping around the condo near my stereo equipment when I'm not here."

Inside there was a note taped to the hallway mirror. It was from the dog walker. The note said she had Gyp and they were on a long walk in Rock Creek Park.

"Hello?" Nik called out, sounding perplexed.

"In here." It was Sam. She was sitting in an armchair by the living room window overlooking the building's tidy courtyard, dressed in jeans and a peach-colored cotton sweater, a magazine resting in her lap.

"Sam," Nik said, relief in his voice, "what a wonderful surprise. I've been trying to reach you for days to apologize and make things right."

She gave him a faint smile. "That's not why I came by, Nik."

"Oh," Nik said and sank into his couch, a worried look on his face. "Why, then?"

"To return some of your things that you left at my house," Sam said and motioned to a box on the far side of the room that Nik had not noticed, "and to explain to you, even though I don't believe I owe you an explanation, why Chase was at my place that day."

"I see. How's he doing?" Nik asked and winced.

"He's better. He's scheduled to get a walking boot. Doctors told him the steel plate would make his ankle even stronger than it was before the break."

"I feel terrible about what happened. Give him my best."

"Not sure it'd be appreciated," she said.

Nik asked, "Want something to drink?"

"Sparkling water would be nice, if you have any."

Nik got two bottles out of the refrigerator, opened them, and handed one to Sam. "So, Chase?"

Sam took a slow drink from the bottle and set it down on a side table. "I don't know if I ever told you, but when I quit my job at the *Washington Post*, I left without giving notice. Fact is, I walked out one day and never went back."

"I knew it was abrupt," Nik said.

Sam had been romantically involved with another *Post* reporter, Gregg Robbins, who was killed when he stepped off a turboprop plane and inexplicably walked directly into the aircraft's churning blades. Sam had not seriously dated anyone for two years after that, until Nik came along.

"I left everything behind at the *Post*. My editor kept my desk untouched for a couple months in case I came back. Eventually the company moved all my belongings to storage. From time to time over the years, someone from the *Post* would call and leave a message asking me what I wanted them to do with my things. I never returned the calls."

"I wasn't aware."

"After I saw Chase at your baseball game, I phoned him and asked if he'd go into storage and retrieve some of the more personal items I left behind. That's what he was doing. Returning my things to me. As a favor."

Sam sighed and turned back to the window. She knew she could have asked any number of former colleagues to collect her belongings, but she'd chosen to call Chase. That was no accident, and she was all but certain he'd jump at the chance to hand deliver the items to her home. At least, that's what she suspected and even, at some level, anticipated.

"Sam . . . ," Nik began.

"Not now, Nik. I put your clothes, a couple books, DVDs, dog leash, toothbrush, a baseball glove in the box. I think that's everything."

Sam stood and headed for the door, but before walking out, she dropped Nik's apartment keys on the coffee table. She felt vaguely sad, but mostly what she felt was relieved.

CHAPTER 45

July 20

Teo had zero interest in visiting Mount Vernon, the National Historic Landmark and home of George and Martha Washington. For one, the slave-owning Washington didn't appeal to the first-generation Cuban American, and for another, Teo didn't own a car and the Metro Blue Line would only take him as far as McPherson Square, and from there, he'd have to hop a bus. There was a ferry, but that was a four-hour excursion. He could Uber, but it would be a sixty-dollar fare, round trip. It wasn't worth it.

But Mount Vernon was where Elizabeth Blake insisted Teo meet her. The television reporter was certain they would be indistinguishable among the mobs of church groups, bus tour retirees, day-trippers, and preservationists roaming the five-hundred-acre estate.

Teo glimpsed Blake, her profile to him, at the entrance of the reconstructed Washington distillery. She was wearing a broad-brimmed straw hat, white shorts, sandals, and a loose-fitting turquoise top that was fluttering in the gentle summer wind. She had what appeared to be a map of the property in her hand and was talking to a guide who was pointing at the document and seemed to be tracing a route for her with his finger. Blake was nodding to the guide when Teo approached.

"You didn't tell me it was going to cost me twenty bucks to get in here," Teo complained.

"Teo, there you are," Blake said, thanked the guide, and refolded the map. "It's a donation that goes to a good cause. The Mount Vernon Ladies' Association maintains the estate and doesn't get a penny from the federal government. I bought an annual membership."

A line was forming to enter the distillery where employees produced small batches of rye whiskey that sold for thirty dollars a bottle in the Mount Vernon gift shop. Blake cocked her head and motioned for Teo to follow her down a graveled lane.

"The guide said this path circles the estate. I thought we could walk and talk."

"I don't want to stay here any longer than I have to," Teo said and fell in beside Blake.

"Relax, Teo," she said, running a hand along his back. "It's a beautiful day. Enjoy it." A clear blue sky had emerged midday after the sun had burned off an early-morning fog, but a smoky mist still hung just above the Potomac River that ran along the property's boundaries.

Teo shrugged off Blake's light embrace. "You said we wouldn't stand out here and would be lost in the crowd, but I don't see many dark-skinned folks around."

"That's why we're walking the grounds and staying away from the buildings where most of the tourists are," Blake explained. "Did you bring what we discussed?"

Teo slung a North Face backpack off his shoulders and unzipped a side pouch, reached his hand in, and pulled out a thumb drive. He held it up for Blake to see.

"What's on it?" she asked.

"A password-protected link that will take you to a secured server in the cloud. You will find everything stored there. Working notes, Yukon scripts, completed podcasts, source contact information, story budgets for the next six months. The password is 'goldmine,' one word, all lowercase, and the files are read-only."

Blake reached for it, but Teo yanked his hand back.

"Not so fast. I want some assurances it's over between us. I don't want this hanging over my head for the rest of my life."

"What kind of assurances, Teo?"

Teo whipped out his smartphone and opened the video player and handed Blake a prepared script. "A statement from you, on camera," he said and hit the Record button. "Read it."

Blake recited the short message crediting Teo as a first-rate, ethical journalist who always upheld the highest professional standards, and then returned the paper to Teo. "Satisfied?"

Teo gave her the thumb drive and slipped the backpack over his shoulders. "Enjoy your stroll around the grounds. I'm outta here."

"Don't take it personally, Teo," Blake called out as he started to walk away. "It's how the game is played in this town. A smart boy like you, I would have thought you would have learned that by now."

Teo popped open the passenger door of the Honda Element and dropped inside.

"How'd it go?"

"Good, I think."

"She read the statement?"

"Yup."

"And you recorded it."

"Uh-huh, just like we talked about," he said and let out a

nervous yawn, tossing his knapsack in the back seat and strapping on his seat belt.

Mia started the engine, shifted the vehicle into first gear, and turned right out of the parking lot, an eye on her rearview mirror in case Blake were back there somewhere watching.

Mia looked over at Teo. She could see the reflection of his downcast face in the passenger window. He was staring out at the boaters, kayakers, and the people fishing from the bank on the Potomac River as she headed north on the George Washington Memorial Parkway.

"This is on me as much as it is on you, Teo," Mia said. "I should have intervened that day when I saw you having lunch with Dick Whetstone downtown. Had I known the woman you were meeting with was Elizabeth Blake, I would have."

"Hindsight." Teo shrugged.

"You need to trust Nik's instincts on this," she assured him. "He's put together a solid plan, and you did the right thing, Teo."

"Did I? 'Cause it's hard to know anymore."

CHAPTER 46

July 21

Despite his pledge to cut back on sweets, Nik found himself at the Sugar Shack drinking coffee, polishing off a chocolate-coated donut, and ruminating over the jigsaw puzzle that was the Yukon story. The bakery's air conditioner wasn't working, and employees had propped open the front door to let in what little cool breeze there was. Mostly what it accomplished was to allow a river of steamy air to flood the tiny eatery.

Mia had asked Nik for an update on the story, and as he sat at the counter, swabbing his forehead with paper napkins, beads of sweat staining the lenses on his glasses, he struggled to construct a handful of declarative sentences that easily summarized the status of the plodding investigation. His head was crammed with information but not necessarily intelligence. It was a familiar feeling. He had been at this place with stories before—neither at the beginning nor the end, but mired somewhere in a middle no-man's-land.

He needed a road map to get to the other side. Nik reached in his satchel, withdrew a journal he kept, flipped open the cover, wrote "Solving Yukon" at the top of the page, and began jotting down a series of steps and questions, the answers to which might help unlock the story:

1. Faud Asma: Who is he and what is his connection to Yukon and Dwayne Mack?
2. Rupert Olen and Allan Trumbo: Why were they killed and are their deaths related to the Bullwhip contract? Seems obvious, but no hard evidence.
3. Retired general Alexander Hiatt and Thomas Polk, former co-chair of the National Security Commission on Artificial Intelligence: Did they personally or financially benefit from Yukon landing the Bullwhip contract?
4. Butch Colson: What is the significance of the baseball card someone sent me and what possible link could he have to Yukon?
5. A Patriot: Who is the anonymous Pentagon source that wrote the note and placed the zip drives in the military documents?

As it turned out, the last piece of the puzzle fell into place first.

———

Louisa Dills was a battlefield-tested quartermaster in the United States Army who had moved to a desk job in the Pentagon after two tours each in Afghanistan and Iraq. During active duty, she had overseen logistical airdrops of millions of pounds of supplies, rations, armament, and ordnance to troops often caught out in blinding desert sandstorms, mountainous whiteout conditions, and on ships at sea in gale-force winds.

Inventory shrinkage, a polite way of saying theft, is the

quartermaster's constant and unwelcome companion in the military, but Louisa Dills was hell-bent on rooting out corruption, and she all but eliminated pilferage through enhanced oversight and a sophisticated software tracking program, a nearly unheard-of achievement, especially in frontier war zones.

Dills treated any theft, no matter how minor, as a national security breach. Behind her back, colleagues teased her and called her "Blanche" after the popular mystery writer Barbara Neely's acid-tongued and streetwise African American sleuth, Blanche White. Dills was aware of the nickname and wore it like a badge of honor. But unlike Blanche, Louisa Dills was not middle-aged, plump, or an amateur. She was, in fact, thirtyish, taut, and every bit the professional soldier.

It had been months since she had responded to Nik's Freedom of Information request for the Bullwhip documents and had anxiously awaited the resulting stories, but when none appeared, she finally decided to launch her own offensive. She created a fictitious email account on Yahoo and, from there, used the alias to open separate social media profiles on Facebook, Twitter, Instagram, and TikTok.

From this perch, she tracked Nik online for several weeks, getting to know his habits, interests, and background. When she felt like she had a clear picture of the reporter in her mind, she reached out to Nik and invited him to join Balls to the Wall—a website she established for DC-area baseball players. She populated the page with made-up names and profiles of local baseball enthusiasts, and Nik accepted her invite.

When Dills sent out an invitation for a group meetup at a local bar where two seats for a sold-out series between rivals the Washington Nationals and the LA Dodgers would be raffled off, Nik couldn't resist and immediately registered to attend.

CHAPTER 47

July 22

Yukon's first test of its AI autonomous and unmanned fighter drone for the military, nicknamed Gunslinger, took place outside of Angel Fire, New Mexico, on a clear, windless day in near-perfect conditions. Despite several spectacular failures in the run-up to the demonstration, recent reports that had reached the Pentagon were more promising, and Dwayne Mack was telling anyone who would listen that he was optimistic the company would pass the milestone.

Top brass from the army, air force, and navy were crammed onto a viewing platform that Yukon had built in the steppes of the Sangre de Cristo Mountains. A series of props had been constructed throughout the area to replicate a conflict zone where an enemy combatant had embedded itself among a civilian population. There was a makeshift hospital, school, factory, mosque, and grocery store, along with two operational military fortifications.

The drone's stated mission was simple yet extraordinarily complex: discern, without human intervention, the difference between the military and civilian installations and then neutralize the enemy's position.

The drone lifted from the valley floor and circled overhead for five minutes. A lone operator tracked Gunslinger's movements on a radar screen and stood ready to hit the kill switch to deactivate its weapons system in the event it went rogue and actually started firing on a real civilian population or, God forbid, the viewing platform where the military chiefs were assembled.

Suddenly, and without telegraphing its flight path, Gunslinger banked hard left and started climbing. When it was just a dot on the horizon, it fired its first missile, leveling the larger of the two enemy bunkers. A lusty cheer erupted on the viewing stand.

Gunslinger dipped between mountain peaks and then reemerged in the eastern sky, hovering for a moment before unleashing its second salvo. There was a bright flash, and when the smoke cleared, the factory prop was reduced to cinder.

Other than some nervous throat clearing, the viewing platform fell silent, but only for a moment. Gunslinger triggered its final missile and vaporized the second bunker.

"Two outta three ain't half bad," the air force general proclaimed. "Hell, I'll take that any day of the week and twice on Sunday."

The navy man said, "I'm impressed. I've seen our pilots level real hospitals and schools by mistake. It happens."

"There're some kinks to still work out, no doubt, but I'd say you pretty much nutted it, Mack," the army general said, and clapped Yukon's CEO on the back. "Congratulations."

Mack breathed easily. Success meant the military would release the next multibillion-dollar payment, Yukon's stock price would begin to recover, Yukon's Boston suitor would be forced to increase its buyout offer, and the Saudis would see the real promise of the technology.

Mack was also painfully aware of what failure meant: government money drying up, further collapse of the stock price, no buyout offers, and the Saudis hunting him down like a wounded animal and taking their revenge.

It wasn't an outcome he could afford to leave to chance. He needed an insurance policy, and that's why he had installed a secret command center in a remote bunker deep in Virginia's Blue Ridge Mountains, thousands of miles away, staffed by ex-military personnel who were experts in drone warfare.

"Kill the targets," he had instructed the six-man squad, "but also lay waste to the factory. I don't want anyone thinking this is too good to be true."

CHAPTER 48

July 23

Nik arrived a little early at the Hot Corner pub—a reference to the third baseman's position—only to find the place nearly empty and dark as a grave inside. It took a minute for his eyes to adjust, and after they did, he found a seat at a booth and looked around, wondering if he got the wrong location, wrong time, wrong date, or possibly all three. He checked his email for verification. He had not misread the Balls to the Wall invite.

"Nik?" a husky voice came from behind him. He turned to see a slender, soft-eyed Black woman, her skin the color of cinnamon, wearing a Nats desert camo jersey and hat and holding two mugs and a pitcher of beer, a purse slung diagonally across her chest.

Nik tilted his head quizzically. "Yeah?"

"Lou," the woman said, and placed the pitcher and glasses on the table and held out a hand.

"Ahhh, sorry, I was expecting a—"

"Guy?" she said, with an easy laugh.

"Yeah, or, at least, that's what I inferred from your name

and what you posted in the baseball group. Clearly I was wrong. My apologies."

"None necessary. Lots of people make that mistake. Lou, it's short for Louisa." She motioned to the booth where Nik was seated and said, "May I?"

Nik nodded. "Of course. I'm really looking forward to meeting the rest of the group," he said and filled the frosty mugs with beer. He scanned the bar. "By the way, shouldn't the others be here by now? The invitation said seven o'clock."

"Gonna get to that in a minute," Louisa said, and pointed her index finger in Nik's direction. "But first, a toast"—she hoisted her mug—"to the Nats," and clinked his glass.

Louisa took a long pull on the beer. "Damn, that's good," she said and smacked her lips and smiled at him. "Well, see, the deal is, Nik, we're it. Just you and me," she said. "We're Balls to the Wall."

"Just us?" Nik said, confused. "I don't understand. What happened to the others?"

"There isn't anyone else. Never was," she said.

Nik glared at Lou, but before he could respond, she said, "You might know me better by another name. A Patriot. I'm the anonymous military source who sent you those Pentagon files."

Nik stammered, "Y-you?"

"Yup, me."

Nik leaned back in the booth and studied the woman across from him carefully and more than a little suspiciously. "Why the charade? Why not just call me?"

"It's not that simple. I have top-secret clearance. I was taking a helluva risk sending you those documents, and if they found out I was talking to a reporter, I could be court-martialed. I needed to be convinced you were a serious re-porter, so I followed you online for several weeks. Gotta tell you, I had my doubts."

"Oh, yeah, why's that?"

"Maybe because you never did anything with the material I provided."

Nik grimaced. "Got sidetracked."

"I all but gave up hope on you," she added. "You sure do take your sweet time. Are all reporters so slow?"

"No, I'm kind of unique that way," Nik confessed, not bothering to defend the pace of his work. "Slow but steady."

"Slow for sure," Lou said.

Louisa then filled Nik in on the highlights of her military career—Officer Candidate School, Fort Benning, Georgia; quartermaster officer training at Combined Arms Support Command, Fort Lee, Virginia; two tours of duty each in Iraq and Afghanistan before transferring to the Pentagon, where she was handed the Bullwhip contract.

Or more precisely, tracking all the details and fine print in the thousand-plus-page original request for proposal and making sure the bids and final contract complied with military regulations.

"I wanted to get up to speed on the Pentagon's artificial intelligence programs, so I pulled all the AI contracts for the past several years. Weren't that many, and none anywhere near the size of Bullwhip, so it didn't take long."

"Learn anything interesting?"

"Couple things. US military needs to get its shit together or risk falling behind Russia and China in artificial intelligence, that's for damn sure."

"I interviewed Tanner Black. He's a military expert. Said Russia more or less lit a fire under the Pentagon."

"Yeah, I saw his name in the files. He's persona non grata over there for bad-mouthing the brass."

"He'd be pleased to know. Is that it?"

"Nope. Something else jumped out at me."

"What was that?"

"Not what, who."

"Okay, *who* was that?"

"Hold that thought. We need a refill," Louisa said and held up the empty pitcher. She boosted herself out of the booth and headed to the bar, and Nik watched her stride off. His first thought was she was attractive. His second was he'd better slow down his drinking or he might say something embarrassing.

He was relieved when he saw Louisa clutching a couple bar menus along with a second pitcher of beer when she returned. Food would help dilute the alcohol in his bloodstream. She scooted into the booth and pushed a menu at Nik.

"You wouldn't know it, but the food in this place is pretty decent. Oyster po'boy is exceptional."

"You were saying," Nik said as he studied the menu.

"Right. All the AI contracts I looked at had one common denominator. Care to guess what?"

"Geoff Tate?"

"Strike one."

"Allan Trumbo?"

"Strike two."

"Dwayne Mack?"

"Single, but you should have been thinking double."

Nik smiled.

"It wasn't just Mack. Every AI contract Blue Sky lobbied for had Lieutenant General Alexander Hiatt's fingerprints all over it. Hiatt used to oversee all of the military's technology budget."

"Yeah, I know who Hiatt is," Nik said disappointedly, and asked Louisa if she was ready to order. Their waitress was sitting on a stool at the end of the bar, sipping a drink, chatting with the bartender, whose arms and neck were covered with tattoos. She seemed put upon when Nik called out to her. "Excuse me. We'd like to order now."

"Whatcha want?" she said when she finally ambled over to their table.

"Two po'boys and fries?" Nik asked Louisa.

"Perfect."

The waitress sauntered back to the bar, plopped down on the stool, and started talking to the bartender again.

"Food's good," Louisa said. "Service sucks."

"So, Hiatt?"

"He left the Pentagon just before the Bullwhip contract was let for bid. I thought the timing was curious, so I started digging into the archives, rooting through his old correspondence, searching his files that were still in storage, and this is what I found," she said and withdrew a sheaf of papers from her purse and slide it across the table to Nik.

He recognized the documents immediately. They were the Pentagon's internal cost projections and specs for the Bullwhip contract, prepared by the Pentagon's analytics division, and were identical to ones he had back on file at his apartment.

"I've seen them already. In fact, I have these same exact documents back at my place. You should know that since you're the one who sent them to me."

"Not these, you don't," she said. "Take a closer look."

Nik squinted at the pages and studied them for several minutes. He shook his head. "I don't get it. What am I looking for?"

Louisa turned her smartphone's light on and aimed it at Nik. "Hold the pages up to the light," she suggested.

Nik did as he was told. "Wait a second," he said, his voice rising.

"Bingo." She nodded. "Those are Blue Sky Consulting documents. You can see the company's faint watermark when you hold the paper up like that. Dwayne Mack and his boys cooked up those numbers and then handed them off to Hiatt just before he retired. Little wonder Yukon won the bid, since the military used Mack's calculations to model the contract."

"This is the smoking gun, then," Nik said.

"Not quite. More like ammunition. You'll notice there's no

date on the documents. They could always claim they arrived after the contract had been awarded."

Their waitress appeared at their table with a heavy tray and plunked down condiments and two oversized plates brimming with fries and oyster po'boys in front of them. The pair hungrily attacked the food.

After they were done eating, Nik looked across at Louisa contemplatively, lips pursed.

"What?" she asked between sips of her beer.

"Umm, those Nats tickets you mentioned, that was just a ruse, then?"

"Ha," Louisa barked. "'Fraid so. Series has been sold out for weeks."

Nik stumbled out of the Hot Corner just before closing time with a slight buzz, a dull headache, and pockets stuffed with napkin scribblings from the all-night session with Louisa Dills.

"You gonna be awright, hon?" she asked as they walked out of the bar together.

"I'm fine." Nik waved her off, but thought, *Man, that woman can sure pack it away.*

Nik crawled into the front seat of his Land Cruiser, powered down all the windows, and steered the vehicle toward Courthouse Road, praying he didn't run into a cop.

He jogged left on Nutley Street before jumping on the I-66 ramp east toward the District of Columbia. He stayed in the far-right lane and kept his speed at a steady fifty-five miles per hour all the way home. When he got back to his condominium, he found a note tacked to his door. It was from Reese, his neighbor. She said she heard Gyp barking, looked in on him, discovered he had somehow locked himself in the bathroom, and took him back to her place to calm down. "Drop by when you get home. I work late," the note read.

CHAPTER 49

July 24

The executive news director for Channel 13 blocked off a coveted nighttime hour slot for Elizabeth Blake's exclusive report on the death of Yukon's CEO Geoffrey Tate and the troubling questions swirling around the Pentagon's half-a-trillion-dollar Bullwhip contract, information Blake and her producer had cherry-picked from the *Newshound* files Teo had handed over to her.

Blake had kept her superiors in the dark about the provenance of her information, but she promised them a blockbuster story, and the station had been promoting it nonstop all week long. "Lizzy Blake blows the lid off Yukon cover-up," promised one over-the-top promo, with a shot of the reporter standing alongside the distinctive prospector sculpture outside Yukon's downtown headquarters, a fake bundle of dynamite in her hand.

Throughout the day leading up to the report, other promos flashed pictures of Geoff Tate on his yacht, Jewel Tate entering the courthouse in her tight-fitting outfits during the trial, and snippets of Jewel's call to 911. All indications pointed to a program that would shatter the news operation's previous rating records.

Lizzy made sure to email and text her network contacts to remind them to tune in or record the program. It was her ticket out of the small, stagnant pond that was local television news and into the bigs, and she planned to punch it in prime time.

She debated what to wear, finally settling on an expensive but conservative low black tunic jacket, zippered in the front, a single strand of pearls at her neck. She had her sandy-colored hair highlighted and professionally blown out; brows plucked; red raspberry lip gloss applied, one coat at a time, with a needle-nosed brush; nails buffed to a crystal sheen.

She chose her favorite pair of rust-colored Bruno Magli Galena pointed-toe pumps, to better accentuate her legs, no stockings, and applied an extra layer of bronzer to her calves, thighs, and face. The makeup artist in the greenroom told her she looked stunning, and, for once, it wasn't an exaggeration.

With forty-five minutes to go to airtime, Lizzy sat down at her computer to give her jealously guarded script one final read before sending it over to the teleprompter.

She keyed in her password—"Cronkite"—and began reading silently to herself: Good evening. In an exclusive exposé by this reporter, I will reveal tonight for the first time the truth behind the death of the late Yukon CEO Geoffrey Tate and his company's connections to a shady Eastern European oligarch, wild cocaine parties on his private island that went on for days on end, and Tate's gambling addiction, which nearly bankrupted Yukon.

When she was finished, she hit Send and shot the transcript over to the teleprompter desk.

No sooner had Lizzy walked off the soundstage after airing the Yukon exposé than the phone lines in the studio lit up. Every light was blinking, and her cell phone was exploding with incoming text messages, calls, and emails. She was overcome by a feeling of power and prestige. *Elizabeth Blake has arrived, damn it!*

Lizzy was sitting at her desk when her producer materialized at her side. "We kicked ass, Tony," she said, a smug, satisfied *Mona Lisa* smile on her lips.

"The whole network is in an uproar," the producer huffed.

"It's what we expected, right? Look at my cell phone. It looks like Grand Central."

"No, Elizabeth, it's not what you think. Lawyers, politicians, foreign embassies are all calling. They're demanding an immediate retraction and full apology."

Huh, what did that dipshit just say? Did I hear him right? she thought. "Retraction, full apology," she repeated hazily.

He nodded. "Yes. They claim none of it was true. The documents are phony, the information bogus, the pictures photoshopped."

"That can't be."

Lizzy plugged Teo's thumb drive into her computer's port and clicked on the link to the secured cloud server. Instead of an index of folders and files opening on the screen, an image of a Guy Fawkes mask appeared before dissolving into a message: These files have been permanently encrypted and are no longer available to the user.

The fog in Lizzy's head lifted. "Fuuuuck," she shrieked and pounded her keyboard with both hands, sending splintered nails sailing through the air. She grabbed her cell phone and punched in a number.

"Teo, you no-good piece of . . ."

"This is Mia," Mia said. "Teo is busy right now. Can I help you?"

"You did this," Lizzy screamed. "Byron is behind this. He had the kid set me up."

"Elizabeth, is that you?"

"You'll pay for this."

"Is there a problem?"

"You're trying to sabotage my career, ruin everything I've worked for. I'll never get a job at one of the networks now."

"Calm down, Lizzy," Mia purred. "Don't take it personally. It's how the game is played in this town. Smart woman like you, I would have thought you'd have learned that by now. Isn't that what you told Teo?"

CHAPTER 50

July 26

Detective Goetz met Nik on a steamy late-week afternoon in Dupont Circle. They were sitting on a bench feeding the pigeons while halfway paying attention to a dozen games of speed chess that were going on around them in the little park. City workers had recently refurbished the two-story marble fountain in the middle of the park, and its water was bubbling over the top and cascading down the sides, sending a plume of spray in a wide arc and drowning out Nik's and Jason's voices. They had to shout to be heard.

"Come on, Jason, what's the use in denying it? I know Faud Asma is a suspect in the Allan Trumbo investigation," Nik said over the crashing water.

"I don't know where you got that," Goetz said, reaching into a sack and scattering seed to the pool of birds cooing and pecking around his feet.

"I saw you and Detective Jenks follow him out of the Tombs," Nik reminded him.

Goetz looked over his shoulder before answering. "Oh, so

you recognized Asma? Okay, but he's not a suspect. He's a person of interest."

Nik was bluffing, but there was no way the young detective could know that. Try as he might, Nik hadn't been able to find any information about Asma online, and his political contacts in DC had stared at him blankly when he mentioned the name. Even Maggie, who'd made a few calls on Nik's behalf, came up empty.

"But we're having a hard time getting him to cooperate because of diplomatic immunity."

Nik sat up a little straighter. "Hmmmm, I could see how that could be a problem," he said, hoping to draw Goetz out even further.

"Yeah, the Saudis are refusing to play ball," Goetz said.

"What did they list as Asma's official position with the embassy?" Nik asked casually. "I wasn't able to pin that down." Not a lie, necessarily, but not exactly the truth, either.

Goetz bent over, reached down, shooed the pigeons away, and retied the laces on his heavy black cop shoes. "Attaché, that's what the documents on file at the State Department claim. We suspect he's security."

Nik decided to roll the dice. "And you think there's a connection between Trumbo's involvement in the Pentagon's Bullwhip project and Asma?"

Goetz stood and brushed the birdseed off the front of his trousers. "That's all you'll get from me, Nik. I've already said too much, and if Detective Jenks found out I even talked to you, she'd have my scalp," he said and smoothed down his dark pelt-like hair. "The woman really doesn't like you."

"Yeah, that's the vibe I get."

Goetz consulted DC's transportation app on his smartphone. "Next metro is in ten minutes. If I hustle, I can make it," he said, and started off at a fast pace toward the entrance of the Dupont train station and then stopped and turned back toward Nik.

"Rumor has it Asma was mixed up in the Khashoggi thing," Goetz said, referring to the *Washington Post* columnist whom Saudi intelligence agents had killed and dismembered in Istanbul, allegedly at the request of the royal court. "Better watch yourself, Nik," Goetz called out before leaving the park.

Nik remained sitting on the bench awhile longer, quietly reminiscing about how he and Sam used to soak their feet in the cool waters of the Dupont Fountain after taking Gyp for a long walk. He sighed, stood, and returned to his lonely apartment.

CHAPTER 51

July 27

It was past midnight, and Thomas Polk and Faud Asma were alone at Asma's uncle's restaurant in Adams Morgan, a thick layer of gray smoke hanging just above their heads like a storm cloud from the nonstop chain of cigarettes Asma had consumed.

"You get a chance to watch the video I sent over?" Polk asked.

"Yes."

"Impressive, no?"

"Perhaps."

"Perhaps? What do you mean, perhaps?"

Faud sucked on his teeth. "If it is true."

Polk said, "You saw it with your own eyes. An unmanned and autonomous drone identified and destroyed two military installations. We've just surmounted a huge AI obstacle. What that video demonstrates is nothing short of revolutionary in the realm of artificial intelligence."

"Maybe so, but we still don't have the technology you promised us."

"No, you don't, that's correct, and that's why I needed to talk to you in person. I had hoped the video would prove to you the great strides the program is making and our commitment to developing world-changing AI platforms."

"The video proves nothing, Thomas."

Polk weighed his next statement carefully. He suspected Asma of being a cold-blooded killer, and he didn't want to unintentionally set him off.

"Faud, we need to discuss deliverables and future remuneration," Polk said as calmly as he could.

Asma blew smoke out his nose and slowly turned his head toward Polk, his eyes dark, lifeless, like a shark's. "You want us to give you more fucking money for something we haven't yet received but have paid for?"

"The two hundred million was a down payment, just for the first phase of Bullwhip's technology. That was clear to everyone from the start. The first phase is now concluded."

"This is bullshit. It was not made clear to His Highness."

"I get it. If you don't want the next iteration of the software, that's okay. Entirely your call, but, just so you understand, it's impossible to slice and dice the algorithm and expect it to function properly."

"What are you telling me?"

"I'm saying we can hand over the code, as we said we would, but it's useless by itself. It won't work."

"You are stalling."

"I'm not," Polk lied.

Polk assumed the Gunslinger test drone he had witnessed was legitimate and had no reason to suspect that Dwayne Mack had rigged the demonstration. Mack had instructed Polk to tell the Saudis that it was impossible to disassemble the software code and expect the system to function properly. If they wanted a fully operational Bullwhip platform, they would have to wait, and it would cost them an additional $200 million.

"You and your friends are playing with fire, Thomas," Asma warned, "and if you are not careful, it will burn down your house."

That's when Polk decided to play his trump card.

"The vice president has taken a real interest in this project," he confided, even though Mack had explicitly told him not to mention Pound's connection to the project.

"What vice president?"

"Ours," Polk said and then realized that Asma, not being an American, might be confused. He clarified, "The vice president of the United States, Matthew Pound. Of course, he has to remain in the background, out of necessity, but he's on our team now."

Asma lit yet another Marlboro and absorbed this piece of news. He asked, "What is this we hear about some other company buying Yukon?" he asked.

"We're entertaining offers, but don't let that worry you. Under the terms of the Bullwhip contract with the Pentagon, any new owner is required to keep existing management in place until all the work is completed. Same song, different verse."

Asma stood and walked toward the front of the bodega and stood at the window. He parted the curtains slightly and looked out. He could see the light-gray sedan parked halfway down the block, its lights off. He couldn't make out any figures inside the vehicle, but he knew they were there, waiting, watching.

He returned to the table. "You should go now, out the back. I will talk to His Highness and let you know his answer."

"Please give the prince my regards. I think he will find what we are proposing reasonable."

Asma ushered Polk out the rear exit. He didn't like the man, he was weak and a liar, but, still, Asma had warned him twice now. What else could he do?

CHAPTER 52

August 8

A stable hand found the body swinging from a rafter in a horse barn on the 220-acre estate just northwest of Sperryville, Virginia, in the foothills of the Blue Ridge Mountains in Rappahannock County, a length of bridle leather knotted expertly around his neck, a kicked-over feed bucket at his feet.

The news of retired army Lieutenant General Alexander Hiatt's death came as a shock to nearly everyone who knew him. They struggled to accept the suicide of a man who had faced death many times over on the battlefield in his long and distinguished military career. But mostly what they couldn't comprehend was how someone who they thought they knew intimately, many of them for decades, could own a multimillion-dollar Arabian horse farm ninety minutes outside of Washington, DC, and never breathe a word of it to a soul.

That discovery was only made more mystifying by subsequent disclosures that the general, a lifelong soldier living on a military pension, also owned, or had an interest in, a ski chalet in Telluride, Colorado; a hunting lodge in Montana; a cigarette boat in the Florida Keys; and a vineyard in Sonoma, California.

Some of his friends speculated it was family money, on his late wife's side, or that the general had gotten lucky in the stock market, or perhaps he had a rich benefactor. None would entertain the notion that the money might have been ill-gotten.

Even Nik, who had reason to suspect that the general was corrupt, was stunned by the lavish lifestyle Hiatt had carved out for himself.

With the assistance of his secret Pentagon source, Louisa Dills, Nik retraced the general's history, from his appointment to West Point as a cadet, to a tour of duty in Vietnam as the conflict wound down, to his heroic efforts on the battlefield in the first Gulf War, and eventually his ascension to a top job in the Pentagon.

To the public, Hiatt was a blunt-talking war hero with a chiseled jaw and a chest full of medals, but behind the scenes, he used his position as the overseer of the military's vast technology budget to feed classified military contracts worth hundreds of billions of dollars to cronies who, in turn, rewarded the general with handsome kickbacks, exotic parties, and female escorts.

As Nik began to unravel the general's cozy relationships with defense contractors, Silicon Valley tech giants, Pentagon lobbyists, political operatives, and foreign interests, a picture began to slowly emerge of a military-technology complex that was taking root in the United States and how that organization used its influence to sell the country on a $500 billion artificial intelligence gamble known as Bullwhip.

CHAPTER 53

August 12

"You got visitors," Corletta Ramsey, DC's chief of detectives, said as she rapped on the doorframe and stepped inside the small office Detectives Jenks and Goetz shared on the second floor of the downtown precinct.

The pair sat in worn swivel chairs facing one another, two gunmetal desks shoved tightly together. A fake potted plant stood in one corner of the room, and two heavy wooden chairs in another. A man and a woman crowded in behind Chief Ramsey and peered over her head.

"These are Agents Luck and Sawyer," Ramsey said and motioned first to the woman and then the man. The woman stood rigid, a grave look etched on her face, and barely nodded. The man raised his hand to acknowledge the introduction. He was nondescript, clean-shaven, a bit of a choirboy look about him. "They got a few questions they'd like to ask you."

Goetz stood and shook the guests' hands, while Jenks remained seated, an indifferent expression on her face. "FBI agents?" Goetz asked expectantly.

"Well, they sure the hell ain't real estate agents, Jason," Jenks said. "How can we help you?"

Ramsey shook her head and turned to leave but was hemmed in by the agents, and all three had to step out of the small office and into the hallway to allow the chief to depart. As they did, Jenks told Goetz, "You lemme handle this. Your job is to watch and keep your mouth shut." The young detective slinked back to his desk and slouched in his chair.

The agents stepped back into the office, seemingly waiting to be offered a chair. When no invitation was extended, they remained standing. Sawyer cleared his throat, but before he could speak, Luck said, "We need you to back off your stakeout of Faud Asma."

"Not sure what you're referring to," Jenks deadpanned.

"It's come to our attention, Detective Jenks," Sawyer started in, "that you and your partner have been surveilling Saudi national Faud Asma in conjunction with your investigation into the deaths of Allan Trumbo and Rupert Olen. We came by your office today to request that you cease and desist your operation as it relates to Asma."

Sawyer's voice had a Midwestern twang to it, like a banjo. "Why?" Jenks asked.

"Now, that's not really any of your business, is it," Luck cut in, "but since we want to remain on good working terms with local law enforcement, let's just say it has to do with issues of national security and leave it at that."

"National security," Goetz said and let out a low whistle.

Jenks threw him a sharp look.

"Please, Special Agent Luck, there's no need to be antagonistic," Sawyer chimed in again. "We can't go into details, Detectives, but I give you my word that we will do our utmost to keep you in the loop, and if anything major should develop, we will notify your office."

"How much notice?" Jenks asked. "Two minutes or two days? Makes a big difference."

"I can't tell you that, standing here just now, but as much time as the bureau thinks prudent. And I will request that you be allowed to participate in any formal action by the bureau regarding the subject," Sawyer promised.

Luck bit her bottom lip, dropped her chin to her chest, and mumbled, "Why don't you just give 'em your goddamn badge and gun while you're at it."

"I heard that, Special Agent Luck," Sawyer said. "Well, Detective?"

"Awright," Jenks said, "it's not like we've had much success penetrating Asma's diplomatic shield."

"Wow, FBI," Goetz said after Luck and Sawyer departed.

"Yeah, FBI," Jenks said. "Fuckin' Bureau of Idiots."

CHAPTER 54

August 16

Nik's investigation into the Bullwhip project, so full of promise one moment, came to a complete standstill the next when
the Pentagon, White House, vice president's office, and Yukon
executives effectively stonewalled his inquiries. Nik was convinced it was a coordinated effort. His calls, emails, and messages went unanswered, and when he did get through to a
human, he was routed from office to office, placed on intermi-
nable hold, or palmed off on some public relations shill whose
only job was to refuse to answer direct questions.

With the investigation stalled and Sam still not responding
to his appeals, Nik was spending more time in *Newshound*'s
recording studio moping around, his dark, negative energy
infecting everyone on the podcast team. Even Teo, who was
habitually in a state of sullenness, begged Mia to ban Nik from
the building because of his sour mood.

"Might be a good time to take a little R & R," Mia suggested
when they were alone together in *Newshound*'s recording

studio. "You rarely take time off, and you got plenty of vacation days in the bank."

"Where would I go?"

"The Grand Canyon."

"Really. You think so? This time of year?"

"Hell, I don't know, Nik, and it doesn't matter. Throw a dart at a map and, wherever it lands, go there, but just go."

"I dunno, Mia," Nik said. "Doesn't feel like a good time to be away."

"It's August in Washington, DC, for Christ's sake. It's like walking through a Turkish bathhouse outside, and it isn't any picnic being cooped up with you indoors. You're starting to get on everyone's nerves."

"Gee, thanks."

"Just saying."

"Maybe I could drive to Rehoboth Beach for the day," Nik mused.

"I got it. Why don't you and Mo take that road trip you've always talked about and go visit major league ballparks on the East Coast?" Mia said, figuring it would get Nik out of the office for at least two weeks.

"Hmm, that's not a bad idea." Nik nodded. "My baseball team's regular season is over, and playoffs don't start for a couple weeks." He shot a quick text to Mo. He got an immediate response. Mo couldn't make it. Dick Whetstone, the chief editor, was on vacation for three weeks, and Mo had been put in charge of running the newsroom.

"No-go," he informed Mia. "Mo's on call for the next several weeks."

"Fine. Stay here and drown yourself in your sorrows for all I care, just don't sink the rest of us," Mia said before she left for an interview.

Nik remained at his desk halfheartedly pecking away at his keyboard, answering a handful of emails, checking his voice-mail box for messages. He called the White House and vice president's office again but got nowhere. He decided to pack up and go home.

He was shutting down his computer when Mia's suggestion spawned another thought. He retrieved his wallet from his satchel and fished out the baseball card of Dale "Butch" Colson that he'd been carrying around ever since he found it inside the envelope.

He picked up his phone and scrolled through his contacts, and when he came across the name he was searching for, he clicked on it and hoped she hadn't changed her number after all these years.

"Talk about ghosts of Christmas past," Leah Kovach said when she answered.

"Hey, Leah, good to hear your voice. Been a while."

"A while? More than seven years, give or take, Niky."

"Has it been that long?"

"You know it has. Don't tell me you forgot our last get-together in New Orleans."

Nik and Leah had dated their senior year at the University of Michigan. Nik was an editor on the *Michigan Daily* and Leah worked as a sports information specialist in the Wolverines' Athletic Department. After they graduated, Nik remained in the Midwest working on newspapers, while Leah headed to the East Coast and a job with the New York Yankees organization. They hooked up off and on over the years when they were in the same town together, but Nik went dark when he and Maggie started getting serious. Leah was now a vice president with the MLB Network.

"Howya been?" Nik asked.

"I'm good. Married, one kid, another on the way. Husband, Dan, works on Wall Street."

"Boy or girl?"

"Girl, Kate. Expecting a boy. You?"

"Single, no kids, and none on the way that I know of."

"What happened between you and Maggie?"

"Short version, bad chemistry. You don't have enough time for the longer version."

"Sorry to hear it."

"It was for the best. We remain friendly, after a fashion."

"You seeing anyone?"

"I was, former reporter. Another long tale."

"Aw, Niky."

"Yeah, I know, story of my life. Should have stuck it out with you when we were dating. Missed my chance."

"Ha, that's a joke, Nik. You acted like commitment was an infectious disease. Our so-called dating was takeout dinner from a Thai restaurant, a roll in the hay, and maybe coffee in the morning if you hung around that long."

"Sometimes we went to a movie."

"One time. We went to a movie one time, and it was a war movie. I hate war movies. They're so depressing."

"You happy now?"

"I am. I'm a great mother, and I love having a family, but I know you didn't call to ask about my personal life after all these years. So what's up, Nik?"

"I got a favor."

Leah paused. "Let's hear it."

CHAPTER 55

August 22

If Nik thought DC's humidity and weather were oppressive, it was nothing compared to the blast furnace that greeted him when he stepped out of the Miami International Airport terminal to hail a cab. The bestial heat seared his skin and made his teeth sweat, and he immediately questioned his decision to take time off from work to track down Butch Colson, the former major league pitcher who might, or might not, have information related to the Yukon story.

It had taken some time, but Leah Kovach was eventually able to get a line on Colson for Nik. A guy Leah used to work with in the Yankees organization roomed with Colson when they both were rookies on the Toronto Blue Jays. He had lost track of the pitcher, but he had kept in touch with another Toronto teammate who, along with Colson, was traded to the St. Louis Cardinals. That ex-teammate, a shortstop, had seen Colson at a Blue Jays reunion and remembered he was working as a pitching coach for a junior college in Tennessee and as a part-time scout for the Cincinnati Reds.

When Nik called the junior college in Chattanooga, he was told the school had discontinued its baseball program and didn't have any contact information for Colson, but the Reds had kept Colson on retainer, and he periodically filed scouting reports to the team and sent the occasional big-league prospect their way.

"Last I heard, he's living somewhere in the Keys and running a camp, mostly for Puerto Ricans, Dominicans, and the occasional Cuban player," the manager for the Daytona Tortugas, a single-A minor league team in the Reds' farm system, told Nik.

Nik wasn't able to locate Colson's phone number, but he had a name, Riptide Baseball Academy, and a location, Islamorada.

He checked into the Delano Hotel in South Beach and booked a room for two nights. He figured he might change hotels once he made contact with Colson. His room was bleach white, spacious, with a large sitting area that overlooked the pool. He showered and went downstairs for a drink.

Nik wandered into an Asian-themed restaurant, decided the Zen-like interior wasn't what he was in the mood for, and walked over to the art deco Rosebar across the lobby.

He sat at the bar, ordered a Budweiser, and pulled out a paper map from his satchel, unfolded it on the bar, and studied it. Islamorada was two hours south of Miami Beach on Highway 1, about a quarter of the way down the Keys. It was officially part of Plantation Key.

The place was off the beaten path for a baseball camp, that was for sure. Hell, it was off the beaten path for most things.

The bartender's name was Robyn. She had short red hair and freckles, and she vaguely reminded Nik of Sam. She poured Nik's beer into a fluted glass and placed a bowl of warm cashews in front of him.

Nik grabbed a handful of nuts. "Anybody ever call you Red Robyn?" he asked.

"Not since middle school."

"Noted," Nik said. "You got a minute?"

It wasn't yet six p.m. and the bar only had a few customers. "Do I look busy?"

"You ever been to Islamorada?"

"Sure."

"What's it like?"

"Quaint. Quiet. Too slow for my taste. Bored out of my skull if I have to spend more than an afternoon there. Why, you thinking about moving to Islamorada? You look a little young to be joining the seniors' Tuesday bridge club social."

"No, I'm trying to find somebody who lives there, or, at least, I think he does. Or did. Runs a baseball camp."

"Wouldn't think it'd be too hard to find him if he's there. It's pretty small, and it's one of those places where everybody knows everybody else's business."

"Good. That's what I was hoping."

Robyn said, "Islamorada calls itself the Sportfishing Capital of the World. Ted Williams used to live there."

"Seriously? Didn't know. Place is sounding better by the minute," Nik said. He finished his beer and ordered another one and asked to see a menu.

"It's just bar food," Robyn said, "nothing too fancy."

"It'll do," Nik said. He studied the menu and again wondered if this trip to southern Florida in search of a washed-up baseball player was a complete waste of his time.

Guess I'll find out soon enough, he thought.

If nothing else, he'd check out where Ted Williams used to live. He considered the Splendid Splinter the best baseball player of his era.

———————

Enterprise Rent-A-Car dropped a white Toyota Camry off at Nik's hotel in the early morning, and he plugged Islamorada into the Waze app on his iPhone. He made the eighty-six-mile trip in just under two hours, arriving shortly after eleven a.m. Nik's first stop was at Bad Boy Burrito for lunch.

The hostess asked Nik if he wanted to be seated outside under an open-air canopy overlooking the ocean on the back patio or indoors where it was air-conditioned. He chose indoors and ordered a plate of the fish tacos, lemonade, and asked his waiter, a deeply tanned, raggedy kid with half-hooded eyes, if he knew where Riptide Baseball Academy was.

"I don't, but Felipe might. His kid plays ball, I think. Hey, Felipe!"

"*Sí,*" came a voice from the kitchen in the back of the restaurant.

"*¿Dónde esta la academia de béisbol?*"

"I think it moved to Southwinds Park near the old Boys and Girls Club, bro," Felipe said, and added, "You say rice and beans with those tacos?"

"Rice and beans?" the waiter asked.

"Sure, why not," Nik said, "and thanks for the information."

"Yeah, rice and beans," he said to the cook. To Nik, he said, "No problem, mister. Just remember me when you go to leave a tip."

The kid started to slink off when Nik called after him, "Wait. Could you ask Felipe if he knows a Butch Colson?"

The kid sighed. "You know Butch Colson, Felipe?" he shouted out.

"Who wants to know?"

"A customer."

Felipe stepped out of the kitchen with a plate of tacos and set them on the bar. He had a white apron tied around his waist, a buzz cut, and a diamond stud in his left ear. He hesitated for a moment before answering. "Yeah, I know Butch. You thinking maybe you want your kid to take pitching lessons from him?"

"No, nothing like that," Nik said. "I'm a reporter and am working on a story about ex–major league players. You know, kinda like a 'where are they now' human interest piece."

"Awright," Felipe said. "Well, if you want to interview Butch, you better get there early. I hear he starts drinking around noon."

Nik paid for his food, left the kid a twenty-dollar tip, thanked Felipe for his help, and climbed back into the baking Camry to make the twelve-minute drive to Southwinds Park.

He found a shady spot, parked the car, and followed the signs to the ball fields across the park. Except for a groundskeeper hosing down the dirt infield, the place was deserted. He waited until the worker finished watering and then asked him if he knew where the Riptide Baseball Academy held its camp.

The man pointed toward the buildings on the other side of the park and said, "Old Boys and Girls Club."

As Nik stepped inside the run-down building, he could hear the piiing of balls flying off metal bats, the thud of baseballs slapping leather, and the clang of barbells dropping onto racks. The gymnasium in the former club had been converted into a training facility and was encased in netting and outfitted with a half-dozen batting cages and a weight room. Off in one corner, Astroturf covered the floor, and kids were taking turns fielding ground balls. Industrial-size floor fans stationed around the facility whirled away, blowing hot air over the stripped-down, sweat-covered ballplayers.

Nik slipped off his sunglasses and looked around. The manager of the Daytona Tortugas wasn't exactly correct. It looked to Nik like half the kids were Latin, one-quarter Caucasian, and about one-quarter Black. He guessed they ranged in age from about twelve to eighteen.

Nik didn't see anyone who even vaguely resembled Colson, but then again, the baseball card he had was more than a decade old now and the guy could have changed dramatically.

A teenager was standing behind a makeshift counter, a TV suspended overhead tuned to ESPN, the sound off. Nik asked for Colson, and the teen nodded to a metal staircase on the far end of the building that led to an upper floor and walkway.

Nik mounted the stairs, and when he got to the top, he saw a young, broad-shouldered, shaggy-haired blond right-hander standing on a sloped platform made to approximate a pitching mound. He was throwing to a catcher sixty feet, six inches away. It was noticeably hotter upstairs, and the sweat started pouring out of Nik.

About halfway between the pitcher and catcher, on the sidelines, sat Butch Colson on a folding chair, a five-gallon bucket of baseballs near his feet, an iPad balanced on his lap. Colson tucked a pinch of snuff in his bottom lip and spit a stream of tobacco juice into an empty Starbucks cup he was holding. He was wearing a faded Rolling Stones T-shirt, shorts, and flip-flops. Except for a pair of reading glasses balanced on his nose, and a goatee, Colson looked remarkably the same. His hair wasn't as bushy, but he still resembled the player on the Topps baseball card. Nik figured him to be late thirties, early forties.

Colson reached into the bucket, pulled out a ball, and flipped it to the kid, who came off the mound to retrieve it. "How many does that make, Guillermo?"

"Twenty-five."

"Fifteen more. Five fastballs, five changeups, and five curveballs. Okay?"

"Okay, Butch."

"Stay on top of your changeup and benders. Remember, same arm motion for all three."

Nik watched the pitcher go into a windup and fire his fastball. The ball sounded like a whip cracking when it struck the catcher's mitt, and the radar panel above the backstop blinked "87."

"Oooooh," a chorus of voices sang out from a row of chairs opposite Colson, where a handful of teens waited their turn to throw. "Eighty-eight, eighty-eight, PR, personal record," they chanted in unison.

"Ignore those yahoos," Colson said. "Trust your mechanics."

Guillermo walked off the makeshift mound five minutes later, his last fastball having touched "88."

"Pick 'em up," Colson called to the boys, and they scrambled from their seats to retrieve the balls that were scattered around the floor. "Juan, you're on the bump next. Guillermo, run your laps. Flush that lactic acid out of your system."

Colson was making notes on his iPad when Nik approached. "Give me a second," he said, and when he finished, he glanced up, a blank look on his face. "How old's your boy?"

"What?" Nik said.

"Your kid, how old is he? I don't take on anyone until they're at least in eighth grade. Bones in the arms haven't fully formed before then," Colson said.

"Butch," Nik said, "I'm not here for pitching instruction. I'm a reporter for *Newshound*. I'm working on a story about former Major League Baseball players, and I wonder if you might give me a little of your time when you're done here today?"

They agreed to meet at the Shrimp Shack on Overseas Highway in Islamorada at five p.m.

CHAPTER 56

August 23

Alexander Hiatt's murder—and Thomas Polk was positive it was a murder, never for a moment believing the general hanged himself—unnerved Polk and hardened his resolve to extricate himself from Dwayne Mack, Yukon, and the Bullwhip project while there was still time. A person couldn't turn on the TV, pick up a newspaper, or open up a website without the news of the deaths staring them in the face.

Polk was convinced Faud Asma and the Saudis were behind Hiatt's death, as well as those of Rupert Olen and Allan Trumbo, and he was equally convinced he was next, despite assurances from Asma that he had no hand in the killings.

Polk bitterly regretted ever getting tied up with Mack, Rupert Olen, and the Saudis. He only did so, he now told himself, because he was frustrated that the US military was sitting on its hands while Russia and China, especially China, surged ahead in deploying artificial intelligence in weaponry. He knew joining forces with Mack wasn't ideal, but if that's what it took to get the United States into the AI game, then so be it.

As an ex–Silicon Valley tech entrepreneur, Polk was independently wealthy and could claim there was no compelling reason for him to seek kickbacks from the Bullwhip project. That would be his line of defense: *Yes, I used my position as co-chairman of the National Security Commission on Artificial Intelligence to jump-start AI adoption and steer the Bullwhip contract to Yukon, but only out of a sense of patriotic duty that the Pentagon was falling behind its adversaries, and not for any personal gain.*

But Thomas Polk was savvy enough to realize that the narrative he was weaving was only credible to the extent he was out in front of the story, not behind it, and the way to achieve that was to leak it.

He would swear that he'd only discovered after the fact Mack had bribed military personnel and politicians and sold the Bullwhip technology out the back door to the Saudis. He would assert he had no prior knowledge of the rigged contract and kickback scheme, and with Trumbo, Hiatt, and Olen dead, it would be his word against Mack's. Maybe their deaths were a blessing in disguise after all.

It was a risky strategy, but it might just work, and with his life on the line, he reasoned he had nothing to lose.

Polk stood looking out over the Washington skyline from his Watergate apartment, a half-empty bottle of brandy on a side table, and thought carefully about his next move. He nervously threaded the string of mahogany worry beads Asma had gifted him through the fingers of his left hand and, with his right, punched in the phone number of the reporter who had been hounding him for weeks.

CHAPTER 57

August 23

Nik ignored the buzzing cell phone in his satchel and walked to the far end of the Shrimp Shack's bar and settled onto a stool. The room's interior was dimly lit, its walls covered in varnished knotty pine, and the bar's back wall was lined with various bottles of rum. It smelled like an outgoing tide, and Nik felt like he was stepping back in time to when the Keys were home to men and women who made their living on the water and served as a hideaway for Beat writers, musicians, and artists.

He hooked his satchel on a peg under the lip of the counter and ordered a Sandbar Sunday, a microbrew from the Islamorada Beer Company, a pelican on the label, breaking his own rule about not drinking craft beers. *But when in Rome,* he thought.

The beer was a degree or two above freezing, and it gave Nik a brief but intense brain freeze when he swallowed his first sip. He thought it was the near-perfect temperature.

The cell phone in his satchel started buzzing again, and

he was just about to reach for it when Butch Colson, with a professional athlete's natural carriage, walked into the bar and took the stool next to Nik. Colson was dressed the same, except he had changed out of the Rolling Stones T-shirt and now was wearing a bright-tropical-print short-sleeved button-up.

"Whaddya have, Butch?" the bartender asked.

"Usual, Jimmy."

The bartender set a glass of ice, a bottle of Coke, a thimble of lime juice, and a healthy shot of rum in front of Colson. "One Cuba libre," Jimmy said. "Want me to mix it for you, Butch?"

"I got it, thanks."

Colson poured the Coke over the ice, added the lime juice and rum, and held up the glass to Nik. "Salute."

"Cheers," Nik said. After he took a swig, he added, "Thanks for taking the time, Butch."

"No problem. What is it you want to know?"

"Fact is, Butch, I'm working on a couple of stories. The first is about the lives of former major leaguers, the second has to do with artificial intelligence. If you don't mind, I'd like to talk baseball first and then explain the other story afterward. Sound good?"

"Sure, I guess, but I don't know squat about, whatchamacallit?"

"Artificial intelligence."

"Yeah, that. Is it like sabermetrics? You know, *Moneyball*?"

"A little bit, but not exactly. I'll get to that in a bit. First I want to hear about your career."

"Okay," Butch said. "Jimmy, another Cuba libre here, please."

"I was a late bloomer and didn't play high school ball until my junior year, and even then, I didn't make the varsity team until the tail end of the season. I was blessed with a live arm and was throwing in the nineties, but I really didn't know how to pitch. It wasn't until my senior year that I came into my own, but by then, all the big Division One schools had committed to incoming players and there were no slots or scholarships left."

Butch paused to take a drink of his cocktail and let Nik catch up with his note-taking. Nik was also recording the interview for a podcast he hoped to produce.

"So, I walked on at Mississippi State and made the team. The coach was going to redshirt me, but before the season opener, two of his starters got hurt and a third got mono. Next thing I know, I'm pitching for Mississippi State my freshman year."

Nik said, "A walk-on freshman, pitching at the D One level, that just doesn't happen."

"Nope, not very often, that's for sure. But here's the real crazy part. I had a great fucking season. I didn't win many games, but my ERA was 2.25, and the next two years, I was a starter. I went 6–5 my sophomore year and 8–2 my junior. I got drafted after my third season and signed with the Blue Jays. I need to pee," Colson said, then pushed off the barstool and headed to the restroom.

When he returned, he asked, "Where was I? Oh, yeah. The Blue Jays. I was with them for a couple seasons but never made it out of the minors and got traded to the St. Louis Cardinals. By this time, I was converted to a middle reliever and got called up to the big club by the Cards at the end of the season. I pitched a couple innings and did awright. The next season, I made the opening-day roster out of training camp. That's when the trouble started."

It was Nik's turn to use the restroom. When he returned, he ordered another round of drinks, a basket of the fried shrimp, and, on Colson's recommendation, the Gator Bites Cajun, breaded pieces of alligator tail deep-fried and served with remoulade.

"Tastes like chicken," Nik said after biting into one. "So, troubles?" he prodded.

"You know who Daniel Bard is?" Colson asked.

"Name's vaguely familiar."

"He's a pitcher. Played for Boston, out of the University of North Carolina. All of 2010 and part of 2011, guy was unhittable, and by that, I mean one of the most, if not the most, unhittable pitchers in the show during that stretch. His stuff was filthy."

"So, what happened to him? He get hurt?"

"Nope, worse. He got the yips. Developed a mental block the size of a Mack truck," Butch said and polished off another Cuba libre. "Can't remember his exact numbers, but there was one game in his downward spiral where he walked nine batters and hit three others, and that was only in a half inning."

"Jesus," Nik said. "You want another drink?"

Butch thought it over for a second. "Sure, why not. I'm not coaching tonight."

"So, what's the point of the story?"

"Same sorta thing happened to me. My problem was, once I got up in the count on batters, 0–1, 1–2, I couldn't buy a strike. If the count was even, or if I was down in the count, not a problem, but once I got ahead, I was a hot mess. Couldn't put batters away. Couldn't find the plate with a compass."

"What did you do?"

"I did what every dumb fuck does in that situation, including Bard. I threw harder. I wound up injuring my arm. Bounced around with other clubs for a while, spending a lot of time in the minors and then here in Florida in the winter rehabbing. That's when I discovered this place and decided it was where I wanted to live when my career was over. End of story."

"Well, at least you got your shot. That's more than most guys can say," Nik said.

Colson said, "That's true. Now, what about this other story you mentioned?"

Nik explained to Colson about the baseball card someone had left for him, Yukon, the Bullwhip contract, artificial intelligence, and ticked off the deaths of Geoff Tate, Rupert Olen, Allan Trumbo, General Hiatt. None of it rang a bell with Butch.

"You have to understand something, Nik, I moved to the Keys to escape life. I don't follow current events. I don't do social media, watch the news, read newspapers. If it ain't on ESPN, the MLB Network, or the Golf Channel, good chance I haven't heard of it. Sorry you went to all the trouble," Colson said.

"No worries," Nik said and picked up his empty bottle of beer and thought about ordering another, then decided against it since he had a two-hour drive back to South Beach. "It was a long shot. Anyway, wasn't a total waste. I got some good material for the podcast on ex–ball players."

"You should hang around," Colson said. "Couple summer teams stocked with talent are playing nearby tonight. I've been scouting this southpaw for a while now. I think he's got real potential."

"I'd love to, but I really need to hit the road," Nik said. "Some other time."

He paid for his and Colson's drinks and left the bartender a hefty tip. Nik slid off his stool, shook Colson's hand, grabbed his satchel, and started walking away, but the satchel's strap snagged on the peg and snapped back, yanking the bag out of Nik's hand, scattering its contents across the barroom floor.

"Aaaah, shit," Nik said.

"Here, let me help," Colson offered and bent down and started scooping up pens, notebooks, power cords, loose change, sticks of gum. He handed the debris to Nik, who stuffed it back in the bag and closed the flap.

"Thanks," he said and headed again toward the door.

"Wait," Colson called. "You didn't get all of it." And he bent back over and picked up what looked like a small index card that had lodged under his stool. He turned the card over in his hands and recoiled as if doused with pepper spray. "Where did you get this?" he finally managed to ask.

Puzzled, Nik said, "Get what?"

"This," Colson said and flipped the card over. "A picture of Pearl, my ex-fiancée."

It was a color mug shot of Jewel Tate the night she was brought to the Northern Virginia County Sheriff's Department after the attack by her late husband. Nik had forgotten he had the photo. Jewel had a wild-eyed look, her neck bruised, her face a palette of red and purple splotches.

Colson collapsed back on the barstool and studied the photo of the disfigured woman and asked, "If Pearl looks this bad, what'd the other person look like?"

"Dead," Nik said.

CHAPTER 58

August 23

Faud Asma slipped out the back entrance of the embassy of the Kingdom of Saudi Arabia and hugged the shadows. The light-gray sedan was parked out front of the embassy when he'd last checked, two figures inside.

Asma's route was well planned, down to the smallest detail. Still, that didn't ensure success. A thousand things could go wrong, any one of which could get him exposed or killed. One was the same as the other as far as he was concerned.

He chose tonight to make his move because the prince was hosting a large gathering of children from local mosques and Asma's absence would likely go unnoticed.

He picked his way along a footpath that ran next to the embassy's white marble building until he came to New Hampshire Avenue. He headed northwest on New Hampshire, and when it intersected Virginia Avenue, he turned west, his destination the Watergate apartments, only a five-minute walk away.

He knew where many, but not all, of the surveillance

cameras were hidden along his route and instinctively gave an extra tug to the bill of his cap and dropped his eyes to the ground when he passed them. There were dozens of cameras—mostly operated by the United States, but by other countries, too—Russia, Israel, China, Pakistan, Germany.

He circled the Watergate complex, saw lights on in Thomas Polk's apartment, even thought he caught a glimpse of Polk staring out his window. Asma quickly glanced over his shoulder. He had been followed, as he anticipated. He then made his way back down Virginia Avenue.

At Twenty-Third Street, he turned north and walked to the Foggy Bottom Metro station, stepped onto the escalator, and rode it down three-quarters of the way before hurtling the divide and joining a crowd riding the escalator back up to the exit. "Forgot something," he said sheepishly as he bounded forward. The heavyset woman who had been following Asma didn't attempt to jump the divide. Instead, she spun around and started slowly clawing her way back up the down escalator.

At the top, Asma raced out of the station and quickly made his way to the adjacent George Washington University Hospital. He ducked into a men's restroom on the first floor next to the understaffed information desk, entered the third stall, stood on the toilet, lifted a ceiling panel, and brought out a small bag.

He removed a shirt, light jacket, and hat that read "GW Emergency Response" and stuffed the shirt and hat he was wearing in the bag, replaced it overhead, and closed the panel.

He departed the restroom and walked down the corridor to the emergency room and exited the hospital and climbed into a waiting ambulance.

"Tail?" the driver asked.

"Yeah."

"Where from?"

"The embassy. A woman on foot, her partner nearby in a car."

"They see you case Polk's place?"

"Yeah. Made sure of it."

"Good. Shake 'em?"

"Yeah, the Metro, on the escalator."

"Okay, you ready?"

"I'm here, aren't I?"

"Just checking."

"Let's do this," Asma said.

CHAPTER 59

August 23

Butch Colson told Nik that he first met Pearl Waters at Hotwired, a gentleman's club in Jupiter, Florida, during one of his rehab stints. She worked at the club as a greeter and a private dancer, and told Butch she was twenty-two. He'd later discover she was barely seventeen and Pearl Waters was her stage name.

Butch said he went to the club several times before he got up the nerve to ask Pearl to do a private dance for him. They got to talking afterward and realized that they had something in common—Butch played college ball for Mississippi State, and Pearl was from Pascagoula, Mississippi, on the Gulf Coast.

He became a regular at Hotwired, spending a good chunk of his weekly paycheck on private dances from Pearl.

"Some of the girls just kinda bump and grind and flop their tits in your face," Butch explained to Nik. "Not Pearl. There was something different about her, dangerous even. She'd pound you like a jackhammer and squeeze like a python. You'd be doing good if you could walk out of that room under your own power when she was finished with you."

Wasn't long afterward that Butch and Pearl started seeing each other secretly outside the club. They had to keep their relationship quiet lest their respective employers found out and put a stop to it.

When spring training ended and the ball club pulled up stakes, Butch promised to return as soon as his season was over, and he was good as his word.

Butch and Pearl picked up right where they left off, and they wintered together in Florida as Butch prepared for another spring training and a shot at rejoining the big club.

But Butch couldn't help notice something had changed with Pearl while he was gone. She had always been partial to rough sex, he knew, but she started insisting on aggressive role-playing in the bedroom. He didn't object because, well, she was an adult entertainer, after all, and, besides, he enjoyed it. At least, at first.

Butch considered the handcuffs, various leather restraints, and gags harmless enough. It was only when Pearl suggested that Butch knock her around a little and that she fight back that he became truly concerned.

"We didn't make love so much," Butch told Nik. "It was more like a cage fight. But I gotta be honest with you. It was a turn-on, and I could see how some guys might get addicted to that sort of thing."

Butch had a strong spring-training camp that year and was invited to join the Rockies when they opened the major league season. At the end of camp, he asked Pearl to marry him. She said yes.

"I left the next morning with the club. I reinjured my arm the twenty-first game into the season. I called Pearl and told her I'd be home in a couple weeks before I had to report to rehab. When I got there, she had cleaned out the apartment, emptied the checking account, and hocked the diamond ring. I never laid eyes on her again until tonight when I saw that picture."

CHAPTER 60

August 23

Yvette Jenks had just finished a Stephen Mack Jones novel she was reading and reached over to switch off the light when the iPhone on her bedside table buzzed. "Yeah," she said without looking at the number, figuring it was the precinct calling, "what is it?"

"Detective Jenks, it's Special Agent Sawyer from the FBI. Sorry for the lateness of the hour."

Jenks propped herself up on her elbows. "Not a problem. I was still awake. What's up?"

"I promised I'd alert you when there was progress in the Faud Asma investigation. We had a significant development in the case this evening, and we anticipate major activity in the next twenty-four to forty-eight hours. If you'd come down to FBI headquarters tonight, I could fill you in on the details."

Jenks pushed the Speaker button on her phone, bolted out of bed, and was hopping around her bedroom on one foot while she wrestled on a pair of jeans. "I'll call my partner and we'll be there in a half an hour," she told Sawyer.

"Drive around to the rear. I will give the guard your names. Just show him your IDs and they'll usher you into the building. We're in the fourth-floor conference room."

Detectives Jenks and Goetz made it to the FBI building in twenty minutes and rushed up the four flights of stairs to the conference room. When they entered, Special Agents Sawyer and Luck were seated on one side of the table, a haggard-looking, handcuffed Faud Asma on the opposite side.

Jenks, short of breath, looked from Asma to the FBI agents, back to Asma. She thought it odd that the prisoner was wearing a "GW Emergency Response" hat and shirt. "What a pleasant surprise," she said.

"Must feel like you know me by now, Detective, given how much time you've devoted to watching my every movement," Asma said and withdrew a Marlboro from the pack in front of him and picked up his lighter. "But you don't know me. Just think you do."

"Looking forward to getting better acquainted, then," Jenks said and pulled a chair out from under the table and sat down.

Asma lit the cigarette and blew the smoke in the direction of a large portrait of J. Edgar Hoover that hung on the wall. "Can we take these off now?" he said, and held up his hand-cuffed wrists to Sawyer.

"Uncuff him," Sawyer instructed Special Agent Luck. "And sorry about that, Faud. Following protocol, you understand."

CHAPTER 61

August 24

The streets and sidewalks of South Beach were swarming with young partygoers, men dressed in linen trousers and silk shirts, and women in short skirts and tight tops, when Nik parked his rental car out front of the Delano Hotel and tossed the keys to the valet. It was a little past one a.m., the temperature a comfortable eighty-one degrees with the ocean breeze, and Nik, due to the long drive and the lateness of the hour, was spent but felt like celebrating after talking to Butch Colson.

He stepped inside the hotel and took a quick peek into the Rosebar and saw Robyn mixing drinks. She looked up and gave Nik a smile and waved him on over.

"How was Islamorada?" she asked when he approached.

"Nowhere near as boring as you made it out to be."

"You must have arrived just in time for the annual shuffleboard tournament, then."

"Ha. Place has its charms."

"You find the guy you were looking for?" Robyn asked, and topped the drinks she was mixing with lemon wedges and

handed the cocktails to an aloof-looking waiter who was leaning on the bar. "Pay attention now, Todd, and don't spill the
drinks this time," she scolded.

"Whatever," Todd mumbled and slunk off.

"Gen L for 'loser.'" Robyn sighed.

Nik said, "Yeah, I did. You were right. Only had to ask
once. A cook at this Mexican restaurant where I stopped for
lunch knew him."

"The trip was worth it, then?"

"As it turned out, it was. Never did get to see where Ted
Williams lived, though. Woulda liked to have done that."

"Well, you'll just have to come back again," she said with a
sly grin.

Todd walked back over to the bar and asked, "Can I leave
now? It's almost closing time."

Robyn looked around. "Might as well," she said. "It's pretty
slow and I can handle it. You'd only be in the way anyhow."

Todd turned and started walking away when he remarked,
"Okay, Boomer."

"You're welcome, Todd," Robyn said, "and, oh, by the way,
no one says that anymore." To Nik, she said, "Can I get you
anything to drink? Budweiser?"

"You got Sandbar Sunday? Had a couple in Islamorada.
Not half bad for a craft beer. Least they didn't give me a headache like most microbrews."

"Let me check," Robyn said and walked to the other end
of the bar, and Nik could hear bottles clinking against one another as she rooted through the beer cooler.

Because he was officially off the clock and on vacation, Nik
had not bothered to check his messages since he had left for
Islamorada. He fumbled through his satchel and retrieved his
cell phone, and when he hit the home button, an alert popped
up on the screen warning him he had less than 2 percent bat-
tery life left.

He had not told anyone about his quest to find Butch Colson, only that he was headed to the Florida Keys to relax, hang out on the beach, read a few books. He figured if anyone knew about his plans, they would ridicule the notion and try to talk him out of it. He wouldn't have blamed them. He would have done the same if their roles were reversed.

A quick glance told him he had fifty or so new emails, a handful of text messages, mostly from Mia and Mo wondering if he had made it to Florida, and several long voice mails, all from the same unidentified Washington, DC, phone number.

Nik noticed he also had a WhatsApp message. It was from Sam. It was the first time he had heard from her in weeks. He clicked on the message and that's when his phone died.

Robyn reappeared. "Your lucky day. You got the last one," she said and held up a bottle of Sandbar Sunday. She snapped off the cap and poured the beer into a glass. When she finished, she said, "I'm free in a few. You wanna stick around and grab a drink with me?"

"Sure."

"Well, you're easy," she said and picked up his empty bottle and placed it under the bar.

"Easy like Sunday morning," Nik said.

———

Nik got two hours' sleep, woke, showered, quickly dressed, and was stepping out of his hotel room when he heard a CNBC anchor on the TV report a breaking-news story. He walked over to the sitting area and turned up the volume.

"*Officials of Yukon, the nation's largest artificial intelligence company and the lead contractor on the Pentagon's $500 billion Bullwhip project, have asked Nasdaq officials to halt trading in the company's stock pending an announcement. Our reporters are working the phones trying to find out more details* *behind the announcement, but we are hearing rumors it could be related to a possible takeover. Stay tuned for more information on this developing story."*

It's starting, Nik thought, and hustled back toward the door when a sleepy voice from the bedroom called out. "Be an angel and turn the television off before you leave, please?"

He stepped back into the room, picked up the remote from the coffee table, clicked off the TV, and hung the "Do Not Disturb" sign on the outside door handle before making a beeline for the elevators.

CHAPTER 62

August 24

With his cell phone recharged, Nik was able to check his messages while waiting to board his flight to DC. The message from Sam on WhatsApp was curt: We need to talk. He called her number and was immediately routed to her voice mail, where an automated message told him her mailbox was full and to try again later. He sent a note back on WhatsApp and told her he was flying to DC and would be back by midday, saying he would try to reach her when he landed, and reminded her that her voice-mail box was full.

Nik then opened the first voice mail from the Washington, DC, phone number and heard a slurred voice say: "They're trying to kill me. They've already killed Rupert Olen, Allan Trumbo, and General Hiatt. I'm next. I know way too much about the Bullwhip project. Call me back at this number if you want the story." The caller hung up without identifying himself, and Nik suspected the call was made from a burner phone.

He scrolled through the voice mails from the caller and

opened the last one he'd received. The man's voice was thicker now, deeply slurred, halting. It began: "Nik Byron . . . I've now left you a number of messages and haven't heard back . . . I would have thought you'd be anxious to talk after you learned what I had to say . . . You call yourself a fuckin' reporter . . . I overestimated you. You got twenty-four hours to call me back at this number . . . or I'm taking the story elsewhere."

In all, Nik had eight voice mails from the caller. He listened to them in the order they came in. When he was finished, he called Mia and told her about the voice mails, Butch Colson, and the rumored buyout of Yukon and laid out a plan.

"This story is moving at warp speed. We need to release the podcasts or lose whatever advantage we have."

"Release them when? Today?"

"Yes. We need to get the ball rolling."

"I dunno, Nik. Seems awful abrupt. I thought you went down to the Keys to relax."

"I'm telling you, we don't have much time, Mia, two days, three at the most. I've busted my ass on this for months, and for what, if we don't push this out. Our efforts will have been a complete waste of time."

"And Colson, you believe him?"

"One hundred percent. He showed me pictures he still had of the day he and Jewel got engaged. They're standing out front of the club where she worked and she's holding up her index finger and pointing at the engagement ring. It's her all right."

Mia switched topics. "Do you know who the caller is?"

"Thomas Polk. He let it slip in the call. I'm sure he didn't intend to, but clearly he'd had too much to drink. I'll call him back as soon as I get off the phone with you, but in his voice mails, he fingered the vice president, Dwayne Mack, politicians, and military personnel. He's ready to talk."

"Okay, what are the next steps?" Mia asked.

"I'll send you my taped interview with Colson and the

voice mails from Polk as soon as I hang up. Give them to Teo to edit. I'll write the Colson and Polk scripts on the plane and email them to you, indicating where to place the audio. Plane has Wi-Fi, so it shouldn't be a problem. I'll head directly to the studio as soon as I land to fill in any gaps."

"Anything else?"

"Yeah, call the vice president's office and tell them what we have and get a statement, even if it's 'no comment.' Same with Jewel. I gotta go. They're shutting the door."

Nik fired off the recordings to Mia and called the number Polk left. He got a recording saying it was no longer a working number. He scrolled through his contact list and found Polk's cell-phone number and dialed it. His call went directly to voice mail. He then called the Saudi Arabian embassy and asked for Faud Asma, and was transferred to the public information officer, who informed Nik that the embassy had no record of a Faud Asma on its staff.

Nik, the last passenger to board the flight, dropped into his aisle seat, popped open his laptop, and started writing. The plane sat on the tarmac while mechanics repaired a cargo door hinge. Nik didn't mind the delay since it afforded him extra writing time, something he was always grateful for, given his slow pace.

On his way to *Newshound*'s offices after he landed, Nik put in a call to Maggie and got a recorded message telling callers that she was on vacation for two weeks and had limited cell phone and Wi-Fi access. He left a short message.

"Maggs, it's me. If you get this, you might want to listen to our Yukon podcasts that are going live shortly. Pay particular attention to the one about Jewel's time in Florida. Some new information has surfaced. Think you'll want to hear it. Enjoy your vacation. Bye."

CHAPTER 63

Producer's introduction: This is the fifth installment of *The Front Page* podcast exploring the life and
death of Geoffrey Tate and Yukon Inc., the company
he founded. The podcast is narrated by *Newshound* reporter Nik Byron. His guest is Butch Colson, a former
Major League Baseball player, and the podcast host is
Mia Landry.

Friendly Fire

Nik Byron: Several years before the late Geoffrey Tate,
one of the world's richest men, was gunned down by his
wife after breaking into their home and assaulting her, a
similar incident played out hundreds of miles away in a
two-story apartment building four blocks from the Atlantic
Ocean in Jupiter, Florida.

On a warm, moonless night, a young Pearl Waters,
who worked as a greeter and private dancer at a gentleman's club, was readying for bed when she was attacked
from behind by a male intruder who wore a woman's nylon
stocking over his head and face to conceal his identity,
much like Geoff Tate did that night. Also like Tate, the
intruder gained access to the apartment through an unlocked window.

Waters, then eighteen, fought off the intruder and escaped to the bedroom, where she was quickly cornered. After another intense struggle, Waters reached under a pillow where she kept a small-caliber handgun and fired two shots, point-blank, at her attacker.

Only, this time, the shots didn't kill the intruder. The bullets were blanks, and the attacker was Pearl Waters's fiancé, Butch Colson, a promising young major league pitcher.

The pair was engaged in a role-playing fantasy, and this story would have ended there had it not been for the fact that Pearl Waters's real name was Jewel Dean, and she was destined to be Mrs. Geoffrey Tate one day.

Butch Colson: Walking into our bedroom was like stepping into the fuckin' octagon. It was a death match. We had more weapons than an army surplus store. Pearl was always into some new, kinky sex thing, the more dangerous, the better. She begged me to indulge her in the gun fantasy. "It'll be a real turn-on. You won't regret it," she told me. I finally agreed to go along, though I gotta tell ya, it scared the living shit out of me, and when she fired those two rounds, I nearly had a heart attack. But she was right. It was a turn-on, and I could see how someone could easily get hooked on it.

Nik Byron: Neither Jewel Tate, nor her spokesperson, would comment on this story or Butch Colson's recollections, and the fact that the two incidents parallel each other so closely is not proof that Jewel Tate intentionally staged the shooting of her late husband, but it does raise fresh questions.

Mia Landry: This story has more twists and turns than a mountain road. So, legally, what can be done?

Nik Byron: Not a thing. Since the court dismissed the charges and found Jewel not guilty of second-degree murder in the death of her husband, she cannot be retried. That would be double jeopardy. If Jewel Tate orchestrated a crime, it appears to have been the perfect crime.

Mia Landry: Why did Butch Colson wait so long to tell his story? Why didn't he come forward sooner, when the trial was underway, when it could have made a difference?

Nik Byron: That's easy. He didn't know about it. Butch more or less lives off the grid. Doesn't follow the news, and he claims the first time he learned of Jewel's real identity and that his former fiancée was married to one of the world's wealthiest individuals was when I told him a couple of days ago.

Mia Landry: And now we hear reports Geoff Tate's company, Yukon, is going to be sold and that Jewel Tate stands to reap billions when that happens.

Nik Byron: If the sale goes through, she will be one of the richest women on the planet. I think most people would agree that's quite an accomplishment for someone so young, let alone a one-time private dancer.

CHAPTER 64

August 24

After making several more rounds of calls, running their story past a phalanx of corporate attorneys, and receiving not-so-veiled threats from the vice president's office, Nik and Mia decided to sit on the final Yukon podcast installment for twenty-four hours.

It was a painful, but defensible, decision given the stakes involved.

They were about to report that the vice president of the United States used his office to conspire to rig a $500 billion Pentagon contract and that a score of politicians and military personnel either directly received payoffs to look the other way or actively participated in the scheme. And if that weren't enough, the story would also allege that Dwayne Mack, CEO of Yukon, one of the country's premier technology defense firms, had secretly and illegally agreed to sell sensitive AI software to the Saudi government.

"You've bought twenty-four hours," Nik told *Newshound*'s attorneys, "but not a minute more."

Nik decided to use the extra time to double- and triple-check his facts, but first he planned to go to his apartment, shower, eat, and grab a quick power nap before returning to the office.

On his drive across town, he called Sam and again got the message that her voice-mail box was full. He tried Thomas Polk. No luck. His last call was to Gyp's pet sitter, Sara. He told her he was back in town and asked her to drop the dog off at his apartment.

———

A Grand Canyon–size fault line was opening under Dwayne Mack, and it threatened to swallow him whole.

Jewel called screaming about "that fuckin' *Newshound* reporter," Thomas Polk had gone dark, Vice President Matthew Pound was demanding a cover story, Faud Asma was out there, somewhere, lurking.

It was decision time for Mack as well. He had anticipated this, saw it coming, in fact, made provisions for it. Stay and fight or cut and run? A binary choice. Door A or Door B. *Either way*, he reasoned, *my odds of surviving increase if I eliminate the threat, which means eliminate the story, which means eliminate the root of the story.*

He made the call.

———

Nik found a parking spot out front of his condo building, collected his mail, and mounted the steps to his apartment, riffling through the correspondence as he walked. Most of it was flyers and junk mail, but there was a hand-addressed envelope. He immediately recognized Sam's distinctive, swooping cursive penmanship.

He put his house key into the lock and turned. No barking. The pet sitter must not have dropped Gyp off yet, he thought. He stepped inside and tore open the letter from Sam. The first jolt from the Taser knocked Nik to his knees, sending the mail swimming down the hallway. The second paralyzed him. The shooter momentarily fingered the trigger for a third shot but reholstered the stun gun instead.

Nik heard low, guttural noises as he was hauled across hardwood floors. He was rolled over on his back, fingers working his clothes. The sound of water. Where was he? He was partially lifted, shirt drawn over his head, his skull slamming into the tiled floor when he was released. Shoes, socks, pants, underwear followed. Loud grunts, then panting, as he was hoisted and tipped over the rim of the bathtub. A splash. The water was warm, but he was immobile and started to slide under.

His eyes fluttered open, his vision blurred. A face floated above him and came into focus. It was Reese, his attractive, helpful neighbor, staring down at him. She wore a determined mask, her warm, friendly smile gone. He worked his jaw. Tried to speak. Bubbles floated to the surface.

His mind and body started to drift off, dreamlike. Eyes, heavy, drooped shut.

CHAPTER 65

August 24

FBI Special Agents Sawyer and Luck and DC Detectives Jenks and Goetz huddled outside the conference room where Faud Asma sat chain-smoking. "Man's a human forest fire. I believe he plans to asphyxiate all of us before this is over," Jenks said.

"Excuse me, but isn't this a no-smoking building?" Goetz asked.

The three of them looked disdainfully at the young detective but said nothing.

"He's fucking with us," Luck said. "And for the record, I didn't like this idea from day one."

"It wasn't your call, Special Agent Luck," Sawyer said. "And clean up your language. Detective Jenks, what do you say? You've observed him the longest."

"Well, if you believe him, he risked his life coming over to our side, and those recordings he made do implicate higher-ups in bribing officials and sanctioning the deaths of Olen, Trumbo, and Hiatt. The evidence is pretty damn compelling."

"Those recordings are probably doctored," Luck said

dismissively. "He claims he refused to have anything to do with the killings, and when he did, his colleagues turned on him. I say that's bullshit and he's up to his eyeballs in this. The only reason he jumped ship was to save his own ass and pin the murders on someone else before it was too late."

Goetz blurted out, "I believe him."

"Yeah," Jenks said and slowly nodded, "I guess I believe him, too."

"That makes three of us," Sawyer said.

"Huge fucking mistake," Luck said. "Pardon my French."

"You're welcome to go back to your office and sit it out, Special Agent Luck, if that's how you feel."

Luck crossed her arms, huffed, and stormed off.

"She's pouty," Jenks said.

"I need to make a call," Sawyer said. "Let my boss know, and he's going to need to call the attorney general. They've been briefed, so it won't come as a complete surprise, but if we're wrong . . ."

"Don't say it," Jenks said. "Don't even think it."

Sawyer advised, "Go home, get yourselves ready, and be back here in one hour."

Jenks asked, "How quick is this going down?"

Sawyer looked at his watch. Agent Luck had rejoined the group.

"It's gotta be a blitzkrieg," Luck said, "or it won't work."

Sawyer gave her a sideways glance.

"What?" she said. "No way I'm gonna miss out on this."

"I'd say in the next couple hours, Detective, give or take, assuming we get the green light," Sawyer said.

"We'll be saddled up and ready to ride," Jenks said.

CHAPTER 66

August 24

Someone was calling out Nik's name, but the sound was far off, like they were at one end of a very long tunnel and he was on the other side. Then the voice moved closer. "Nik." The word hovered over him and he forced his eyes open. A face, but not Reese's. It was Sara, Gyp's dog walker. A hand plunged into the water, grabbed a fistful of hair, and yanked. Nik coughed and sputtered, eyes wide, the size of poker chips. He leaned over the rim of the tub and threw up.

"No, Gyp," Sara said and pushed the dog away from the vomit and out the bathroom door. "What happened?"

Nik tried to answer, retched, and dropped his head back over the tub. He remained there for several moments and then finally lifted his face to Sara.

"Thank you," he exhaled.

"Are you going to be all right? Do I need to call medics?"

"No. Give me a minute."

Sara sat on the bathroom floor and started speaking rapidly while Nik attempted to resuscitate himself. "When I came in, I heard noises and called your name. Someone, a woman, I think, ran out into the hallway and then to the back bedroom. She must have gone down the fire escape. That's when I found you. I thought you were dead."

"Any longer and I would have been. That woman you saw run out was Reese. She shot me with a stun gun when I walked into the apartment and then dumped me in the bathtub to drown."

"Reese? Your neighbor? But why, for God's sake?"

"Think it has to do with a story I'm working on. Could you hand me a towel?" Nik lifted his chin toward a cabinet.

Sara pulled a towel from the shelves and gave it to Nik. He steadied himself and stood. She averted her eyes and said, "Don't step in the puke. I'll wait for you in the living room. And here, I nearly stepped on these." She handed him his glasses.

Nik dried off, wrapped the towel around his waist, emptied the bathtub, placed a floor mat over the vomit, and went in search of Sara and his phone.

CHAPTER 67

August 25

Had animal control not ordered her to euthanize the dog after it bit the Amazon deliveryman, limo driver, and DoorDash girl, she would have been alerted to the intruder in her house, but as it was, she was oblivious, two white earbuds, like tiny icicles, dangled from her lobes blocking out all noise. She didn't hear a thing until the black-clad, nylon-face-covered intruder was on her, and then all she could hear was the thundering of her heart exploding in her ears.

Shortly after midnight, she was at her bathroom sink, music pumping to her brain, in panties and bra, applying a coat of lotion to her face and arms when, suddenly she was violently attacked and in the fight of her life.

She couldn't think, let alone breathe, then survival instincts kicked in. She reached back and gouged the attacker's eye and broke loose. She ran toward the bedroom and was tackled from behind. She kicked free, scrambling to her feet, lunging for the bedside table. She pulled open the drawer and reached in.

"Looking for this?" the attacker asked, and held up the chrome-plated .38-caliber revolver and leveled it at Jewel and shot her twice in the chest, lifting her off her feet and slamming her into a full-length mirror, her blood splattering the walls, bed, and shooter.

The attacker removed the nylon stocking, and Marianne Tate stood looking at herself in the mirror, bloodied but unbowed. She held the gun in one gloved hand and reached into her pocket with the other and removed the cell phone that had once belonged to her late brother and that she'd used to switch off the home's security system.

She dropped the gun next to the body. On her way home, she would throw the phone into the Potomac River. After *Newshound*'s podcast with Butch Colson, she was betting the cops would conclude that one of Jewel's sexual role-playing escapades had gotten out of hand and turned deadly.

Tomorrow, she told herself as she walked out the front door, she would begin the task of retaking control of Yukon, confident the mayhem and potential lawsuits surrounding the company would scare off any potential suitor.

CHAPTER 68

August 25

It was two thirty a.m. when Nik and Mia released *Newshound*'s
final Yukon podcast to apps and broadcast channels nationwide, having notified company attorneys they were breaking
the embargo after an attempt had been made on Nik's life.
Even then, the lawyers tried to stall.

"Chickenshits," Mia said as she hit the Send button on the
podcast that would expose a massive military fraud that impli-
cated the vice president of the United States.

At five thirty that morning, FBI agents had fanned out over
the region and raided Yukon's offices and served search and
arrest warrants on dozens of businesses, politicians, and military chiefs.

Yukon CEO Dwayne Mack was arrested on a charge of trea-
son as he attempted to board a private jet for the Caribbean

with a female companion who was identified as Theresa "Reese" Grosbeak from Chicago, a suspected contract killer.

FBI Special Agents Sawyer and Luck and DC Detectives Jenks and Goetz arrested Vice President Matthew Pound as his motorcade exited the United States Naval Observatory grounds for a sunrise round of golf at the Congressional Country Club.

Thomas Polk's body was found floating in the Potomac River. Police preliminarily ruled the death suspicious, witnesses having reported seeing a heavyset woman and a Middle Eastern–looking man brush past Polk the moment he somersaulted off the Key Bridge and into the water. A toxicology report revealed Polk had ingested large quantities of both alcohol and barbiturates prior to his death.

Elizabeth Blake, demoted to early-morning news reader on Channel 13, reported that confidential sources were telling her that a Saudi national by the name of Faud Asma had entered the FBI's witness protection program and was a key figure in what was now being referred to as the Bullwhip Sting or, as it soon came to be known, BS.

"Asma has reportedly turned over several hours of what is being described as incriminating conversations he secretly tape-recorded with US politicians, business leaders, and foreign diplomats," Blake informed listeners and privately told herself, *I'm back.*

Louisa Dills, Nik's Pentagon source, was driving to her gym for her ritual predawn workout when she heard the news come over the car radio. "Damn, he did it," she said and pulled off to the side of the road to send Nik a text when the report was finished. It read, Balls to the wall.

CHAPTER 69

August 25

Nik finally got home at ten in the morning, Gyp twirling around his legs with unbounded joy, and he was reminded, once again, that the later you arrived, the happier dogs were to see you, unlike girlfriends, wives, and cats.

He thought about breakfast, looked in the refrigerator, saw leftover meat loaf, a quarter of a roasted chicken, and a couple cold enchiladas. Nothing appealed to him. He opened a cupboard and took out a jar of extra-crunchy peanut butter and scooped out a few spoonfuls. That hit the spot.

He stumbled back to his bedroom, stripped off his clothes, and climbed under the covers. He got back up and closed the blinds. When he lay back down again, he started thinking about the events of the past several months.

He wrestled with Geoffrey Tate's role in the whole saga. Tate seemed both a victim, on the one hand, and an accomplice, albeit an unwilling one, on the other.

Based on what Tate's sister described as her brother's "wayward carnal impulses," Nik believed Tate was set up and was voluntarily indulging in one of Jewel's sexual fantasies the night he was killed.

Nik couldn't help but wonder if Tate would still be alive had he not delegated negotiating authority for the Bullwhip contract to Dwayne Mack. Why Tate, a self-described control freak, did that remained a mystery. Had Tate intentionally distanced himself from the project because he privately opposed using AI to wage war? Nik would never know the answer to that question. Whatever the reason, it gave Mack insights into Tate and the company that he was able to exploit.

And how strange was it, Nik thought, that a has-been major league pitcher who now made a living running a baseball camp in southern Florida would be the one to shed light on what actually happened the night Tate was killed. Nik figured he'd probably never learn how Colson's baseball card had wound up in his office mail.

Before Nik and Colson departed the bar they were in, the pair had talked at length about the future of professional baseball. They both worried the sport was at risk of going extinct if it didn't figure out how to shorten both its season and games that were running to four and, in some cases, five hours. And on top of that, players were fatigued by the 162-game schedule, and there were way too many injuries to pitchers. That gave Nik the opening to test out his pet theory on Colson on how to solve the problem:

"Fans and players want fewer and shorter games," Nik explained. "There are roughly six months to the season— early April to early October—and if every team played six doubleheaders—three home doubleheaders, and three away— players would pick up an additional six extra rest days during the season. On top of that, if the doubleheader games were only seven innings, it would be possible to squeeze in two games in a little more than three hours. Over the course of the season, this would shave twenty-four innings off the schedule, the equivalent of 2.666 games, in effect getting the schedule back under a hundred sixty games for the first time since 1961.

"And as for pitchers, the mound needs to be raised back up to fifteen inches, where it was prior to the '69 season."

"I like the idea of raising the mound," Colson said. "But fewer innings means fewer beer sales, which means less money in the owners' pockets. Not sure they'd go for that."

As he drifted off to sleep, Nik's final thought was that he feared journalism, too, faced extinction if it didn't change its ways. And with small-minded editors like Li'l Dick Whetstone, who was threatened by hard-charging reporters, it seemed a near certainty.

CHAPTER 70

September 1

The Washington Cannons were eliminated in the third round of the playoffs by the Supremes, Chase Hurley's team, by a score of 6–5. While Hurley was unable to play in the tournament, Nik, on the other hand, did and led his team in extra-base hits, runs scored, and putouts. It was easily his best performance of the season, and his teammates voted him most valuable player following the game, even though they failed to make it to the championship round.

Nik was sitting in the dugout unlacing his spikes, putting away his gear, and thinking about the next season when a voice in the stands said, "Hey, stranger." He looked up. It was Sam.

He was struck by her radiance. She had a glow he hadn't noticed before. He thought it might be the result of the sun at her back, either that or her newfound relationship with Chase Hurley. He hoped it was the former and not the latter.

Nik said, "You here to root for Chase's team?" and wished he hadn't.

Sam looked out over the field, where workers were preparing the grounds for the next game. "No, believe it or not, I came to see you, Nik."

Nik climbed to the top of the dugout. "I must have called you twenty times and sent at least that many text messages. When you didn't respond, it started to sink in that you didn't want anything to do with me."

"I came because I have a question I need to ask you," she said.

"Oh? Okay."

"Why didn't you reply to the letter I wrote you?"

Letter, Nik thought. *What letter?*

When he didn't answer, Sam said, "So I guess the answer is no."

"No," Nik said.

"All right," Sam said.

"No, I don't mean no. I mean, I don't know what letter you're talking about." He then recalled the letter from Sam he was opening when Reese shot him with the Taser. It must have fallen out of his hands and gone under the hallway table. He explained to Sam what he thought had happened.

"I never got a chance to read it. What did it say?"

Sam hesitated, her answer caught in her throat, tears pooling in her eyes. "I'm pregnant, Nik, and before you say something stupid, it's yours. I mean, it's ours."

Nik's jaw dropped, and he stood there, speechless, gulping air.

"But I thought you and—" he started in.

Sam cut him off. "There is no me and anybody else, and even if there had been, you look me in the eye, Nik Byron, and tell me you didn't see other people while we were apart."

"Well, but—" Nik tried again.

"And who do you think sent you Butch Colson's baseball card? That was the story Chase mentioned to me that day on the hillside. I found one of Colson's old cards on the internet and passed it along to you after Chase lost interest in the story when Jewel was found not guilty."

"That was you?"

"That was me."

"I owe you, then."

"The only thing you owe me, Nik, is an answer. I'm keeping this baby, with or without you."

"Okay."

"Okay, what? What the hell is that supposed to mean, okay? Care to spell it out?"

Nik looked around and swallowed hard. "So," he finally said. "You wanna get married? There, how's that?"

Sam leaned over the dugout and kissed Nik. "Needs work," she said, "but it's a start."

ACKNOWLEDGMENTS

There are currently four books in the Nik Byron series (five if you count the one I'm slowly working on). The book you hold in your hands, *Friendly Fire*, originally was to be the third book in the series. But after much deliberation, the publication sequence got reordered, and the first book, *Newshound*, will now be released as a prequel. The second book, *Hack*, was published in July 2022 as my debut novel. While the decision was wholly mine, I had input from other writers, trusted friends and, in no small measure, Faith Black Ross, my editor at Girl Friday Books. Faith is a wise editor with a sharp eye and a good ear, and she has been indispensable on this journey. After reading all the manuscripts, it was her belief that we could launch the series with *Hack*, which was a favorite of hers. I realize this is somewhat inside baseball, but it is just one of the hundreds of decisions that go into publishing a book, and in this case it turned out to be not only an important decision but the right one.

Speaking of Girl Friday, I also want to give a tip of the cap to Sara Addicott, Georgie Hockett, and Bethany Davis for expertly shepherding my books through the publishing gauntlet. I'm lucky to have such a great team.

And last, I owe deep gratitude to my family—Jennifer, Benjamin, and William, without whom none of this would have been possible.

BLACK BIRD

PROLOGUE

The snowstorm had rolled in a little after noontime the previous day and had continued throughout the evening and into the small hours, turning the Methow Valley into a deep, powdered-sugar landscape. It was the first major storm of the season, and Anne was determined to cut a track in the virgin snow before anyone else had a chance to spoil it. She was up early and had waxed her telemark skis the night before in anticipation; she was now brewing coffee and making a fried-egg sandwich to pack for lunch. Leza Burdock, her partner, wasn't a skier, and Anne was careful not to wake her when she slipped out of bed. The sky was beginning to lighten, and Anne could see the outline of Goat Mountain from her kitchen window off in the distance. That was her destination this morning, a fourteen-mile round trip, give or take, from the cabin. Otto, Leza's portly Dalmatian, stood patiently by the front door, tail rhythmically slapping the pine floor.

Anne had arrived in the Methow Valley in the Pacific Northwest nine months earlier, after she was dismissed from Xion Labs, a biotech and life sciences company located outside of Washington, DC, in Rockville, Maryland. The company informed her that it had lost its government contract and could no longer fund her virology department, which meant firing her core team of research scientists and scattering other associates across the company.

Anne secured severance packages for herself and the three other dismissed colleagues, and after cashing in her settlement and selling a condo she owned in Alexandria, Virginia, she packed up her late-model Subaru and headed west, searching for a spot to set down roots. She found what she was looking for in the remote North Cascades mountain range in Washington State.

Her former colleagues Thom Berg and Deirdre Stewart also fled to out-of-the-way places, Berg to Bokeelia Island in Florida, and Stewart to the Outer Banks in North Carolina. Based on a postcard Anne had happily discovered one day in her mailbox, Puck Hall, the youngest member of the research group, was making plans to hike the Appalachian Trail.

Anne had immediately fallen in love with both the Methow Valley and Leza, a large-animal veterinarian, whom she met one morning while browsing at the local farmers' market in Twisp. On the surface, the two women didn't have much in common: Anne was athletic, whereas Leza was bookish; Anne was a vegetarian, and Leza loved nothing better than a medium-rare T-bone steak; Anne was outspoken, while

Leza was quiet. Anne was a Democrat, and Leza a Libertarian; Anne was urban, Leza was rural.

Nonetheless, they found common ground in their shared love of nature, cheesy eighties movies, road trips, inexpensive wine, and yard sales, and five weeks after meeting, Anne moved in with Leza and Otto.

If there was one area of her life Anne was reticent to share with Leza, it was her past work life in Washington. At first, this reticence troubled Leza—she felt Anne was trying to hide something from her—but as kindred spirits, they had a thousand and one other things to talk about, and Leza didn't dwell on it.

Anne filled her CamelBak with water, wrapped the sandwich in wax paper, poured trail mix into a brown bag, and dropped it all into her backpack. At the last minute, she grabbed the GoPro from the hallway closet that Leza had given to her as a birthday present and crammed it in the bottom of her pack. She hated the damn thing, thought it intrusive and a pain to operate, but felt she at least needed to make a show of using it since it was a gift from Leza. She debated whether to take Otto but, in the end, decided against it, fearing he would sink into the fluffy snow and only slow her down. As it were, she'd be doing well to be back home before nightfall, and that was if she hustled.

"I'll take you out tomorrow for a long run," she promised the sad-eyed animal, and poured a scoop of kibble in his bowl. "The cross-country trails will be groomed by then." She could hear Otto pawing at the door as she stepped outside and closed it behind her.

Anne clicked into her skis and, with a powerful thrust of the long poles, skated down the drive, and in no time she was whistling through a stand of ponderosa pines. She crested a slight hill and nearly toppled over when she stopped suddenly to avoid hitting a porcupine that meandered across her path.

She shoved off again and was instantly lost in the serenity of her surroundings.

After heavy poling over a long, flat expanse, Anne rounded a bend and broke out of the tree line, the base of Goat Mountain coming into view. She calculated she could reach the mountain in less than an hour and, from there, slip the skins over the skis and climb a quarter of the way up, maybe farther, depending on how tired she was, and then ski down.

It started snowing again, lightly at first. By the time Anne reached the mountain, the snow was coming down harder, dry flakes the size of small clamshells covering her head and upper body. She unsnapped her skis, slung the backpack off her shoulders, and sat on a deadfall to eat her sandwich and hydrate before making the ascent.

She had written Leza a short note that morning before leaving but hadn't told her the route she intended to take and now mildly regretted the oversight. Anne finished her sandwich, begrudgingly attached the GoPro to the handle of her ski pole, activated the avalanche beacon she carried, affixed the skins to the skis, and started to climb.

She was surprised at how swiftly she moved up the mountainside. The yoga and running had actually paid off, and seventy-five minutes after starting the climb, she reached the quarter-way point. She was tempted to continue on, but the snow showed no signs of letting up, and she didn't want to press her luck this early in the season by herself.

She turned on the GoPro and looked around in awe. "I have Goat Mountain all to myself. It's a glorious day."

Anne had not seen a single soul on her way out that morning, but now, as she looked over her shoulder, another skier was clawing up the mountainside. "Who can that be?" she said under her breath as she turned around to face down the mountain.

Anne considered skiing downhill, but whoever was coming toward her was directly in the fall line she intended to take off the mountain. Anne shrugged off her backpack again, grabbed a handful of trail mix, and leaned against her poles to watch and, in so doing, knocked the camera loose and into the snow. "Ah, shit. The hell with it," she muttered as she shoved the GoPro back into her pack.

Anne didn't have long to wait. The climber was fit and chewed up the terrain in long, powerful strides.

"Congratulations," the skier said, huffing, when she reached Anne. "You beat me. Doesn't happen often. It's a personal point of pride with me to be first on the mountain after a major dump. Name's Narda."

Narda slid her sunglasses off her nose and perched them on the top of her candy-cane-striped knit cap that had a red pom-pom on top, revealing pale-gray eyes the color of cement, her skin bronzed and shiny as a copper kettle from the sun.

She had an angular face and wide, muscular shoulders. Anne smiled victoriously and reached out her gloved hand. "Anne. Anne Paxton. Nice to meet you," she said.

"Nice to meet you as well," Narda said, quickly shaking Anne's hand before pulling on the sunglasses and starting to climb again.

"You're not skiing down?" Anne asked.

Narda shook her head. "Aiming for the ridge," she said, using her pole to motion across the face of the mountain to a spot about three hundred yards above them. "It's my favorite run. The powder is sublime."

"Never been up there," Anne said.

"Not many people have. That's why I love it. Come on. I'll break a trail and you can follow."

"I don't know." Anne hesitated. "It looks awfully steep."

Narda laughed. "Steep? It's a sheer cliff, but there's a

switchback on the far side that winds around through a stand of birch trees to a nice gradual descent. You can't see that from here, but suit yourself."

Anne checked the time on her smart watch. She might be able to make the ridge, ski down, and still be home in time for dinner if she didn't loiter. It'd be tight, but she could do it, and she'd text Leza when she reestablished cell coverage to let her know she was on her way.

What the hell, you only live once, she thought, and tucked her chin against her chest and plunged forward. The snow was as light as goose down, and she practically floated in the track Narda cut.

By the time they reached the ridge, though, Anne had a dull ache in her thighs from skating up the incline and decided to rest briefly, drink some water, and eat a couple more handfuls of trail mix before starting down. Both skiers stripped the skins off their skis while they caught their breath.

"You ready?" Narda asked.

"Lead on," Anne said and wrapped the pole straps tightly around her gloved hands.

Narda dug her poles into the snow and, with a heave, disappeared around a sharp downhill curve. Anne followed but soon lost sight of Narda as she zigged and zagged down the steep switchback.

Darkness was beginning to seep in around the edges of the sky, and Anne now cursed herself for following Narda in the first place. It was foolish of her, and the terrain was nowhere near as gentle as she had been led to believe. She was becoming exhausted, and her legs were turning rubbery from the exertion.

Anne shot around a hairpin turn and pulled up abruptly, the mountain dropping off below her, thousands of feet of nothingness beyond the tips of her skis.

Her heart was hammering so hard, it felt like it was going to burst from her chest. She closed her eyes and forced herself to inhale deep gulps of cold air to steady her shaking limbs.

Anne finally collected herself, planted her poles, and started to push back from the abyss when she heard a soft cough from behind her.

Narda appeared out of nowhere, skis off, in boots. "You need to be more careful, Anne," Narda said. "You're lucky you didn't sail right off the edge."

"Narda, thank goodness. I thought I'd lost you. You should have warned me about this turn. I might have killed myself," Anne scolded.

"You got a helluva set of brakes on those skis, I'll give you that. What's the brand?" Narda said, smiling. "I need to get me a pair."

"Don't joke. It's not funny, goddamn it," Anne said and started backing away again.

"Sorry, you're right," Narda said, advancing, blocking Anne's retreat.

Anne twisted around. "What are you doing?"

Narda pushed her sunglasses to the top of her head, her eyes like two cold gray spikes now, the smile gone.

Anne, unable to maneuver, panicked, and then it came to her. "No," she begged, ashen-faced. "I swear to God, no one knows anything. I haven't told a soul."

Narda drew closer.

"Please, don't do this," Anne pleaded. "I'll disappear. For good this time. I promise."

"You got that right, sister," Narda said and shoved Anne in the back. She watched as Anne pitched forward, arms and legs helicoptering, fighting unsuccessfully to arrest her descent, until she was swallowed up by the darkness.

ABOUT THE AUTHOR

Mark Pawlosky is an award-winning reporter, editor, and media executive. A former reporter for the *Wall Street Journal*, editorial director for *American City Business Journals (ACBJ)*, and editor in chief of CNBC.com/msn, he oversaw financial news channels in the US, London, Munich, Paris, Tokyo, and Hong Kong. He successfully helped launch several media operations nationwide, including MSNBC, *American City Business Journals*, and *Biz Magazine*. A graduate of the Missouri School of Journalism at the University of Missouri, Pawlosky and his family spent the past twenty years living on an island in Washington State before relocating to the Midwest. He is the author of *Hack*, the first book in the Nik Byron Investigation series.

Visit the author at: www.markpawlosky.com.

— A —
NIK BYRON
INVESTIGATION

"Written with all the speed and blunt force of a high-speed car chase . . ."

—Vincent Zandri, *New York Times* bestselling writer and Shamus Award–winning author of the Dick Moonlight P.I. Thriller series and *The Girl Who Wasn't There*.

Read the series.

Available everywhere books are sold.

Watch for Nik Byron's next investigation,

Black Bird,

coming soon.

CPSIA information can be obtained
at www.ICGtesting.com
Printed in the USA
JSHW010213040123
35619JS00005BA/5